MAFIA DON'S SECRET TWINS

AN ARRANGED MARRIAGE DARK MAFIA ROMANCE

RUTHLESS MAFIA KINGS

VIVY SKYS

Copyright © 2025 by VIVY SKYS

All rights reserved.

No part of this book may be reproduced in any form or by any electronic or mechanical means, including information storage and retrieval systems, without written permission from the author, except for the use of brief quotations in a book review.

PROLOGUE: DINO

8 years ago

Panama City, Florida

My phone buzzes, but this time instead of answering, I shut it off.

Marco is not going to fucking ruin this for me. Not again.

Will he be pissed when I turn it back on? Sure. But honestly, I don't fucking care.

Marco isn't my boss. He's my older brother but acts like he's my fucking keeper. No, Marco isn't going to ruin this trip for me.

If our dad called, then I might be worried.

Dad, however, will absolutely not call. I know that for a fact. He won't call. Not when he can task Marco with it.

Not when he doesn't now, and hasn't ever, given a fuck about me and what I do.

I put the phone in my backpack, where it hopefully will fall to the bottom and I won't have to fucking think about it again until I'm on my way back to New York.

Marco is going to be livid. However, that's a future problem. I'll handle that when the time comes.

But for now?

I'm in a motel. In Panama City, Florida. The room isn't much to look at, but the view?

Damn.

There's a stretch of powdery soft white sand in front of me, curling as far as I can see in either direction. The ocean is a beautiful jewel-toned blue, and I swear to fucking God, there are dolphins just at the edge of the horizon.

I'm on spring break. Like a normal fucking human.

And I'm going to enjoy the hell out of it.

"Yo, D. We doing this or what?"

I turn, leaving the view from the cheap motel's balcony as I look at my friends. They grin back at me, and I'm immediately grateful for both of them.

Jayce and Brent.

They're two completely regular guys that I met playing football. They're both from Jersey, both from regular boring-ass families who don't have to consider whether or not phone conversations or family associations will get them locked up on RICO charges.

The exact opposite of my family, basically.

In high school, I knew that I would rather hang with them than with my brothers. So, I did.

We've been friends, more or less, ever since.

"Fuck you looking at? The view?" Brent grunts.

Jayce laughs, handing me a plastic red cup to mix a drink into. "Yeah man. There's nothing to fucking see right now until we find some fucking girls."

I nod. "Fuck yeah, man." I grab a handle of vodka and start pouring, ready to mix it with whatever the hell we packed to get the party started.

The party is the most important part.

That's the point of this trip. If I'm being honest, we're fucking losers. College drop-outs, or in my case, college non-starters. For whatever reason, Jayce had a football scholarship to Penn and lost it. Brent is... Brent. I don't think he ever applied.

Neither did I.

Having brothers like mine? Yeah. No fucking way was I going to try and stand in either of their shadows. Even my sister is a badass, and I just can't hold a candle to them. Marco just graduated business school. Sal is in fucking Yale. Caterina is probably going to be a lawyer or some shit.

And then there's me.

No one expected much of me, honestly. My mom cried like a baby when I graduated high school a few years ago. I could tell that she didn't think I'd make it.

Neither did I.

For the most part, I don't give a fuck that I don't go to school. I like working on the docks for De Luca Shipping. It suits me.

No one cares that I'm loud and mouthy and as prone to getting in a fight as I am doing my fucking job.

It suits me.

At this point, most of the guys have even forgotten that I'm the boss' son. I should remind them every now and then, but honestly...

I don't want to.

It's kind of freeing to not be Dino De Luca when I'm with them.

I just get to be... me.

And Jayce and Brent are part of that freedom.

But, since none of us actually went to college, none of us had a college-style spring break.

So, we decided to make our own.

This trip?

This is it.

I finish pouring the drink, mixing a soda into it, and the boys do the same. I hold up my red cup. "To failing and still being fucking great," I say.

Jayce and Brent clink glasses with me and we all drink. The vodka burns my throat going down, and I take a deep breath after.

I look at my friends. "Well, let's find the fucking girls, yeah?"

While I typically consier myself to be a pro at day drinking, I have to admit that nine hours later is kind of a long time to be really fucking drunk.

It's getting old at this point.

We've been to the beach. We've had some food at some point, but it's sitting poorly in my stomach. Now, Jayce is somewhere unknown, and Brent has been trying to get the same girl to give him her number for an hour. The club is outside, on the beach, and the pulsing lights and grinding music are giving me a headache.

I need some fucking air.

Slowly, I rise, my feet feeling weirdly unstable under me. I trip forward, tumbling toward the edge of the party, where the crowd wanes and the actual ocean starts.

The music is still loud, but it's fading.

I look to the left of me. The hotels and bars curve away to the right, but to the left it looks.. quiet.

Dark.

While I was deeply engaged in spending my day drinking, the sun slipped below the horizon, and now...

Well I can't exactly see stars, but it's nice to see darkness for a change.

I lurch toward the promise of stars, and the sounds of the party slowly fade away from me.

I'm not sure how long I walk for, or even if I'm allowed on this stretch of beach. But, eventually, something trips me and I fall.

The world is spinning, so I opt to not get up.

This was supposed to be fun. A way to meet some fucking cute college girls and pretend that I belonged somewhere.

Now, though, I'm drunk and I feel lonelier than ever.

I shut my eyes.

If I never got up from this spot, would my family even fucking care?

Everyone wants me to be something I'm not. Marco wants me to go to college and fall in line, maybe live in Italy for the business. My dad doesn't give a fuck what I do, so long as I don't embarass him.

Sal wants me to be "nice'. He wants me to blend in and hide who I am just to get along.

Caterina?

I don't know. Caterina is the person I feel the worst about disappointing.

Her, and my mom.

They've all been able to just... exist. Like they all got programmed with something that I don't.

I feel like I came out wrong. Like there's this ball of anger and pain and something fucking awful inside me that I have to hide to be like them.

I'm so fucking sick of hiding it.

God, I'm a miserable fucking drunk. I need to get my shit together and go find my friends...

I try to get up but I collapse.

Fuck.

I don't even have my fucking phone.

Do I even remember our room? Or the hotel? Fuck, I guess I should have at least asked...

"Are you dead?"

My eyes snap open.

I blink.

Maybe I am dead, because standing in front of me is the prettiest fucking girl I've ever seen in my life

She blinks at me. "Okay. I hope not because if you were dead this would be really weird."

Jesus fucking Christ. Her voice is smooth and sweet, like the breeze on a hot day. I sit upright, well aware that there's sand sticking to my sweaty, drunk skin.

"I'm alive," I croak.

She raises one of her perfectly groomed eyebrows. "You don't seem alive."

"I am now," I say.

It's so fucking true that it rings through me like a bell.

She folds her arms across her chest. She's wearing a white dress that ties behind her neck. I can see that she's wearing a bikini under it, like most girls at the beach, and her torrent of brown curls is tugged up into a braid that I want to unravel.

Her eyes are so brown, they look black in the night. Her skin looks velvety smooth.

Her lips are lush, and they bow into a perfect shape...

Wow.

I'm being so fucking creepy. "I'm not dead," I clear my throat and say again. "Just..."

"You're like falling down drunk."

I nod. "Yeah."

She looks me over. "Are you staying here?"

"Yeah."

"Where?"

I narrow my eyes. "Why do you care?"

"Because, asshole,' she tips her hips, her feet widening like she's squaring up. "I walked out and found someone who I thought was dead on the sand dunes, and I don't really want to walk away feeling like you'll be dead after I leave."

"Why do you care?"

The question is a little harsh, but it's true. She's a total stranger. Why does she care even a little about a stranger on the beach?

She sighs. "Because I'm a nice fucking person. And I can't be a nice person without being nice. And it wouldn't be very nice of me to walk away if I saw a dead body on the beach, now would it?"

I blink.

She stares at me. "So. Are you staying nearby? Do you have friends that could come fish you out of... this?" she gestures to the sand.

"Uh. Yeah."

"Okay. Well, are you gonna call them or what?"

"Don't have my phone."

She curses softly in Spanish, which explains the light accent that I've been hearing. "Do you know which hotel you're in?"

"Uh..."

I can't exactly lie to her. Somethinhg about her keeps me from doing what I normally would, which would be pretend to be fucking fine and tell the other person to go to hell.

Instead, I tell the truth.

"I don't remember," I say.

Her beautiful eyes widen. "So. Your plan was... to pass out here and wait until morning?"

"Yeah," I nod.

The girl heaves the biggest sigh that I've ever heard in my entire life. She curses again in Spanish, and I know enough to recognize that she's calling me an asshole and an idiot.

I'm both of those things.

But for some reason, coming from her, it hurts.

To my shock, she extends a hand to me. "Come on," she says, her fingers flexing. "Let's go."

"What?"

"You're coming with me," she says matter-of-factly.

"Why?"

"So you can take a shower and sleep in a place where you won't die of exposure."

I raise an eyebrow. "Die of exposure?"

"Just get up, okay?"

There's a heartbeat of hesitation. I look at her outstretched hand, which seems outrageously small.

When I slip my fingers into hers, I know that my world is changing.

After her, everything will be different.

Interestingly, she's not staying in a hotel.

She leads me to a little house. It's just a shack on a beach, but it's clean and warm and has a very nice shower. There are sweatpants and a large white shirt waiting for me when I get out.

The idea that another man might have stayed here, or that she might have a boyfriend or someone, makes me unnecessarily angry.

Clean and more or less sober, I follow the sound of dishes clinking together to the kitchen. The girl is in there and something smells amazing.

"Damn," I lean against the door. "What's that?"

"Something to sober you up."

"I think the shower did that," I murmur.

She gives me a curt nod. "You don't smell like a distillery anymore so that's a start."

Ouch.

She points to one of the small chairs. "Sit."

I obey.

She hands me a plate full of rice, chicken, and something that looks like a banana. "Plantains," she says as I examine them. "Best hangover food in the world."

Cautiously, I take a bite.

It's fucking amazing.

I eat in silence. The whole time, I'm aware that she's watching me, but I don't talk to her until I'm practically licking the plate.

"Holy fuck," I groan. "That was so good."

"Good."

I look at her again. The borrowed clothes seem to itch on my kin. "Do you entertain strange men a lot?"

"No."

I chuckle at her succinct response. "So you just have spare sweatpants lying around."

"I do."

She's not giving an inch. I lean back, ready to needle her into a reaction. "How do you know I'm not like some kind of fucking rapist?"

She tilts her head. "You might be."

"That doesn't scare you?"

Slowly, she shakes her head. Her curls bounce, some of them having come free from her braid. "No. It doesn't."

"Why?"

Her eyes gleam slightly. "One, I know how to take care of myself. And two... I've already survived the worst thing that could ever happen to me. Lighting doesn't strike twice."

I snort. "That's... both depressing and optimistic."

"It's real," she says softly.

Real.

That's the word that comes to mind when I think of her.. In our short interaction, I can tell that she's the most real person I've ever met.

And I fucking like that.

"What's your name?"

She smiles, a small curl at the edges of her lips. "Marisol. You?"

No last names. Noted. "Dino."

"Okay. Are you tired, Dino?"

No. I shake my head. "Not really."

"Okay."

I shift. "I um... thank you."

"For what?"

"For.. this," I gesture.

She shrugs. "Like I said. I can't call myself a nice person if I don't act like one, so. Yeah."

That statement is so compelling.

I've met a lot of people in my life. Part of the deal, I guess, because I'm a De Luca.

I very rarely meet people whose integrity matters to them so much. I mean, she took me, a total stranger and potential danger, and she fed me, let me shower, and put me in some new clothes.

Fuck.

That's... the bravest thing that I've ever heard.

"So, Marisol," I smile at her. "Are you just here to rescue sad looking fuck-ups?"

"You're hardly sad looking, and why do you say you're a fuck-up?"

"I..." I don't answer. I can't.

I don't need her to know how I'm not just the black sheep in my family.

It's more like they're a pack of wolves.

And I'm a fucking lion.

"I was asking about you," I recover.

She snorts. "Smooth. But I'm here because one of my friends is going through a really bad breakup and my... I was tasked with making sure that she didn't do anything too stupid."

I arch an eyebrow. "And? Where is this friend?"

"Notably not here. Hopefully making whatever stupid decisions she wants."

I laugh at that. Then, my mind catches on one of her words. "Who tasked you with this?"

"No one you need to know about," she says with a grimace.

God, whoever did this to her... she fucking hates them.

It makes me so weirdly possessive. I want to dig more to find out who the fuck is 'making' her do anything.

And I will fucking end them.

"So, your friend's out making bad decisions... what about you?" I smile at her.

She shakes her head. "No. Not me. Never allowed to do that, for sure."

I laugh. "Oh, come on. Everyone makes some bad decisions in their life."

"I don't," she says quietly.

I look over at her. She's so beautiful that it makes me fucking nervous.

When she looks back up at me though, there's fire in her eyes.

"I don't make bad decisions. I never make any decisions. I'm not supposed to," she says boldly.

I hold up my hands. "Whoa, okay. Well, let's see. If you did want to make a bad decision, what would you make?"

I'm thinking she'll say something standard. Get a tattoo. Get a piercing. Run from the cops.

What happens next, though, shocks me to my core.

She looks me dead in the eyes and says, "I'd kiss you."

Then?

She fucking does.

I'm so shocked that when her lips lad on mine, I'm completely frozen. My mind is a confusing jumble, because part of me wants to wrap my arms around her and kiss her back, and part of me...

Part of me thinks that would be a bad fucking idea.

So when she pulls back, her eyes wide, I'm still trying to decide.

"Sorry," she breathes, her chest heaving as she looks at me. "I just..."

Yeah. While she might not be known for bad decisions, I am.

And I decide.

I curl my hand up the back of her neck and grab a fistfull of her beautiful curly hair. It feels like yards and yards of silk in my hand, and I tug her head back to get better access to her mouth.

She gasps.

And I'm gone.

I devour her. There's no other word for it. I've never kissed anyone like this, and I've never had a kiss like this.

Ever.

This is so much more than just a kiss. It's... an obsession. I'm lost in her. My hands roam her body, greedy to experience everything.

Every touch is a new treasure that I hoard to myself. Her skin is so soft when I free it from her clothes. Her hips curve out before dipping back into her neat waist. When I take her bra and throw it aside, her breasts flow over the sides of my hands.

When I lick her pert brown nipples, she moans and its fucking music to my ears.

Her fingers in the waist of my pants feel cautious, but curious. When she wraps them around my hard cock, I have to take in a deep breath to keep myself from erupting.

Her thighs are so sweet when they part. We've moved from the kitchen onto the small couch in the living room, and it might be tiny, but I've never been closer to heaven than I am right now.

As I fit myself to her entrance, I hesitate.

Does she want this?

I look down at her. Marisol is staring up at me, her eyes wide, her pupils blown with lust.

"Marisol," I breathe. "Do..."

I don't finish, because she tips her hips and presses against me, and then I don't have an option.

I'm inside her, and she's so fucking tight that I have to control myself before I lose it.

Slowly, I pump inside her. The arch of her back as she meets me, the slight jiggle to her full breasts, all of it is more erotic than any porn I've ever watched.

I'm so mesmerized by her that my orgasm catches me by surprise.

She comes a second before I do. She cries my name and it sends me over the edge. I tug her up to kiss me as the orgasm spirals down my spine.

I swear, I can feel it for an eternity.

When I finally let her gently back down onto the couch, we both lay there, chests heaving. I gently tuck a lock of hair behind her ear. "Damn," I whisper.

She smiles. "I know."

"You..."

She shakes her head and presses her fingers against my lips. "Let's just... hold me. Okay?"

I nod. "Okay."

Gently, we shuffle so we're both lying on the little couch. I hold Marisol close, stroking her hair until her breathing evens out.

That's my cue. I fall asleep holding her, breathing in her pineapple smell.

Thank god I came to Panama City.

Because I'm going to marry this girl.

And nothing my family can say will stop me.

But, in the morning, she's gone.

No note.

Nothing there.

I wait for her.

But she never comes back.

1

DINO

Now

There's a heartbeat of terror when I watch her fall. One moment when I feel helpless, like I can't do anything.

Then, my body responds. I rush forward, and something in my heart clicks...

When Marisol is in my arms.

She's covered in cuts and bruises. Her beautiful hair is still long but chopped short on her forehead for bangs, and it's uneven, like she did it herself and in a hurry.

And I am one selfish fucking bastard because despite all of that, I'm happy that she's in my arms, and I fucking hate myself for it.

There are people moving around me. Yelling. I can hear Sal and Gia, and Elio barking instructions.

None of that matters, though, because I have Marisol.

I cradle her closer. Fuck, she still smells the same. It's been eight years and I haven't forgotten how she smells.

I want to kiss her. To scream in frustration. To...

"Dino," I hear Caterina say softly. "We need to get her to a doctor."

There's this insane urge to hold her close and like... hiss at my sister. I feel like I can't let Marisol out of my sight, because if I do...

If I let her go right now, I'll never see her again.

"You can come," Caterina murmurs, seemingly reading my mind. "You can come with, but we have to get her to Doctor Cutrali."

At that, I nod.

Reluctantly.

"He will be here in ten," Elio says gruffly. "Dino, what do you wish for us to do with these children?"

"I've got them," Caterina says quickly.

Children.

My children.

Holy fuck.

"I don't think they know," Gia whispers softly in my ear. "We've got them. Prioritize Marisol."

I give her the sharpest nod. I'm routinely terrified of Gia, but the fact that she's shepherding my two dark-haired children right now...

I tighten my grip on Marisol.

"Dino. This way," Elio barks.

Blindly, I follow him.

Everything except Marisol is a blur.

Thank God Elio's house is so fucking big. He has a whole room that he's kind of repurposed as a makeshift hospital room. It has a bed in it, various medical supplies, and a cabinet full of shit to patch people up long enough to either get to a real doctor... or to get better.

It's where Elio left me after he tortured me. Nice of him, I guess, but at the time I think we both were thinking he was just doing it to rip me apart again.

I'm the only one, I think, who knows exactly how sadistic Elio can be.

Well. I'm the only one who's lived to tell the tale.

But I'd do the same or worse to anyone who tried to hurt what's mine too. Fuck I'd kill me. So I don't blame him. I had no choice but to rat out Luna's location to the Irish Mafia in order to protect my girls.

I wouldn't have done it if I didn't know Elio's power and reach. With my siblings' help I had no doubt he'd get to his little girl before anything happened to her. It's fucking sick that I had to place my niece's life in danger to save my girls and my woman, but that's the savage hand I'm dealt with.

Gently, I put Marisol down on the bed. Her beautiful light brown skin looks so ashy and pale, and it makes me feel like I'm the worst fucking person on earth.

I have zero doubt in my mind that whatever happened to her, happened because of me.

I'm not just bad luck. I'm a fucking curse.

And my heart sinks as I realize that I must have brought Marisol down with me.

"How long until the doctor's here?" I hear Caterina's voice float over my shoulder.

"He's pulling up the drive," Elio rumbles.

I nod. I feel useless. Unsure of what to do now. My hand slides down Marisol's arm, then hovers above her fingertips.

I wish I could just hold her hand.

Studying her in the bed, it's like seeing a ghost. I can see the beautiful girl that I fell for all those years ago, but more than that, I can see the stunning woman that she's become.

Her face has lost all traces of the roundness from when I first met her. She's still got gorgeous hair, so dark brown that it's almost black, and it hangs just past her shoulders. There are new freckles across the bridge of her nose, though, and a scar that crosses one of her perfectly groomed eyebrows.

That little fucking scar makes my chest hurt with anger.

"Dino," Caterina says quietly. "I need you to step back."

No.

I fight down my compulsion to snarl at my sister. "I'll step back when the doctor gets here."

"He's here," she adds softly.

I look up to see an older gentleman standing in the door. I

don't recognize him, but the little twitch of his eyebrow when he looks at me tells me that he recognizes me.

With a sharp jerk of my head, I narrow my eyes at him. "You know me?"

"It's nice to see your neck healed so well," he says in a heavily accented voice.

That's one fucking way to put it.

Elio did a number on me. My vocal cords are still shot, and the way he sliced my stomach open?

I held my fucking guts in my hands.

"Thanks for the scars, doc," I snarl. I look at Marisol then back at him. "Do the same hack job on her and I'll put a fucking bullet between your eyes."

"Dino!" Caterina cries. She spins and turns to Doctor Cutrali, who looks completely unruffled. "I'm so sorry, he's just..."

"I know what he is," the doctor waves her off. "I have been treating mafiosos for years, no? All of you bark, some of you bite, but when you're lying on my table, you all beg."

"Not one fucking scar," I snap at him.

He raises one of his bushy white eyebrows. "Maybe you should threaten me less so my hands do not shake as I examine the young lady, yes?"

The thought of him *putting his hands on her...*

"That is enough, Bernadino," Elio says sharply.

Fuck him. He doesn't get to use my fucking name like that. "I fucking mean it," I growl.

"If you threaten my doctor again, Dino, I won't let him stitch you up after what I do to you."

Elio and I glare at each other. I size him up, taking in the stance of his shoulders and the tension in his jaw.

He's gotten a little soft. I know he knows how to fight, but with the babies...

"Dino, I literally will use this stun gun on you without a single heartbeat of hesitation," I hear Gia call from the doorway behind me.

Fuck.

If it's Gia, it's serious.

Slowly, I turn. Sure enough, she has a Taser pointed right at me.

I glare at her, and she smiles. "I'll do it and you know I will," she says cheerfully.

Sal, holding their baby, gives me a nod. "Leave the room, brother."

Fuck.

If your baby brother is telling you to fuck off, it might be time to fuck off.

I storm out, pushing past Gia gently, and avoiding Sal and the baby entirely. I walk down the hall to my bedroom, which isn't so much my space as it is somewhere for me to sleep sometimes.

Once inside, I slam the door and sit down on my bed.

Only then do I put my head in my hands and grit my teeth

against the shame that's swirling through me in a torrent of emotion.

How the fuck did I even get here?

Marisol is... well.

She's a dream.

One that I've had every night for the past five years. One that I've fantasized about, especially after I found out about the twins. The day that I discovered her, and my kids?

Fuck.

I need to take a shower. I'm fucking... I just need to.

Heading in to the attached bathroom, I strip and turn the water on ice cold. I get in, hoping the shockingly icy water will keep me from thinking about her but....

I shut my eyes, remembering it.

---

5 years ago

I found her.

I thought that Marisol, my dream girl, was lost. After I woke up and never saw her again, it seemed like something that was a complete non-starter. She wasn't with me. I didn't know her last name. I didn't know shit.

Until a letter appeared at my doorstep, with a picture of her.

And two kids who look like me.

There's no fucking way it's her. But here I am, in Fort Lauderdale, looking for her.

Because if she is who I think she is?

I'm in a whole fucking mess of trouble.

I'm outside of the shop that they just went into. The person who sent me the letter told me that if I don't pay, they'll come after her. After all three of them.

And they'll make it seem like it was our family who did it.

Marisol's father will wipe my family from the face of the fucking earth if that's the case. He's so much bigger than we are.

And so much worse.

The little bell on the door rings, and I duck, trying to stay out of their way. Sure enough, Marisol and two kids, twin girls, come out. They chat animatedly in Portuguese, and I regret ever failing out of Portuguese in high school.

Fuck.

There's no denying the kids are mine. I grab my phone and type out a number. There's only one person I know I can count on right now.

"Dino?" my brother rumbles.

I suck in a breath.

And I tell Marco four words that I never thought I'd say.

"I need your help..."

A knock on the door jars me from my memories. My eyes snap open and I shut off the water, grabbing a towel and opening the bathroom. I march to the door of my bedroom, wrapping a towel around my waist.

I open it.

It's Sal.

"Brother," he says simply.

I ignore him, turning to rummage through a drawer. I produce a pair of basketball shorts, then step inside the bathroom, tugging them on without any regard for Sal's presence.

When I emerge, I glare at Sal. "The fuck do you want."

"My wife almost tased you."

I nod. "I have a feeling she would do that a lot if she could."

Sal nods. "You're not wrong. But you can't deny that it's kind of warranted."

"The fuck does that mean?"

He sighs heavily, and sits on my bed. "Dino…"

"What?"

"The attitude, man. It's terrible."

I don't reply.

"I got it when you were a kid. Marco isn't… following Marco isn't a fun place to be," Sal says quietly. "But you're grown. It's time to back off. We're a family, you know. Us and the Rossi's. We're on each other's teams."

Yeah. Fucking. Right.

"So my teammates would fucking tase me if they could?"

Sal looks up sharply. "Dino... "

"Elio and Gia might be on your fucking team, Sal," I snarl. With my damaged vocal cords, the words are barely a whisper, and they hurt as they rasp over my throat. "You and Caterina might get along like a house on fucking fire with them. But I'm not you. I have never been one of you," I hiss.

The last word seems to linger in the air.

Sal's eyes drift over my torso and neck. Both he and Marco are built like our grandfather. Big, with big shoulders, muscles that pile up into pretty shapes.

If they're built like an ox, I'm built like a fucking wolf.

I'm faster than they are. Strong, but more wiry. Both Marco and Sal look like linebackers, and I'm more...

Soccer. My body is suited to a different sport entirely.

That's not what he's looking at, though. He's my brother, he's seen me naked more than once. I also know that he's not interested in the tattoos that cover me so thickly, there's barely any skin showing through the dark patterns of ink on my body.

He's looking at the scars.

I turn and snatch a shirt up and tug it over my torso. "Yeah. I know you know what the fuck I'm talking about, Sal," I snap. "Elio is your fucking brother-in-law. Gia is your fucking wife. They're my bosses."

More than that, I'm alive literally because Elio decided not to kill me out of his devotion to Caterina. If he had his way, I'd be buried in the fucking lake, cement brick around my feet, my corpse a vibrant habitat for some fucking fish or shit like that.

No, Elio and Gia do not like me. They have clearly pointed out that I'm alive because they love Caterina and Sal.

And they never once let me forget it.

Sal looks at me, his lips curling into a frown that makes my gut twist. "You could fix that."

"Yeah, fuck off."

"The attitude, Dino..."

"If you don't like my fucking attitude, then fuck you," I bark.

Sal heaves a sigh. The little muscle in his jaw ticks as he stares at me. "Fine. Whatever. Your kids are in the house, man. If they see you like this..."

"They won't," I respond quickly.

I'm not a fucking idiot.

And, they won't see me at all. Marisol kept them hidden from me. She kept them hidden from everyone, and for all I know, they have no fucking clue who their daddy is.

Unless she tells me otherwise, I'm going to keep it that way.

I spent so much time trying to protect Marisol and the twins from afar. Marco went into fucking witness protection to help me.

And now they're here.

In this house.

What the fuck do I do now?

Sal stands up. "I'll let you know when the doctor has a verdict."

"I'll be there."

"I think it's probably best if you stay here, Dino," he says gently.

I grunt. Part of me wants to fight him on it.

Part of me, however, doesn't care.

"Ok. Stay here," Sal says. He shuts the door to my room, and I sit right back down on the bed.

2

MARISOL

Dino De Luca.

Having a photographic memory isn't a bad thing. It's an inconvenience a lot of the time, sure, but in this situation I'm happy that my mother made me memorize the family trees of every single connected family that she could think of.

Because when I find him on the beach, I know exactly who he is.

And the fact that he doesn't know who I am?

It makes me feel...

Sexy.

Mysterious.

Like for once, I'm the one in charge, and I'm running my life.

Instead of the exact opposite.

He's cute.

If he knew that I was Benicio Souza's daughter, he might... I'm not sure. Run? Kidnap me?

I'd welcome the kidnapping, honestly. If I didn't know my dad would burn down the entire world, and everyone in it, to get me back, I'd happily be kidnapped.

I inch closer.

Why is he lying there? Maybe he's drunk.

Maybe he's dead.

I wonder...

If I could pay money to stop dreaming about Dino De Luca, I would. Literally. Any of the painstaking savings that I've stolen from my father, one piece at a time?

I'd do it if I could just not dream about him.

However, I guess that it's kind of a moot point at the moment. Because unfortunately, this time I need him.

I've spent my whole adult life trying to forget Dino De Luca.

And I've spent the past seventy-two hours trying to find him.

My whole body hurts. I blink, my eyes feeling thick and heavy, as I struggle to wake up.

One thought, however, wakes me right up.

The twins.

Angie and Maia. My babies.

"Where are my babies?" I slur.

I'm not even really sure where the question is going. I have no idea where I am. I vaguely remember the sounds of a party, and screaming Dino's name— but after that—I must have passed out.

"They're safe," a familiar voice soothes me. "They're currently stuffing themselves with pizza and trying to keep Luna from eating an entire chocolate cake by herself."

"Luna?" I croak.

"My daughter," a different voice says. While Gia Rossi is all brass and confidence, this voice is softer. Milder.

This must be Caterina.

My eyes are still struggling to focus, but slowly I can see shapes crystalizing into people. It seems like I'm surrounded by so many faces, for a second my brain clicks and whirrs, trying to place all of them.

Then, I do.

Elio Rossi.

Caterina De Luca, now Rossi.

Gia Rossi, who waves at me and smiles.

Sal De Luca, glowering in the back.

And, an old man with a stethoscope.

"This is Doctor Cutrali," Elio says, his voice heavily accented. *Grew up in Italy,* I remember from his file. It's a credit to Gia's language skills that, while she also grew up with Elio in Italy, her accent is as American as apple pie.

It's even better than mine, and I worked hard to make sure no one knows my first language is Portuguese.

I look at the older man. *Doctor Cutrali.* The name clicks with the face, and my memory registers them.

Now, I'll never forget him.

The doctor smiles. "Hello madam." His accent is thick too, and also definitely Italian. I wonder if Elio brought him from home... "I have been the Rossi family doctor since these two were just small babies," he adds.

That explains that. "Thank you," I whisper.

My throat hurts.

I'm sure I know why, but at the moment, I'd rather not remember.

Because I'm sure it's bad.

"You've had quite a hard time, no?" the doctor leans forward. He nods to my stomach. "Luckily, that knife did not go deeper than your skin. You'll have a nasty scar across the rib, but you know sometimes a scar is just a chance to tell a good story."

I bark a small laugh at that. "I don't want to tell that type of story."

"A wise woman, then."

The doctor nods at Elio and stands. "I'll be back tomorrow. She should rest. She may see her children, and I'd like to make sure they are well."

"They are," I say confidently. "They weren't... there's no physical damage."

The mental stress of seeing their grandmother kidnapped, and running from the men who grabbed her in plain sight?

I'm not sure any of us will get over that.

My heart squeezes, but my mom is a tough woman. She's survived Benicio Souza before. She's actually the only one of his many wives and mistresses who is still standing, probably because shortly after having me, she moved us to her parents' horse farm in Florida.

Well, that, and she's a crack shot. She shot my dad in the chest, once.

I think he kind of liked it.

I thought that the twins and I would be safe with her in Fort Lauderdale. He's never tried to take the twins back to Brasilia, and they've lived there since they were about six months old. I lived with them, and he didn't care until recently. He only came for me, two years ago, because he remembered that as of yet, I am unmarried.

I don't want to get married.

I didn't think that he'd look for me at my mom's, but I guess he did. Why he decided to kidnap her is probably going to be a huge problem, but I can only assume she's alive.

I hope she will survive him now.

I shuffle, and the stitches along my ribs twinge. I gasp and Gia shoos Elio out of the way, coming to sit by my side. "That was a nasty cut, girl."

"Yeah," I grunt. "It wasn't really fun for me either."

Her hand slips into mine. "It's good to see you again."

I grin. Gia and I met about a year ago when my father took her hostage too.

Gia doesn't take kindly to being a hostage. Not even a week in my father's compound in Brasilia, and she got us both the hell out of there.

I had no idea that she was Dino's sister-in-law until she told me. Being trapped in my father's house, I'd missed the Rossi-De Luca nuptials.

Not that I would have been invited.

Being a Souza, I don't get invited.

Ever.

Because people would rather invite a starving tiger to a wedding than anyone who shares my father's name.

"What happened?" Gia asks.

I sigh.

I shouldn't tell them. These people owe me nothing, and I'm the daughter of a man who, for some reason or another, has decided that they need to be wiped from the face of the earth.

They deserve to know, though.

"After we left my father's house in Brazil, I went to go live with my mother and the twins in Fort Lauderdale. Father has never once tried to bother with my mother, not when she lives in the United States."

"He's on the top ten?" the question comes from Sal, and it's referencing my father's place on the DEA's most-wanted list.

I nod. "Yes. He still is. He's wanted and will be apprehended on sight should he get caught."

Despite what the movies say, it's still a pretty formidable barrier to enter the States, especially when your face is an arrest-on-sight mandate. My father is, surprisingly, quite risk-averse for being one of the most brutal cartel leaders in South America.

It's never been worth the risk.

"So you thought you'd be safe in Florida," Sal says softly.

Of course I did. "I never would have put my kids at risk, De Luca," I respond.

The room seems to react to that.

I get the impression, pretty immediately, that everyone in this room would do whatever it takes to keep their kids safe.

"And you're here because.... Holy shit," Gia's eyes widen. "He came for you."

"He did. He took my mom. The twins and I made it out, and drove north. We made it to Hoboken before he found us."

"He?"

God, I'm afraid to even say his name. I harden myself. He's not some kind of spirit; I can't summon him by speaking the word three times. "Andrei. My father's... assassin." For lack of a better word.

I guess you could say he's a fixer. He's my father's go-to guy, and he's terrifyingly amazing at what he does. Had he been present that day in Brasilia, I have no doubt that Gia and I would not have escaped.

I think at the time, he was in Morocco, but I can't be sure.

He's like the Terminator.

We barely managed to escape him, but he's the one who gave me the epic knife wound on my stomach.

Elio's face twists. "Andrei Moretti?"

"I see you've heard of him," I say darkly.

"You're lucky to be alive," he responds. Turning, Elio grabs his phone and starts barking orders in Italian.

I hope he's doubling the guard. Tripling it, even.

Not that it will matter. Andrei is absolutely insane. I've seen him walk into a field of government soldiers and come out alive.

Alive, and the only survivor.

"Whatever you're doing, it won't matter," I call to Elio. "He's after one thing."

Gia's face looks pale. "Let me guess... you?"

I nod sharply. "I.. I didn't know where else to go," I say honestly. "I knew that I needed to get the twins to safety, and..."

And I knew, in my heart, that their father would look out for them.

Or, if nothing else, their Zia Gia would.

"They're safe with us," Gia assures me.

I nod. "They will be. He doesn't want them. He only wants me."

Gia's eyes widen. "No, Marisol. You can't..."

"I can," I whisper. "I have to."

Surely she understands that.

"As soon as I can, I'm going to go find him. I'm going to let him take me back to my father. I just... I needed to know that the twins were safe."

The room is dead silent. I shut my eyes. "I'll go as soon as I can."

"Like hell you will," a voice rasps.

My eyes snap open.

In the doorway, there's a familiar shape.

My heart aches, meeting Dino's dark green ones for the first time in almost a decade.

"You're not going anywhere," he snarls.

Heart thumping in my chest, I hold my head up high.

"You don't get to say that," I respond.

"Yes, Marisol. I definitely fucking do."

The room clears out quite quickly after that.

Gia gives Dino a meaningful glare, while cheerfully informing me that she will happily tase him if she needs to. I give her a grateful squeeze before she files out, the rest of the crew behind her.

Dino shuts the door behind them, but I have no doubt that they're hovering in the hallway.

It's weird. Even though Dino is Caterina and Sal's brother, it's almost like they're closer to their respective partners than they are to him.

For a second, I realize that Dino must be...

Incredibly lonely.

I shift, uncomfortable with the realization. I assumed that if he was here, with his people, then he'd be fine.

Welcome, even.

But I don't know that 'welcome' is how I'd describe their relationship with him.

He stares at me.

And I stare back at him.

He looks… different. Obviously, time has passed since we last saw each other. And I know I look different too.

But where time might have softened some of my edges, they've hardened his.

He's wearing a plain white t-shirt and loose shorts, an outfit that I imagine is something he wears when he's at home or relaxing, but it doesn't make him look vulnerable. Quite the opposite, it makes him look…

Well, he looks like he just escaped jail and threw on the first thing he could find.

His face is all angles. There's nothing of the boy that I found on the beach all those years ago.

Even his eyes look different. They've always been such a dark green they look almost black, but now, there's nothing even hinting at the green.

They seem to burn, like something inside of him is on fire.

Beneath the lines of his face, I can see the column of his throat. It's covered in dark ink, but as he steps closer, I can see something else.

There's a long, twisted scar running across his neck.

The kind you only get when someone tries to cut your throat.

Oh, Dino.

I don't know what to say to him. I've imagined this moment a thousand times, but right now, all of my carefully rehearsed speeches seem to be completely pointless.

I have a perfect memory. I thought I remembered exactly who Dino was.

I was totally wrong.

Suddenly, I'm self-conscious. I know that we never really knew each other, but...

I kind of knew him.

He was my first, after all. The first and only man that I've ever had sex with.

My heart cracks a little with the realization that Dino, the sweet young man who treated me so well that night, might be gone forever.

And I have no clue who this one is.

I'm still wondering what to say when he opens his mouth. "You're not going anywhere."

That voice.

Dino had a deep voice before. But now, I can tell that there's been some damage to his vocal cords. His voice is raspy and low, like every word is an effort. It makes chills break out and race over my skin, and it turns my head so that I'm focused on his lips.

There's a scar crossing his mouth as well, and I lick my own lips as I look at it.

What happened to you?

I blink up at him, realizing that I never responded. "So now you're going to hold me hostage too?"

"Yes," he says without hesitation. "I'm absolutely going to do that."

God, there's not an ounce of doubt in his voice. He really will try to keep me here.

I can't let that happen.

I sigh and shake my head. "No, Dino. You can't. It's not safe."

"It's safer than you walking back out there. Safer than putting yourself at your father's mercy. Safer than surrendering to fucking Andrei Moretti," he hisses.

Every word sounds like an effort.

And, with every sentence, he moves a step closer to me until he's hovering at the edge of the hospital bed.

I can hear the small heart monitor next to me start to kick up.

Oh. That's *my* heartbeat.

Dino notices it too. He looks over at the monitor, then back at me.

"Scared, Princess?"

I shake my head. "No."

"I think your heart says otherwise."

"You don't know anything about my heart, Dino De Luca."

"I think we both know more about each other than we let on, Marisol Souza."

My eyes widen, then narrow. "Gia told you."

"Gia didn't need to tell me," he says quietly. "I knew."

"You... what?"

He extends his hands, placing them against the plastic rail of the hospital bed. He leans forward, until his eyes are so close, I can see the slight ring of forest green around his pupils.

Dark green. I knew it.

The color is somehow comforting to me.

I look down at his knuckles, noticing the tattoos. They cover his hands completely, and then run up his arms. It's unclear to me what they are. A tumble of words and images, some whole, some bisected by scars.

How many scars does Dino have?

He shifts again, this time leaning forward. I catch the very top of a large letter M, tucked right at the top of his collarbone, before I look up at him.

"I knew, Marisol. I knew about the twins. I knew about you. And I know for sure that now that I have you? I am never, ever fucking letting you go again."

The words should scare me. This is not my Dino. Not the man I remember.

Instead, however, I bite my lip.

Because I'm not scared of him.

Or, if I am, there's an even bigger truth.

I like being scared of him.

3

DINO

I don't know what I'm doing.

I'm running on pure instinct. And every single one of those instincts, right now, is telling me that I'm an idiot if I let Marisol walk out on me.

So I won't let her.

She's not going anywhere, a fact that is resoundingly clear to me. I don't care if I have to keep her here under lock and fucking key.

I'm not letting Marisol out of my sight again. It isn't a fucking option.

Her brown eyes narrow as she looks at me from Elio's makeshift hospital bed. "Keeping me here puts everyone in danger, Dino."

"I don't give a fuck." I truly don't. If I need to use Elio's army to keep her here, and every last one of them dies protecting her, I don't care.

I'm not letting her go back there.

"If you know about me and the twins, then you know about my father."

Everyone knows about her father.

Benicio Souza is the nightmare that keeps the cartels in line. He's something else entirely, a monster made human.

When I first found out that Marisol was his daughter, I couldn't figure it out. The difference between the two of them seems completely irreconcilable. Where she is kind and thoughtful, and sweet, he's.. not.

He's a hardened killer. His attack dog, Andrei, is brutal and nasty not because it's necessary to fuck people up the way he does, but because Benicio is entertained by it. I'm sure Andrei has a couple of screws loose, but I'm also certain that Benicio loosened them right up.

He's sick.

He also has lots of children, somewhat scattered all over the world. Being Benicio's wife, mistress, or child is one of the most dangerous roles on the face of the planet, as he seems to kill them without a second thought, and quite often.

Marisol, however, is obviously his favorite.

I nod. "I know about your father."

"Then you know that to keep them safe I need to go."

Just like that first night, Marisol is practical.

"No," I say again.

"Dino. You're being ridiculous. You can't keep me here against my will."

"I can."

She starts to sit up in the bed but I put my hands on her shoulders, pushing her back into the bed.

"You will not leave. The children are safe."

She glares up at me, and the unspoken word that I didn't say simmers between us.

Our children.

"You don't know anything, Dino. You have no idea why my father had me in Brasilia for the last two years. Also, do you think that I escaped him just to be trapped by someone else?"

I snarl at her. "I. Don't. Care."

"He's going to marry me off, Dino."

The silence is so loud, you could hear a pin drop.

Marisol.

Marrying.

Someone else.

"He's in debt. Like, a lot of it. Some of his fields were taken over in a government coup, and he can't persuade the new president for anything to give them back. All of it was confiscated. Thousands of tons of product. He can't make his payments, his shipments are all empty, and every day that he doesn't have it, is another day that he continues to lose money. He's desperate. I've never seen him like this before. He's auctioning me off to the highest bidder, essentially, and I'm the only leverage he has."

Her words cut through the ringing in my ears. I hear them, but I'm still not certain that I understand.

Marisol looks up at me, her brown eyes wide. "Please, Dino. He doesn't care about his grandchildren. He'll do anything to get me back. He has my mother, and I think if I don't go back to him, something awful is going to happen to her. If it hasn't already," her voice drops to a whisper.

My blood feels like it's roaring so loud, I can barely hear her.

"I have to. Or he's going to hurt these people, and I can't let him hurt the people I love. I can't let him hurt Gia and Elio and Sal and Caterina, not when they were so nice and helped me. Not when Gia helped me escape him that first time," she whispers.

I notice that I'm not on the list of people she cares about. It should sting.

But it doesn't.

"You and your goddamn sense of integrity," I growl. When she found me on the beach and told me she can't call herself a kind person if she doesn't act in a kind way, I thought it was cute. A little idealistic, but cute.

Now, it's just annoying.

"It's not integrity. It's common decency. I can't sacrifice people I care about to save myself. Plus," she adds, looking down. "It's pointless. He's going to come for me one way or another. I might as well make it a little less damaging when he does."

Fuck that.

I grunt and push back. She stares at me, wide-eyed, her chest rising and falling as her nostrils flare.

"Don't move," I grunt.

With that, I walk out and slam the door behind me.

I storm upstairs. Gia and Caterina are sitting at the kitchen table. Judging by the amount of food and the silence, they managed to cut the party short. There's no longer a crowd of people floating around, and while I have no idea where the kids are, I assume they've put everyone either to bed or locked them up as well.

I can't talk to the twins yet.

I...

I don't even know if they know I'm their father.

The thought makes my stomach twist with anxiety. Instead of uncovering why I feel so sick at the thought of meeting my own children, I square my feet and look at the women sitting at the kitchen table

"Where's Elio?" I bark.

Gia frowns at me. "He's at the front gate, checking on the guards..."

The rest of the sentence doesn't matter to me. I turn and spin, marching down toward the gate house.

The air is warm, unseasonably so, but that's fine with me. It echoes the heat I feel from the hatred in my heart.

Marisol can't marry someone else.

It's been years. I never really thought that there was a future for us, sure, but she never so much as looked at another man. When I rediscovered her a few years ago, I was so fucking happy that she didn't have a boyfriend or a husband.

I've been watching her ever since.

She hasn't so much as gone on a date. Hell, I don't think she's even glanced at another man.

So for her to get married?

It's not fucking happening.

She can't marry you, idiot.

The thought nearly stops me in my tracks.

I'm not good enough for Marisol. I know that, beyond a shadow of a doubt.

But at the very least, I can make sure she doesn't marry anyone else.

The gate house is full of people. I step inside, quietly filing in behind Sal.

Elio's speaking.

"There are round-the-clock patrols. Do not let a single person enter this area who is not approved. No one goes in or out," he says to the crowd. "We are on total lockdown. Nobody will come into this place of ours without our knowledge, and no one will leave. Do not underestimate the threat before us. Andrei Moretti has been trained as an assassin since he had his feet beneath him as a baby. Benicio Souza... I do not need to tell you what a threat he is," Elio says calmly to the gathered crowd. "He will stop at nothing to get what he wants. Until Marisol can leave, and feels able to, we will ensure that our family, our people, and our organization remain safe. This is not our battle," he says to the crowd.

Anger flares in me. Not our battle?

Marisol is mine. The twins are mine.

Here again, the difference between us stands. When it is Elio's family at risk, it's all hands on deck.

But when it's mine?

Not our battle.

I feel Sal shuffle next to me, and I want to turn and slam my displeasure into his face. However, he merely nods, agreeing with Elio's words.

As he always has.

Elio finishes giving his orders.

The gathered soldiers nod before filing out.

After a moment, Elio gestures to Sal and me. "Come. Let us see if there are any weaknesses in the fence."

Walking the fence seems like a weird way to spend the time, especially considering that Elio likely wants to be inside checking on his family, but I follow all the same.

Outside of the iron fence that guards Elio's home, the New York forest is oddly quiet. The air is still, almost like there's nothing moving in the woods, and even the normal noises you'd expect, like bugs or frogs, are muted. I don't hear anything except the crunch of gravel under our shoes as we walk the path that goes around the perimeter of Elio's compound. We make it the whole way around and back to the gravel road when Sal finally speaks.

"You can't keep her here," Sal says quietly.

I stop. "You don't get to fucking tell me what to do."

"It's not safe."

"She's not safe out there."

"Souza wants her," Elio says calmly. "He's her father. She knows him best. Perhaps we...."

He pauses.

There's a shape walking up the road.

The three of us react. I reach for the knife in my belt. Sal shines a flashlight on the person.

And Elio sprints for them.

The split second before Elio flies in, arm poised to punch the stranger in the face, is when I realize who it is.

"Marco?"

4

MARISOL

After Dino leaves, it's blissfully quiet.

Well, I guess that it's certainly quiet. The blissful part is up for debate. Because while I'm happy that he's gone, my heart feels like it's aching with all of the thoughts swirling around.

Seeing Dino again is shocking in ways I hadn't anticipated. I feel like a snow globe. I had years to settle my emotions around him, years to let them drift down and sit at my feet where I would never have to see them again. I could ignore all of those feelings there, where I didn't have to examine them in the light of day.

But now?

My whole world has been shaken up, and all I can do is examine the fallout.

Dios Mio, he's so handsome.

All of the scars make me itch to follow them with my fingers. I want to map out the new terrain on his skin, ask him how each one came to be. They show me a brutality that I hadn't considered in him before, which makes the memory of our night together, and the tenderness that he showed me, even more fascinating.

A chill skates over my skin. Is Dino even capable of such thoughtful, emotional connection again?

Why do I want to find out so badly?

I can't think like this.

I take a deep, shuddering breath as despair grips my stomach. What Dino is or is not going to do is not any of my concern. My kids are safe. They're here, and they're out of the clutches of my dad. Without me here as the prize, he might think twice about coming to raid the somewhat well-fortified Rossi home.

He's never cared about my kids, something that irks me to no end, but is absolutely par for the course with him. I'm well aware of the fact that out of the dozens of bastards he's sired over the world, he seems to be somewhat obsessed with me.

Somehow, however, that obsession does not extend to my children.

Their safety is my priority. And right now? They're safe, which takes that off the list of problems.

Much as I would like to spend time just thinking about Dino, I have to face the problems in front of me.

When you're Benicio Souza's daughter, you learn very quickly that you can't spend too much time perseverating on what might be or what could be.

For one, things change quickly. It might not even matter to spend all your time making plans for one thing, when something else entirely could pop up.

Which, of course, leads me to my next point, which is that being Benicio Souza's daughter means learning how to deal with complete and utter chaos.

I need to figure out how to get back to him. Before he hurts my mom, and before he comes after the Rossi clan.

Gently, I unhook myself from the IV, taking care to extract it from my vein. I've had training in how to do this, again, as a side effect of the father who brought me into this stupid life.

I'm in what looks like a regular guest room, except that it has a high-end hospital bed in it. The bed, and surrounding medical equipment, are clearly top of the line.

I shake my head. "Mafia families are just built differently," I mutter.

There is, however, an attached bathroom and shower. While I have no doubts whatsoever that someone in the house has a key that will open this room, I lock both the bedroom and bathroom doors. I shower, fully prepared to put on my old clothes, when I notice a little free-standing drawer set in the bathroom. I open it and find it fully stocked with light, airy clothes, most of them somewhat close to my size.

I have a feeling I have Gia Rossi to thank for this one.

Showered, freshly clothed, and feeling better than I have in days, I creep out of the room. The house is pretty quiet; you can hear the distant murmur of voices, but nothing specific.

I want to find the kids, tell them goodbye, and then I can go.

I pad upstairs. I have no memories of the house whatsoever, being that I was passed out when I was last taken this way, and it's a huge house.

Part of me just feels... bad. Like, looking around, these are glimpses of what I could be offering my children. A large house, a stable family, lots of cousins to grow up around...

Instead, I have given them a relatively stable childhood in Florida. I won't say it was terrible for them, because it wasn't.

But that little bit of guilt still punches into me at what I could be doing for them instead.

Eventually, I do hear the sound of voices. It sounds like they're coming from the hallway to my left, so I softly follow. Eventually, the hall opens up into an open space, a combined kitchen and living room, that's brightly lit. Windows, from ceiling to floor, let in an amount of light that's impressive given that we're in upstate New York, and the furniture is an easy, light color that's homey despite being expensive looking.

This is where the voices are coming from.

And, I recognize two of them.

I step into the room, watching for just a minute.

There are three babies, playing together on a tasteful looking blanket in front of a couch. Two of them look to be about a year old, and they're twins, a boy and a girl. A third, slightly younger baby babbles at them, and they all seem to be managing an interaction, common among familiar babies.

Then, there are three children. Three girls.

Two of whom are mine.

"Luna," Maia says, always the bossy one. She puts her hands on her hips, looking at a dark-haired little girl. "It's your turn to be the dragon."

"I was the dragon last time," Luna whines.

"I can be the dragon," Angie, my other girl, says, trying to mitigate the attitude of her twin.

I smile. The girls continue to argue, but it looks like they're figuring it out. Eventually, they settle, and Maia surprisingly zooms around, arms outstretched, roaring while she pretends to be the dragon.

This is exactly what I was envisioning when I thought of my girls having cousins. They have friends, of course, but Mama and I are very cautious when it comes to their playmates. We often wished that they would have cousins to play with, because the power of your primas?

It's better than just a friend, that's for sure.

"Looks like you're feeling better," I hear Gia say softly.

I turn to the right, where she and Caterina are sitting at the kitchen table. They can easily see all the kids, and the babies as well, but they're definitely giving them some space to play.

I really wish I'd had that as a younger mom.

"Come sit with us," Caterina says, waving to a chair. "Do you drink? I could get some wine."

"One glass, please," I say with a little smile. Both Caterina and Gia have been nothing but wonderful to me, but their treatment of my children, who are so engrossed in their play they haven't noticed me yet, is what makes me trust them instantly.

Hearing my voice, my girls instantly stop. "Mamá!" Angie says with a shriek.

Seconds later, both girls are in my arms, and I hug them close. "Oh, pequeninas," I smile. I breathe them in, holding on as they hold me tight. "How are you?"

"Zia Gia and Zia Caterina said you were sleeping because running away from the scary people made you sick," Angie pulls back, looking at me with an accusing eye. "Are you better now?"

"I'm much better, thanks to your Zias. They did a lot to help me."

"Whose clothes are you wearing?" Maia says with a frown.

"I got her some extras, since everyone deserves to wake up looking fabulous," Gia laughs.

Maia, who is far more fierce than her sister, seems to accept this. ", do we have to leave?"

My heart sinks a little. I'm not sure how to tell her that she's going to stay here without me.

I don't want to tell them yet.

Seeming to sense my hesitation, Caterina steps in. "Girls," she says, her voice full of kindness, "why don't you grab the babies and bring them over here? We probably need to feed them."

Maia's eyes get big. "Like, hold them?"

"I can do it!" Angie hops up, and together with Luna, they carefully lift each baby before bringing them over.

Caterina nods at me, holding one of the two twins out. "Can you hold him?"

"Yes," I say, accepting the wiggling baby boy.

Task accomplished, Maia and Angie look lost again. "Come on," Luna announces. "Let's go play dress up. Dad just bought me a new castle!"

"A castle?" and with that, the girls are gone.

Caterina sighs. "I had no idea he bought them that. Did you?" she looks at Gia.

Gia shrugs. "I know better than to stop Elio when he wants to buy Luna something."

The baby in my arms makes a garbled noise, and I look down. "Okay," I say, looking back up. "Now it's time to tell me whose baby I'm holding."

Both Gia and Caterina laugh. "These are my two," Caterina says, indicating the twins, "and that one belongs to Gia."

I smile at her. "Ah, I see. The baby you brought with us on your wild escape."

Caterina gives her a questioning look, and Gia sighs. "Marisol took one look at me and could tell I was pregnant when her dad kidnapped me."

"That's pretty good," Caterina grins.

I shrug. "Well. I guess I was also pregnant with De Luca babies at some point. Maybe I just sensed it."

Catarina laughs. "That makes three of us. Luna's mine too," she says by way of explanation.

"Someone needs to study how many twins we have in this family," Gia says, her eyes rolling. "It seems like slightly more than normal."

"Is anything normal about being with a De Luca or a Rossi?"

Caterina's comment makes Gia smile. "Fair point."

I nod. "Well. Sounds like we all need to stick together, then," I smile.

Caterina reaches a hand out and takes mine. "I grew up with three brothers. I can't tell you how happy it makes me to have another sister-in-law."

"Oh, I can't... um..." I pause.

Gia and Caterina look at me expectantly.

I sigh. "It's more complicated than that."

"How so?" Caterina tilts her head to the side.

Heat floods my cheeks. "Um... Well... Dino... Dino and I..."

"We know they're your kids. The two of you. You don't have to hide that," Gia says softly.

I take a breath. Of course. "Well, I guess I should share the story." Or at least some of it.

It's a little embarrassing. That's the only reason that I don't like to share it.

"My dad... well. You should know that my dad has a lot of connections. And a lot of children. For some reason he's very obsessed with me, and one of my half-brothers. But, back then, he was trying to get the favor of... someone he needed to have the favor of in order to do this like, business deal. He wanted to use me as part of that. I was supposed to go to Spring Break with this girl who had just gone through a breakup, as a favor to her father, and I was supposed to show her a good time."

"Why you?"

I snorted. "I grew up in Florida with my mom. My dad would actually come visit and be kind of cool. Like, he would bring presents and stuff and he and my mom would kind of get along until she would kick him out again, or he would disappear. So I knew Florida, and he thought I could show this other girl around."

"Why your mom?" Gia asks.

I shrug. "I don't know. He's killed most of his other lovers. I think he was a tiny bit afraid of my mom. She shot him with a shotgun, once."

"Oh my god, I love her," Caterina gushes.

The ghost of a smile crosses my lips. "Yeah. She's pretty great. Anyway, this friend immediately ditched me so I just kind of hung out and I found Dino on the beach."

"What do you mean, you found him?" Gia asks.

"Exactly what it sounds like. I literally found him. He was piss drunk and basically half alive."

They exchange a look. "Sounds like a teenage Dino, to be honest," Caterina sighs.

I blink at her. "What?"

"Dino… he's always had kind of a chip on his shoulder. For a long time I thought it was like a second son thing, but lately…" her voice trails off.

It doesn't look like she wants to say anything else, so I let it go.

"Dino and I met. I liked him. And I just… I felt so dumb because all these other girls were like, living their Spring Break dreams, and I was just… there," I mutter.

Both Caterina and Gia are quiet. "So we had sex," I add softly.

"He didn't…"

"No," I cut Gia off. "It was my idea. I wanted to feel… sexy. Cute. Powerful. I'd never had sex with anyone before and I was like eighteen and I just... I thought it was a time in my cycle that was safe," I shrug.

Caterina sighs. "I know how that goes."

"So. Anyway, I walked away and never talked to him again. Didn't have his number, didn't have anything. Found out I was pregnant, my mom and I raised the babies, and now..."

"Wait. Why were you in Brasilia?" Gia asks.

I shut my eyes. This is the part I hadn't really wanted to talk about. "Well. I have to go back."

"No!" both women practically shout, startling the babies.

I nod. "Yeah. I do. My dad... he's not going to stop coming for me. He needs me. He's broke and he's offering me up to be married."

"And what? People have to pay?" Gia snarls.

I shrug. "Yeah? I guess."

"Marisol, you don't have to do that," Caterina says softly. "What about the girls?"

Tears tug at my eyes. "You'll help them get to know Dino, right?"

"Marisol..."

There's a loud bang from the front door. "Gia!" we hear Elio yell.

Gia sighs and hands me her son. "Coming!" she yells.

I turn back to Caterina. "Promise me you'll take care of them. Promise you'll help Dino get adjusted to being a dad."

"You don't have to go back," she whispers. "We can help you. Keep you safe."

"You won't," I say softly. "Maybe someday after, maybe my future husband will be less... aggressive than my father. I will have to wait to see, but until then, I can't. It's safer for the girls to be here, with their... with their father," I end on a whisper.

God, this hurts so much.

"I'm sorry. I'll try to write, try to send them money for their care. I'll do my best but I just don't know how to do this otherwise."

"Marisol, we can protect you."

I shake my head. "No. You have babies, Caterina. The Rossi's are great, you're a big family, but you're not on the same level as my dad. Benicio Souza is a monster," my voice is shaking now with conviction. "He's a vile, awful man. He won't stop until he has what he wants, and what he wants is me."

"Marisol..."

I stand, putting the baby I've been holding into a high chair. "Promise me you'll help him. When I get my mom back, when she goes back to Florida, you can send the twins there. He has no interest in the girls, for whatever reason. It's always only me," I say bitterly.

Caterina's eyes are wide. "How will we know?"

"My mom will contact you. She's the woman who shot Benicio Souza in the chest with a shotgun. She'll figure it out," I give her a small smile.

Caterina studies me for another minute before finally, she nods. "Okay," she murmurs. "But if you ever need help, if you need anything, we're here. I won't let one of my sisters suffer."

"I'm not…"

She waves her hand, interrupting me. "You are, Marisol. You're one of us now. I understand that you know what you're doing, and that you want to keep us safe. I appreciate that," she says, looking at the babies snoozing in her arms and in the high chair. "But you have to know that we protect our own. You're one of us now. Let us help," she murmurs.

I wish I could.

"I'm going to tell the girls. The plan is that they'll be here with their dad until their avó can come get them," I add, making sure she knows the Portuguese word for grandmother.

The girls will know it, so it's good to be consistent.

Caterina nods. Tears gather in the corners of her eyes, but I shake my head. "Trust me," I whisper. "It's better this way."

However, I don't know who needs to hear that more. Caterina…

Or me.

5

DINO

Elio takes all of us down to his basement offices.

Marco included.

I still can't believe that Marco is here. How the fuck did he get out of Ireland?

And, does this mean that the protection he got for the girls and me in exchange for being in witness protection is done?

That, more than anything, makes me restless. Despite the fact that they all seem to think they have a better grasp on the situation, better than Sal or Caterina, I know Marco. I've lived with him as my barely-older brother for my entire life.

I know that Marco is significantly colder, more calculating, and less trustworthy than anyone thinks he is.

So if he's here, with us...

Something changed.

In the office, there's silence, until Elio looks over at Marco. "Well?"

"What, Elio," Marco says, his lips pulling into a frown.

"What the hell do you have to say for yourself?"

Marco looks up, a glimmer of defiance in his brown eyes. "Absolutely nothing."

"You've been missing for long enough that you have new nieces and nephews that you know nothing of," Elio snarls. "And yet here you sit, in front of me. Not dead. Not even a fucking scratch on you."

I look over at Sal, who is starring as passively as he can forward.

Clearly, Sal didn't tell Elio everything about his time in Ireland.

Good.

Now I can use this against Sal, if I need to.

Having some ammunition against my brother feels good. I don't know if I'll need it, but if I do...

I'll use it.

"I had my reasons," Marco says stiffly.

"Your reasons? To abandon your family? To let us think that you were dead?"

Elio's accent is so thick you can barely tell he's speaking English. He's about two seconds from disappearing into a cloud of Italian curses and murder threats... at best.

The scar on my neck, and the one across my stomach, itch.

I remember what Elio is capable of when he's in that kind of a mood.

"I don't ask you how you run your family, Elio," Marco says cooly. "However, from where I stand, it seems like you, at some point, decided to maul my brother and kidnap my baby sister to get revenge on me for something I did not do."

Sal's trying extremely hard, but I can see a twitch in his eye.

I don't give a fuck. This is great.

Elio growls. "She was, and is, my wife."

"And that makes it better?"

Elio releases a string of curses and jumps forward, but Sal catches him. I give Sal a look. "Let him go."

"No, he's not... in his right mind."

"That's why you should let him go. I'll go pop the popcorn and we can watch our very own cage match," I say.

I can't help it that I'm somewhat gleeful. Watching Elio and Marco tear each other to pieces would be fucking fantastic.

Except, I think I do need at least one of them in order to make sure Marisol doesn't get back to her father.

Unfortunately, I'm not the head of an organization like Elio or Marco. We've been running the De Luca Shipping business, and its associated criminal shit, as part of the Rossi Imports for a while now.

If Marco's decided to show up and fucking run it again, that means that he and Elio are going to have to figure some shit out.

Fast.

Elio and Marco stare at each other. Marco looks away first, turning to look at me. "I heard."

I blink. "How the fuck did you hear?" and, more importantly, *what* the fuck did you hear.

"It's not important."

"If someone does not tell me what the actual fuck is going on I will shoot the both of you," Elio growls.

Sal looks like he's sweating bullets.

Fine, little brother. I'll cover for you.

I glance at Elio. "Marco knew about Marisol and the girls."

Elio does his best to not look surprised. "He knew... what?"

"He knew that they existed. I told him, after I found them, and asked for his help."

"Help with what, Dino," Elio says.

My throat itches again. I rub at it before I continue. "He helped to make sure they were protected from Marisol's father."

"So for how long..."

"A few years," I interrupt.

I don't want Elio to know more than we're giving him. At this point, it doesn't fucking matter.

Marco shifts. "I heard that Benicio Souza's daughter is eligible. That he's going to host a series of trials, and whoever wins them will have access to his daughter."

Series of trials? I shift. "Marisol said that he's flat broke. Motherfucker needs cash, fast."

"It appears, Dino, that he might be broke, but some part of him still wants to use this to his advantage. It's assumed that, since Marisol is quite clearly his favorite child, anyone who marries her will be heir to the entire cartel, all its holdings, and its extensive network." Marco's eyebrows lift. "I also believe that while you know there are some significant financial issues within the organization, that is hardly common knowledge. Word on the street is that the cartel is doing as well as it ever has, meaning the man who achieves this goal of marrying Souza's daughter will also become insanely rich."

The silence thunders around my ears.

"Every fucking cutthroat in the world is going to try and win," I eventually manage to grit out.

That means Marisol is going to get married to someone who is...

Fucking brutal.

The idea of her getting married was bad enough. The idea of her getting married to someone who's enough of a killer that Benicio Souza approves of them?

I feel like I'm melting from the inside. My rage feels nuclear, and it bubbles against my chest, eating at my bones.

Benicio Souza is fucking dead.

Anyone who touches Marisol is going to be *fucking dead.*

"She can't go back," I snarl. The words are so raspy they're hardly legible, and I see a flicker of something cross Marco's face. "She can't fucking go back there. I'll keep her here. I'll fucking lock her in this motherfucking house..."

"This house?" Elio says.

His words glimmer with darkness.

"This is not your house, Dino," He adds.

I turn on him. "I don't give a fuck. I will take her and run. We'll go anywhere that they can't find her."

"There is nowhere that Andrei Moretti cannot find her," Marco says evenly. "You're welcome to attempt to use the house in the city…"

The fucking house in New York that our grandparents lived in?

No fucking way.

It can't be secured. On one of the busiest streets in Brooklyn. Under an overpass that someone could literally drop a bomb from and no one would know.

"And what about your children?" Elio says quietly. "Would you separate them from their mother in perpetuity?"

"She'll be alive," I bark. "If she's with one of those motherfuckers…"

"Marisol is smart, and she's walked out of basically her entire life with him alive," Sal adds.

Sal's words drive a knife through my heart.

I spin, my hands raised. He manages to stop me right before I smash my knuckles into his eye. "Shut the fuck up, traitor," I hiss. "I'll fucking…"

"Touch my husband again and I'll shoot," Gia's voice echoes calmly through the room.

It's followed by the sound of a safety clicking off, and that's the only reason I back off.

Chest heaving, I stare at my brother.

Sal's face is impassive. His hands, though, are clenched into tight fists at his sides.

"Back off, Dino," Gia snaps.

I don't, but I don't go after Sal again either.

"All of you need to stop. Marisol's gone," Gia says.

My mind screeches to a halt.

I spin. "What the fuck?"

"I will shoot you, Dino, if you don't calm the fuck down," Gia says softly. "Try that fucking sentence again."

My chest wheezes, the air barely making it through the tightness in my throat. "What. Did. You. Say," I grunt.

"Marisol's gone," she repeats.

My eyes narrow.

"What did you do?"

After another thirty minutes of conversation and a look at the security footage, I'm still convinced Gia did something.

Sal can tell.

He rolls the footage back. "Look, Dino. You have to look."

I don't want to look, so I stare into the corner.

Sal sighs, and I flick my attention back to the screen. He points to it. "Brother, she came in and talked to the girls," the camera cuts to a new angle of the hallways. "She walked down here," he points, "and then here," the camera cuts again, to the outside. "She walked there."

Meaning, down the driveway.

To where a man wearing all black stands at the end.

I narrow my eyes and glare at Elio. "Your guys didn't get that one?"

"Some of them are dead. Some of them do not remember," Elio mutters.

I can see that he's clenching his jaw.

Moretti must have done a number on them.

Fucking useless. That's what they are.

The thought of her with that motherfucker...

"She asked us to take care of the girls," Gia says softly.

My head whips around. "The fuck are you talking about?"

"Before she left. Marisol asked us to watch the girls. I think her plan is to let herself go back to Benicio, and then in exchange, he's supposed to release her mother, the girls' grandmother. Once the grandmother is safely back in Florida, Marisol wants the girls to go live with her."

Rage darkens my tone. "They wouldn't live with their fucking father?"

Gia's face hardens. "They don't know that they have a father, Dino."

Something inside of me cracks. "They know about me."

"Marisol didn't tell them that you're they're father."

My mouth opens.

Shuts.

It feels like my chest is being ripped open again by one of Elio's knives.

How could they not know about me?

Is Marisol ashamed that we...

"I have to give it to her. It's a tough choice she made, but it's the right one," Sal says near Gia's shoulder. "She knows exactly what she's working with, and she knows how to protect the girls."

The girls.

Who don't know that I'm their father.

"I want to see them," I say abruptly, looking at Marco.

He frowns. "Dino, I don't think that's a good idea."

"I don't give a fuck what you think. They're my girls. My daughters. My children," I snarl at him. "I want to fucking see them."

"Dino..."

"Elio. You didn't know about Luna. You know exactly what the fuck I'm going through right now," I say. I give him a meaningful stare, hoping that he'll fucking get with the program.

That he'll know what I'm asking, because I'm not going to beg him.

This is the closest to begging that I'll ever come.

"It seems that you did know about your children, Dino. You simply did not attend to your duties once you did."

I'll fucking kill him.

I throw myself at Elio, only aware that I can't punch his smug fucking face because there are two sets of arms holding me back after some of the rage fades from me.

"Get him out of here," Elio snarls.

I throw off Marco and Sal. "Fuck you," I bark.

If they don't want to help me get Marisol…

I'll fucking do it myself.

I'm heading up to go get Marisol back from Moretti when I hear the sound of children's voices.

I pause.

Slowly, I creep to one of the open doors in the long hallway. Inside, I can hear them.

Three little girls. Luna, my niece.

And my daughters.

"I didn't know Elio was my dad," Luna says casually. "But he was gone for a really long time and then he came back for me."

There's an awkward silence.

My heart gets that stabbing, aching feeling again.

"Our mom says we don't have a dad," one of my girls whispers.

I shut my eyes. *Fuck me.*

"But she said we have a guardian angel."

Opening them again, I frown.

"Yeah, she says that he's like super strong. That he looks like us, and has dark hair and dark green eyes."

"Your mom has brown hair and brown eyes," Luna points out.

"Well she says we look like the angel. His name is Dino De Luca. And that if we're ever in trouble we just need to find him and he'll help us."

"Will he help you find your mom?"

There's that silence again. "I think so," one of the girls says.

"Yeah definitely. We just need to figure out how to find him!" the other one responds.

Quickly, I step away and walk to the front door. My hand on the handle, I pause.

That aching, stabbing feeling is... a little better.

Marisol did tell them about me.

She didn't tell them that I was their father.

She said we have a guardian angel.

Fuck.

I drop my hand from the doorknob. I pace, backwards, then toward the door again.

Fuck, fuck, fuck.

"Going somewhere?"

Marco's voice makes the hair on the back of my neck stand up. I turn and glare at him. "The fuck do you care."

His eyes flash. "I think at this point it's probably pretty

evident that if anyone cares about you and your fucking terrible attitude, it's me."

"I didn't ask you for that—"

"You did," he cuts me off. "Remember? The day you found out about the twins."

I stare at him.

Marco glares back, then sighs. He runs a hand through his hair, and for the first time I notice that my older brother looks...

Tired.

"I've been keeping your secrets for longer than you know, Dino."

I tilt my head. "The fuck does that mean?"

"Nothing. Someday everything will be clear. I think. But for now, you want to get your girl back?"

I nod.

Marco looks me up and down. He sighs.

"This is going to fucking suck."

6

DINO

Sal, Elio, Marco and I are sitting at the kitchen table. Caterina, having put the kids to bed, and Gia, who sits back with a taser like she's some kind of sheriff, are lurking nearby.

Caterina refuses to speak to Marco. Ever since he showed his face, she's absolutely refused to look at him, or talk to him. It's clearly bothering Marco, and I heartily approve.

Good job, little sister. Don't let him off easy.

I would be just fucking fine if I never talked to Marco again. Caterina, clearly, feels the same way. However, Marco has decided that this particular issue is of interest to all of us.

So, here we all fucking are.

Marco leans forward, putting his hands on the table. The gesture is so reminiscent of our dad that my eyes slide to the side.

I see Sal looking back at me, and I know he's thinking the same thing.

If I'm going to experience Marco's bullshit, at least it's nice to have someone who knows what I'm going through.

Marco shifts, clearing his throat like he's a king about to announce something. "Obviously I've been gone," Marco starts.

I snort.

I can't fucking hold it in. Marco saying that he's been 'gone' is like saying a hurricane is a rainstorm. He vanished, completely and totally, and left us all in varying states of discomfort because of it.

I at least knew why, but it took a while to find him.

Annoying prick.

"If gone is what you wanna fucking call it," I mutter under my breath.

Marco gives me a glance but doesn't address the statement.

Somehow, that makes it even worse. I'd rather have him rage at me than just.... Sit there.

I drum my fingers against my arm. I'm not about to say where Marco's been, and add even more chaos to this fire.

Since he's supposedly been doing it to save my ass.

Marco shuffles, his hands resting gently on the table. "A while back, Dino came to me and told me that he had children with Marisol Souza."

The room, which was already quiet, suddenly drops into dead silence.

My rage feels like it's choking me. It tugs at my throat, and it's all I can do to not hurl myself across the table and grab Marco by the throat.

How dare he fucking tell my business like this?

"Relax," Caterina whispers to my ear. "If he's doing this without a good reason, I'm going to scream at him."

My anger diminishes slightly, with gratitude for my sister filling some of the space.

She brushes against me, offering me more comfort and I let her.

Marco levels Caterina and I with a stare.

I refuse to cower in front of him, and from Caterina's stiffening next to me, I can tell she feels the same way.

He looks away. "Given that Benicio Souza is who he is, I approached the situation with the utmost care. In exchange for international police protection for Marisol and her children, I offered to become a witness for Interpol against the Irish."

You can practically hear Elio's brain start to melt.

A string of curses in Italian flows out of him so quickly, even I am kind of impressed. Caterina drifts over to him, patting him gently on the hand. It doesn't really seem to help.

The whole scene would be kind of comical, if I wasn't also certain that Elio is already plotting a thousand ways to have Marco killed quickly after he's done.

I exchange a look with Caterina, who is still saying soothing things to Elio, and gently rubbing his arm. Elio's redder than a tomato, so I'm not entirely certain it's working. The room is dead silent except for his breath, which is sawing in and out of his lungs, making him sound like a bull.

I guess I'll defend Marco, if Elio tries to throttle him. But I think Sal would probably, like a traitor, back Elio up. I'm going through the mental calculations of whether I could beat Sal and Elio together when Elio finally murmurs something to Caterina, and shakes his head. He takes one more deep, wheezing breath.

Finally, he looks up at Marco. "So why the fuck are you here then? Here to find more of our secrets so you can sell them?"

Marco's eyebrows shoot up. "I heard that my nieces were on the run from their ruthless grandfather, who sent his best and most terrifying assassin after them. There are also some..." his voice trails off, and he glances to the side. "Complications with the bargain," he finishes.

I narrow my eyes. "Complications?"

"There are other actors at play, and Interpol is not immune to the influence from dirty cops," he says darkly.

A fissure of concern races down my spine. "Are the girls in danger?" I growl.

"Not if they're here," Elio rumbles.

I settle slightly at that. I know that Elio wouldn't let anything happen to his family, so mine being here puts at least a little umbrella of protection over them.

Until it doesn't.

I squint at him. He better fucking mean it.

Or there's going to be hell to pay.

"Benicio Souza has never taken an interest in his grandchildren, for whatever reason. Marisol, however, is clearly his favorite daughter, and favorite child among the horde of bastards that he's sired over the years," Marco continues. "So, when he announced that he's ready to marry off his favorite child, you can imagine the impact on the international community."

My insides feel like they're seizing up. "Marisol isn't going to marry anyone," I growl at him. "She's fucking *mine.*"

"Except she very much is not," Marco responds. "And while she's here…"

"She's gone," Gia interrupts. We all shuffle to look at her. "She's gone," Gia announces again and I think she's repeating it for my sake, my jaw works, my chest tightens, fuck! "Left a while ago."

"Do we know if Moretti found her?" Marco asks.

I growl again at the thought of that psycho coming close to my Marisol.

"One can assume. Moretti isn't exactly easy to find unless he wants to be found. And," Gia adds softly, "Marisol was highly motivated to leave."

I feel the weight of everyone's stares as they turn to look at me.

I bristle. "I don't fucking care," I bark. "She's mine. She doesn't belong to him, or to them—"

"She doesn't belong to anyone, Dino," Marco cuts me off. "But she does get to choose the future that she wants."

I narrow my eyes. "She would never choose him." She would never choose anyone other than me.

"I think she made that choice already," Caterina says softly.

Caterina looks at me with so much sadness, I feel the truth of her statement echo into my bones.

Gone.

It's too fucking hot in this room. I can't fucking breathe. I can't...

I can't lose her to someone else.

Not again.

Gone.

I turn and grab the door handle, ripping it open. I don't give a fuck that it bounces off of the wall as I fling it open and I storm into the hall.

I keep going until I make it out to the garden. To the front gate.

Then, I pause.

It's dark. The woods around Elio's estate are silent.

The night is so quiet, it feels like it's suffocating me.

I open my mouth and I yell as loud as I can with my damaged vocal cords.

It's a primal, feral sound. All of my rage, all of my anger, it's all there, echoing out and ripping the silence of the night apart.

I don't give a fuck that Elio's security guards hear. I hope they do.

I hope the whole fucking world finally hears me for once.

When I'm done, my chest heaves and I stare down the driveway. I'm not sure exactly what I'm waiting for.

Because it's not Marisol. Marisol, who walked away. Marisol, who left me.

Again.

"Well, I hope that felt good," I hear Marco say from behind me.

I spin. "The fuck do you want?" I spit at him.

He stares at me, his eyes glimmering in the dark. My own anger, diffused by my random scream, seems to claw at me again.

It's hard for me to look at Marco without becoming angry, if I'm being honest.

Dad always took much more time to spend with Marco than me. Hell, even Caterina and Sal got more attention from our sperm donor than I had.

Mom was a different story. But still, seeing Marco glare at me in the darkness...

He's much more of a father figure to me.

And he looks so much like our actual father, broadcasting that same disappointment in me with every fucking muscle in his body, that I just want to wipe the expression off of his face.

Right as I'm about to scream at him, however, Marco's face shifts slightly. He sighs.

"You're going to go after her, aren't you?"

I nod.

Marco's face takes on an expression that I don't necessarily recognize. It's a shadow between his eyes that fades nearly as quickly as I notice it.

I'm still trying to figure out what that expression means when Marco sighs.

"You're going to get yourself killed if you do it alone, you dick. Come with me."

I narrow my eyes. "The hell is that supposed to mean?"

"It means that I'm your brother. I'm not going to let you die. So come with me, and we can make sure that you at least stand some chance of making it out of this with your fucking life."

Despite my clear reluctance, Marco takes me back into Elio's house. No one else is in the kitchen; it's just the two of us.

I'm aware that anyone could be listening, but I have a feeling that Marco's handled that as well.

I can't think about the details, anyway. All I can think about is Marisol, and the way that Caterina looked at me with so much pity in her face.

The fact that she looked at me like it was a done deal. Like Marisol wasn't going to come back.

Like it was over for me, and she was getting ready to watch my heart break.

Before I even knew what was coming.

Marco gestures to the kitchen table. I fold my arms and stare at the chair he's indicating, and he huffs.

"You don't have to be so disagreeable," he snaps as he settles into a seat.

"What the fuck do you want with me, Marco?" I growl.

His eyes narrow. "You're acting awfully testy for someone who doesn't have a lot of fans to begin with."

Well.

Thanks, brother.

I glare at him.

Marco sighs. "Dino. If anyone deserves the hatred, it's not me."

"It isn't?"

"No."

I growl. "How can you say that, Marco? You're the one who lies to your family constantly."

"Have I lied to you, Dino?"

I narrow my eyes.

Marco tilts his head to the side slightly. "There are many times, I admit, that I am not entirely forthcoming with the information that I have. But I have never once misled you. I have always protected you, brother, even when you came to me with your biggest mistakes."

"Marisol and the girls are not a mistake," I seethe at him.

He shrugs. "They may not be. But there have not been many intentional decisions made on your part around them."

"You mothefuc...."

The insult dies in my throat as Marco silences me with a glance.

I hate that he can do that to me.

"My point, brother, is that you do not make a great deal of decisions with purpose. You often act, and then deal with the circumstances that arise. Or, you ask for my help in doing so."

"And you hate that, don't you?"

Marco shakes his head. "Dino, if I hated it, I wouldn't help."

I don't know what to say to that.

"Did Dad help, when you found yourself in situations like this? When your mouth wrote a check that you couldn't cash?"

Studying him, I consider his words. Dad didn't help me at all. He looked down on me, always angry with me. Always making an effort to point out how I'd fucked up.

He never offered to help.

"No," I mutter reluctantly.

"I know. I was there. The point isn't that Dad was cruel to you, Dino, even if he was. The point is that I am not."

"But you..."

"I never said I didn't keep secrets from Elio. Or Sal. Or Caterina," he says softly.

That does make me pause.

Marco looks at me for a second. Marco and I are close in age. Close enough that it's almost suspicious. He's older than I am, but only by ten months, and that's where the similarities between us end.

Marco is built like dad. Thick. Broad. We're both tall, but he's slightly shorter than I am, with thick brown hair and heavyset eyebrows.

We have our mother's eyes, I guess.

But I've buried every genetic similarity I have to my siblings under tattoos. I've never worked out like Marco, or even done sports like Sal, but I've spent every fucking second I could in my life learning how to fight.

I might not look thick like Marco, but if you're going to get punched by one of us, you don't want it to be me.

It won't just be a punch. I'll have a knife in there too. That's for damn sure.

Still, when Marco looks at me with that glare, it reminds me so much of dad that I...

I glance away.

"I don't keep secrets from you, Dino. I never have."

His voice is... different.

I look back at him.

Marco shuts his eyes and pinches the bridge of his nose. He inhales, exhaling in a long sigh.

He looks tired.

For the first time in a long time, a fissure of concern about my older brother spikes through me. I went to find him when he went into hiding because I had to. I had to know what he was doing, had to know how I could continue to protect my girls.

Had to know if he was going to ruin my life.

But Marco did go into hiding... for me. He chose to work with Interpol.

I think.

"You look bad," I say.

It's the closest I've ever come to asking my older brother if he's okay.

Marco's eyes snap open. "Did I ask you to be a fucking beauty consultant, Dino?"

"You didn't ask me for shit," I snap back.

Marco leans forward, his elbows on the table. "I know you're going to go after her."

"I am," I say flatly.

He nods. "Good."

"Good?"

My brother smiles at me. "For the first time in your life, Dino, do something with intent. Instead of just dealing with the situation as you make it, let's actually get you into a place where you're in control. You're the one determining what you want. You want her?"

I nod.

"Then you need to fucking get her."

I sit. "I don't know how to defeat Moretti," I state.

He shakes his head. "That's the wrong question. You don't need to ask about how to defeat Moretti. There's a way to win everything, without having to take down Benicio Suarez and his den of killers."

"How?" I ask.

I need to know.

Marco nods. "You need to win the competition. You need to win, fair and square, so Marisol is yours."

I huff. "Yeah fucking right."

"Don't, Dino."

Marco's face is dead serious.

"Don't what?"

"Underestimate yourself. You always do."

"What..."

"The first problem is that you can't enter the competition for Marisol's hand without leading an organization."

I roll my eyes. "Well I'm fucked from the beginning then."

"No, you're not."

"Come on, Marco," I scoff. "Everyone knows you're the head of our family. Elio and Gia own the Rossi empire."

Marco hesitates, uncertainty flickering across his face.

I tilt my head. "What?"

"There is an option," he says quietly.

Confusion makes me frown. "What do you mean?"

Marco takes a huge breath, then lets it go. "There is a business. An organization that you stand to inherit."

"Marco, you're being fucking stupid, I already told you..."

"You are not our father's son, Dino," he says quietly.

My jaw drops.

The world spins.

"The fuck did you say?"

7

MARISOL

Moretti finds me about a mile outside of the Rossi's home.

It's amazing, truly, how fast he is. One second I'm walking down the road, completely alone, and then the next, there's a dark shape in front of me.

If he wants to startle me, though, he's going to have to work a hell of a lot harder than that.

"I'm here," I say softly. "I'm here, and you can take me to him."

Predictably, Moretti doesn't say anything.

I'm certain he is capable of speech. He's spoken in front of me before.

I think.

He doesn't often do it, though. Moretti is a man of few words, which works for me.

He doesn't need to speak.

And neither do I.

Without another word, he escorts me to a blacked out Dodge Charger. I raise my eyebrows at it. "Seems a little obvious, no?"

"It's a police vehicle," he says, his words heavily accented, showing his Italian upbringing.

I raise my eyebrows. "And that's less conspicuous?"

"They aren't looking for it," he replies.

Okay then.

Moretti opens the passenger door for me and I get in. I buckle, and he slides into the driver's seat, starting the vehicle with a throaty roar.

He slams his foot down on the accelerator, confident and controlled, and we're out.

We don't speak.

The private airstrip is an hour away. I'm surprised Moretti hasn't blindfolded me, but I'm not going to say anything about it.

I guess it would be kind of weird if he had to explain it. Especially since the passport he hands me lists that we're married, a couple heading back to Brazil after our honeymoon.

God.

It's like some kind of sick joke.

What's amazing is that as soon as it's assumed I'm Moretti's new wife, no one looks at us twice. They don't notice that there's absolutely zero affection between us. No one makes any comment on the fact that Moretti and I barely speak.

I don't know why I'm expecting more.

I've never seen a marriage that has affection, so I guess it's normal enough for everyone.

That's not true.

Elio and Caterina seem to like each other. Same with Gia and Sal, who I know are more than just affectionate.

Sal was willing to take on my father to rescue Gia.

That's more than just affection. That's devotion.

Moretti jerks his head, signaling that I need to get to the plane. We board, with suitcases that contain absolutely nothing for me, but make a convincing enough front that again, no one says anything.

When the plane takes off, my thoughts return to Sal and Gia.

Devotion.

Could Dino be capable of...

No. Stop. It doesn't matter.

I shut my eyes tight, trying to hold back the tears pressing against my lids.

It doesn't matter what Sal and Gia have, or if Dino is capable of giving *that* to a lover.

It doesn't matter because I can never be his.

And he can never be mine.

When we get to Brasilia, my mood darkens.

I don't realize how evident it is until Moretti turns to me, one hand on the wheel as the car curves towards my father's estate.

"Stop," he says quietly.

I tilt my head. "Stop what?"

"Being nervous."

"I'm not nervous," I respond. I am, but I don't want my father's guard dog to know that.

He looks at me, his dark eyes too astute, too knowing, and I look out the window.

The road rushes by, but I can't stop myself. I pick at the edge of my pants. My father needs me, I know, but that doesn't mean he's going to be happy to see me.

I need to get myself under control. We're entering the final checkpoint when Moretti speaks again.

"I will stop him if he tries to hurt you."

My head snaps back to look at him. "What?"

But Moretti doesn't respond. He rolls down the window to talk to the guard, and doesn't say anything to me.

Andrei Moretti is a robot. He doesn't have feelings. My father hired him as his assassin and go-to support because if there's one person on earth more unhinged than my father, it's Andrei Moretti.

I will stop him if he tries to hurt you.

We're basically at the front gate. Andrei turns the car off, and goes to unbuckle.

"I need to free my mom," I whisper.

His hand pauses on the buckle.

Neither of us are looking at each other.

I don't even know why I'm saying this. Moretti could be lying to me. He could have said that to me to gain my trust, so that I don't try to run again.

However, given that Moretti hasn't hurt me yet, and the fact that he's been... It feels like the bar is in hell to say that he's been kind, because he hasn't.

But he's a man of so few words, I can't imagine that he would use them on a lie.

So I take a deep breath, and say what's on the tip of my tongue. "I need to get my mom out of here. That's my plan. I'll come willingly. I'll do whatever I have to. I'll be his doll. But I need my mother to walk out of this place. Alive," I add.

His hand wavers. "I don't know..."

"That's what I'm doing. You can try to keep him from hurting me if you can, but if it comes down to pain in exchange for my mother's freedom, I'll take the pain," I whisper.

I don't give him a chance to respond. I unbuckle, open the door, and pause.

The door snaps open and Moretti follows me.

I take two seconds to adjust myself. I'm still wearing the same clothes from when I left the Rossi estate. They're nothing but workout attire.

However, that doesn't mean I'm going to walk in like I'm ashamed.

I throw my shoulders back, tilting my head forward. When I stride into my father's home, it's as though I own the place.

As if I am the Mafia princess he's making me out to be, and this is the castle that I've always been promised.

The guards melt to the side, and I feel Moretti at my back like a stalking panther. When I push the doors to the house open, there's no lock on them.

They bang against the walls.

"Papai," I say, the cutesy term sour on my tongue. "I'm back."

For a minute there's silence.

Stunned, presumably.

Then my father belts out a laugh.

I take the time to assess the situation. My mother, to my relief, is sitting at the dining room table with him. She looks pale, but unharmed, and she's looking at me with an arched eyebrow.

I smile at her. "Mãe, you're looking well."

"And you, my beautiful daughter," she purrs.

Benicio finally stops laughing. "And you think you can just what? Waltz back in here and pretend that you did not run from me? That you did not cause the death of so many of my men?"

"It's hardly my fault that they were incompetent, Papai," I snort.

This is the game with my father. Any sign of weakness, which he can sniff out like a bloodhound, he will take and he will squeeze between his fingertips until he pops it like a pimple.

His specialty is to cause pain, which he seems to take pleasure in doling out.

My mother warned me of this, many times.

So yes. I am absolutely going to pretend that I didn't run. I'm going to make the whole thing seem like a game. He has largely forgotten that I have two children, after all.

I'm going to make sure he doesn't remember.

With my shoulders still held back and my head up high, I sidle into the seat next to my mother. She leans my way, her knee barely brushing mine.

She's shaking.

My heart sinks.

"Papai, how am I to trust that someone can well and truly win my hand if it is so easy for me to escape?" I ask casually.

He snorts. "Easy? No, Marisol. It was not easy."

"It was easy enough."

"Only because that Italian bitch brought you out of here!" he snarls.

My mother freezes, and I bump her knee with mine.

I know well how to handle his rages.

"Easy enough. And I'll do it again, if I have to prove my point."

"And what point is that, Marisol?" he sneers.

Casually, I pick up a fork and stab the chicken sitting in the middle of the table. "That those guards were not worthy of your employ."

"Marisol," he growls. "I am not in a position to lose the men I have, which you well know."

I do.

I shrug. "Then I will leave again."

"Your mother will die if you do."

Mãe laughs at that. "You couldn't kill me if you wanted to, Benicio."

"Watch me, Isadora."

My mother mutters in her native Spanish, which usually means she's plotting something.

She told me she thinks better in Spanish.

That's good.

"How about this, Papai," I say casually. "If you let Mãe go, I'll agree to your stupid plan."

"You'll agree to it either way, you ungrateful, unworthy child," he spits.

Interestingly, my father never calls me names. Not truly. He calls me all kinds of things, but he'll call my half siblings 'bitch' or 'bastard' about a hundred times in a sentence.

Again, for some reason, I am his favorite, and we have no idea why.

"Perhaps. But imagine, when I escape again, and Mãe stabs you through the heart, how you'll feel then, knowing you could have simply made this deal."

"There is no deal to be made," he growls.

I look at my mother, who shakes her head slightly.

Then, my eyes slide to Moretti.

I take a deep, steadying breath.

Please forgive me, Andrei, and please, for the love of God, don't betray me either.

"Let mother go."

"No."

"Let mother go, and I'll make your marriage competition even more interesting."

Benicio looks at me.

I can feel Moretti's eyes burning a hole in my shoulder. I slice my chicken, neatly and into small pieces, showing off the fancy etiquette lessons my father paid for me to attend in Paris as a teenager.

"Let mother go, and I'll add a complication to your trials. Moretti will serve as my champion. Anyone who gets through your games has to get through mine," I say softly.

There's silence in the room.

"Think of it, father. It was so easy for me to leave. So easy for the Rossi's to find me here. So easy to just walk out. The rumors. The holes in your security. You wouldn't want them to think you weak. But with Andrei as my champion, he'll be unstoppable. Truly, the only ones who can defeat him would be the ones you'd want as a son-in-law, no?"

His eyes narrow. "What makes you think that I had not planned to do that anyway?"

"It doesn't matter. Moretti already swore his loyalty to me, and agrees that this idea will be the best for the organization."

This is where I need Andrei to follow my lead. *You told me you wanted to help. You told me that you would keep him from hurting me. This is the only way. Please,* I mentally beg him.

It's a leap of faith. Moretti doesn't owe me anything. He has no reason to do this.

But my relief when he speaks is so great, I almost sag in my chair.

"I will do this," he says in that thick Italian accent. "It will make it seem as though you are stronger than you are. The security is too weak. If I walk among the competitors, I can find the strongest one. And then they must get past me," he adds.

I look at my mom. Her eyes are round.

Benicio nods. "Isadora, pack your things. Marisol, you have a deal."

Thank you.

8

DINO

YOU ARE NOT OUR FATHER'S SON.

I'VE BEEN through a lot of shit in my life. Lots of bad shit. A lot of shit that I'm not proud of, but I got through.

This?

I feel like the center just fell out of my world, and I don't have a fucking clue what to do with the hole that it left.

My ears are ringing. Marco's mouth is moving, and I have no fucking clue what he's saying.

All I hear is the same thing, over and over again.

You are not our father's son.

"Dino," I finally hear, the sound distant. "Bernadino," Marco says, louder this time.

I look at him, but I have absolutely no idea what to say.

How could I?

How is there any possible response to what he just told me

that doesn't include me melting my brain from the inside fucking out?

You are not our father's son.

"Breathe, Dino," Marco says.

I glare at him.

"I promise, it will be better if you breathe."

"Fuck you," I snap. "There's no fucking way this could be better, Marco."

He raises his eyebrows.

I feel the rage boiling inside of me, a lava flow of darkness that's pounding at my skin. I want to stand and punch him in his smug fucking face.

If he can't talk because his jaw is broken, then he can't say stupid shit like...

"I understand that this is a lot. But it's true."

If I had claws, I'd rip into him with them, right now.

"The. Fuck. Are. You. Saying," I manage to grit out from between my teeth. My jaws are clenched so hard that I'm pretty sure one of my teeth just cracked.

I could just rearrange Marco's face...

"No one knows, except Mom and I," he says quietly.

I freeze.

Marco takes my sudden stillness as a sign to continue. "Dad wasn't mom's first choice for a husband. Right before she was supposed to get married, she went on a vacation to Greece with Zia Priscilla, and she met someone there."

"How. The fuck. Do you…"

He holds up a hand. "Let me finish. She met someone there. I don't think it started out as anything but a friend to talk to. She married dad. Then, after I was born, she ran away for a while."

"What's a while?"

Marco shrugs. "Long enough that she came back, and I had a baby brother before I was two years old."

Oh.

"How the fuck do you know this?"

"Apparently you look like him," Marco says softly. "She wrote about it in her journals. I read them all, after she died. I was cleaning out their stuff and I found every single one, and I read them."

Jesus fucking Christ. The amount of pain in Marco's expression makes my chest ache. "Fuck, Marco," I spit.

"She thinks Dad probably knew, but never said anything."

"And she just… wrote this down."

Marco shrugs. "Mom liked to journal."

"What the fuck else did she write about?"

His face drops, and his eyes look kind of hollow and distant. "You don't want to know."

I'm still so stunned, I have no fucking clue why we're even discussing this.

Until I remember.

"How the hell is this supposed to help me get Marisol back?"

Marco nods. "There aren't that many families who she would have known when she was there."

I shudder at the word *known*, which feels pretty fucking biblical in this sense. "You're talking about my... biological family," I spit at him.

"Don't fucking say it like that."

I glance at him, surprised. Marco leans forward, his eyes on mine as he intensely stares me down. "Don't ever fucking think that, Dino. I don't give a fuck who your dad is. I don't give a shit about what happened back then. You're my fucking brother, you understand? You're my family. Biologically. In every fucking way that counts."

"Half-brother," I whisper.

God, it's so fucking weird to say. The words are almost bitter on my tongue, and I feel like I'm swallowing thorns when I shut my mouth.

How the fuck did this happen? My whole fucking life.

A lie.

Marco leans back. "You're my brother, Dino," he says fiercely. "No matter what anyone says, you're my fucking brother."

I don't have anything to say to him. I just stare, noting the twitch in Marco's jaw and the way his hands flex on the table.

For years, my big brother has been the only person who seemed to give a shit about me. Even then, I haven't always liked the type of protection that Marco offers.

He's been a dick. He's been a controlling asshole. He tells about a quarter of the truth every time he speaks, and the rest he keeps to himself.

But he does always have a fucking plan.

I jerk my chin down in a nod.

Marco studies me for another minute, then continues. "Like I said, there are a select few families that she would have aligned with. I believe that I know which one. You can compete for Marisol's hand as their heir," he says.

I raise an eyebrow at him. "And they'd be fine with that? Some fucking kid from the states, pretending to be their previous fucking son?"

"Let me handle that," Marco says smoothly.

I roll my eyes. "Come the fuck on, Marco. Ain't no fuckin' way that some group of people I've never fuckin' met is going to play along with this bullshit."

"I said I'd handle it," Marco repeats, his voice low. "It's not like you can make the necessary arrangements or requests, and it's not like he'll look. The family that I think we're dealing with is old, and they are not active any longer, but it's a name that Benicio Souza will not walk away from."

I narrow my eyes. "This is fucking stupid."

"It's your only chance, Dino."

The sincerity of his statement hits me like a ton of bricks.

He's right.

He's absolutely fucking right.

This is my only chance at getting Marisol back. At making sure the girls are safe, and cared for, and...

"The only other question is, do you want your girls to know who you are?"

I look over at Marco.

He's staring at me, and the way his eyes are digging into my skin, I feel...

Exposed.

I look away. "They don't know I'm their fucking dad," I mutter.

"Yes."

It's just one word, but it feels like a bomb in my mind.

I shut my eyes. "Marisol didn't want to tell them about me."

"Perhaps."

"Why the fuck would I go against what she said, and why the fuck do I want them to know who I am?"

"So they can know who's going to save their mother."

My eyes snap open and I stare at my brother. For a minute, all I can do is look at him.

What if I fuck it up?

The thought is too fucking scary to say out loud. I can't. I don't want to.

I don't want the girls to rely on me when I don't even know if I can fucking pull it off.

Disappointing them...

"You're going to save her," Marco says softly. "I know it, Dino."

"I don't."

He sighs. "You've always believed so little of yourself."

"The fuck?"

Marco looks me dead in the eye. "You've always thought poorly of yourself, Dino. Always had a chip on your shoulder that worked against your own fucking point. You're a good man. You'll be a good father. You'll be a good husband. But you can't do any of that shit without a wife, and you certainly can't be the father to your children without her either. It would fucking kill you and you know it."

"I..." my jaw snaps shut.

He has a point.

"I know that you're sitting there listing all the ways you think you're going to fuck this up. But Dino, I promise you that you won't. You're a much better man than you think you are, and while you don't always have the best way of going about something, I know you. I know that when push comes to shove, you're not going to shove wrong. You're going to save her, if it's the last thing you do."

I narrow my eyes at him. "When did you become some fucking expert in me?"

"I've been your brother for your entire life, asshole. You think I haven't spent enough time watching you be fully capable of all kinds of shit, then backing off of it because you thought you couldn't do it?"

"You spent most of our lives trying to clean up my fucking messes," I growl.

"Sure. You had a lot of them. But every single one of them, you could have fixed on your own."

I glare at him, and he stands. "Enter the contest. I'll give you a name. Promise your kids you'll get their mom back."

"No."

"Then lose her forever," he shrugs. "But you said you were going to get her."

I seethe, staring at him. I don't want to do what he's saying, but deep inside me, I recognize why.

I am afraid to fuck it up.

I am afraid to promise my daughters that I'm going to get their mom back, and then fail at that.

I'm afraid that once I show up, Marisol won't want me.

Or, even worse...

That I'll show up, and she will.

And I'll fuck it up and lose her again.

"It's a leap of faith, Dino. No one can predict the future. But I sure as hell know that you won't get what you want sitting on your ass here," Marco says.

He leaves the room.

I stare at the kitchen table. It's dark, and I can hear Elio's people moving softly around the house. Idly, I wonder if the girls are asleep.

I shouldn't wake them up. Right?

I have no fucking clue how to be a dad. Clearly, my own role model thought I wasn't even his kid, and put exactly zero effort into fucking helping me become someone.

Slowly, I put my elbows on the table and let my head sink into my hands.

Do I even call him dad anymore?

I snort. Even as a kid, I knew something was fucking off. Dad always fucking had it out for me. I couldn't so much as walk by without him finding something wrong with me, and then he would send Marco to hammer down on whatever the fuck it was that he took an issue with that day.

Dad never thought I would amount to shit.

Mom...

I squeeze my eyes shut.

Mom did.

She was always on my side. Always in my fucking corner. Always making sure that Dad and Marco didn't make me too miserable.

I miss her.

It's been years since their death. When they died after Caterina's engagement party, every part of me wanted to find Elio Rossi and beat him to death. It was obvious, after all, that he'd organized a hit on my parents, and somehow had fucked it up to kill his own in the process.

The years, and Caterina's reassurance that it wasn't Elio, haven't really done much to dull that pain. Working with Elio has been... calculated. A necessary risk, something that I've been angry about for a long time.

I don't fucking like Elio.

I don't fucking like Marco all the time, if I'm being honest.

Sal and Gia have their own thing now. Caterina and Elio do too. Marco is... Marco.

And I'm alone.

Always.

My tongue tastes bitter again.

If I'm being honest, I want what they have. I want someone to fucking belong to. Someone to come home to at night. Someone that I don't feel like a fucking outcast around.

Right now, I am an outcast. I'm a stranger to my own children, and Marisol, the love of my fucking life...

I look up.

Marco's right.

I have to do something about this, about her. I have to fucking make a choice.

I might not be my father's son. I might not be my siblings' brother.

But I'm their fucking dad.

And I'm going to get Marisol back. I belong one place in this world.

With her.

So I need to fucking make it happen.

9

MARISOL

"Marisol. My love. What the hell have you done?"

Behind closed doors with my mother, I finally let myself fall apart.

The question is harsh, but as soon as the tears start to flow out of my face, my mom makes a soothing sound. She comes over to pat me on the back, and I fall into her embrace. "It's okay," she murmurs in Spanish. "It's okay, my love. Tell me everything."

I pull back. I reply in Spanish, the language she taught me as a kid. It fits between us... our special, secret code. Spanish and Portuguese are similar enough, and I'm fluent in both, as well as English, but it still feels like some kind of secret code when my mom and I use it to talk to each other.

It feels safe.

"The girls are safe. They're in the states, at their father's home."

Her eyebrows skyrocket, and she swears softly. "Does he know?"

"He does now. But Gia... she's..." I stop.

She's not my sister-in-law. Saying that is just plain silly, even if it's wishful thinking. Gia would be an excellent sister-in-law.

"She's the friend who helped me escape the first time," I add lamely. "And she's married to his brother."

My mom doesn't need to know more. We've kept it this way, so that she doesn't have too many questions, and she can maintain some kind of plausible deniability when it comes to things about the girls.

We try, as hard as we can, to make sure that the girls are safe. Protected.

And that my dad can't find them as easily as he can us.

"They're safe," I finish, despite the fact that my mom's eyebrows are pinching together with skepticism.

"And you trust these people because..."

"There were a whole crowd of babies and kids there, Mamá," I clarify quietly. "They're not going to let anyone in that they don't want to."

"And the security?"

"So tight, you couldn't slip a credit card under it."

She huffs. "And yet your father's hound was able to find you just fine."

"I volunteered. I told the girls that when you were able, you'd send for them. Then I walked out onto the road and he was waiting for me."

She nods. "And their father?"

I look away.

My mom sighs, pulling me close. "Oh, my sweet girl. Tell me what happened."

"I just... I thought it wouldn't matter, really. That seeing him wouldn't be a problem because it was just so long ago, you know?"

"It is not such a long time," she says with a little tilt of her lips. "I became a grandmother before I was ready."

"I know. But I just... I thought that seeing him again wouldn't do that to me."

"Do what?"

I tuck myself smaller, burying my nose in her shoulder. "He's basically a stranger, Mamá. We didn't date. We didn't know each other. There's nothing there between us."

"And you felt like there was?"

I nod into her shoulder.

She sighs. "Ay. Well. You did have his children, you know. You know him through them."

"I never told them that he's their father."

"Does he know that?"

I nod again.

She clucks her tongue softly, squeezing me. "What a mess, my Marisol,"

"I know. I messed it all up."

"You didn't, my love. You didn't even a little bit mess anything up. Is he going to watch over them? Does he want to be…"

"I don't know."

"Well. Did he ask you to stay?"

I pull back and wrinkle my nose at her. "Not really."

She raises her brow again. "What does that mean?"

"Well, he didn't ask. He just kind of... demanded."

"Demanded?"

I nod. "Yeah. He told me that I was going to stay, and that he was going to... keep me there."

She swears. "He sounds like your father."

"No!" I say, a little too loud. My mom pulls all the way back and gives me a look. I shake my head and repeat myself. "No. Not like dad. It's like he..." I stop.

The words that are on the tip of my tongue are *it's like he cared about me.*

But that can't be true.

I'm not anything to Dino. He's not anything to me. We made two beautiful girls together, but only because we were so irresponsible that night all those years ago.

It's not like we're in a relationship. We literally don't have one.

So he can't care about me.

It's kind of familiar. I have to remind myself of things like this a lot, because other than my mom... people can't care about me.

I'm not *someone* to anyone. I'm Benicio Souza's daughter. I'm a pawn, something that people move around on a board to get what they want.

I'm not just... me.

Well, except to my girls and my mom, I guess.

Still, the idea that Dino would be interested in me for who I am is silly. It's a fantasy that I've entertained for way too long.

He doesn't know who I am.

I keep that information under lock and key, and I don't know that I've ever really been my true self around anyone...

Except Dino, that one night.

"Okay. So," my mother's voice interrupts my thoughts. "This man who sounds alarmingly like your father, he is protecting the girls."

"Well, he's definitely at the house..."

"Marisol," she admonishes. "You think the girls can just—what? Wait for me there?"

"Gia will take care of them," I add confidently.

She sighs.

"We need to get you out of here, okay? So let's pack, and..."

She waves her hand at me. "Your father was going to let me go when you came back. I had already scared him into it."

"Mamá!"

She shrugs. "You just walked in and negotiated this! I couldn't stop and pause you!"

Ugh. "At least Moretti will keep the worst of them away, I guess."

Another one of her scathing looks. "That boy wants more than just to be your father's guard dog. Or yours," she adds.

"What does that mean?"

Putting her clothes into a bag, my mom throws me a look. "Don't tell me you haven't noticed, mi Corazón."

"I really have no idea what you're talking about."

She heaves a sigh, muttering in Spanish, then turns back to me. "Well, I think it will just have to stay that way then."

"Stay what way?"

"Amor, I must go. I have someone waiting for me."

I blink. "Who?"

"Don't worry about that. But tell me how to find the girls, and I will find them."

I go through the directions to the Rossi estate in New York. I also give her Gia's contact information, which I memorized earlier, and my mom memorizes it as well.

Sometimes you learn certain things when you're connected to this life.

Like how to memorize information before it disappears forever... or keep someone else from seeing it written down.

My mother confidently takes the information from me, then wraps me in a huge hug. "You didn't have to bargain for me, mi corazón," she whispers. "I would have been just fine."

"Well I didn't know that," I grumble.

"After all this time, surely you know that your father and I will do many things to each other, but him coming close to hurting me is not one of them."

"Again. I didn't know that."

She sighs and pulls back. Her brown eyes are pinched with worry, and she lightly plays with a tendril of hair. "Did you really think he was going to do something to me?"

I nod. "How could I not? He stormed the house in Florida with basically an army. He took you from me, and there was gunfire and the girls..." my voice tails off and my lips tremble.

It was terrifying.

I've been through a lot with Benicio as a dad. I've been through a lot of stuff with my mom.

Seeing her taken at gunpoint from the house is not something I want to repeat.

Ever.

Nor do I want my girls to see that ever again.

"Even if that's the case, my love, don't you think that I would rather put myself in harm's way so that you and the girls would be fine?" she says, her eyes kind.

"I won't let him hurt you. I won't," I utter.

"Ay. So fierce. You might be named for sunlight, but I think sometimes there's a storm in you that few understand," my mom says with a smile. She holds me close again, and I spend a last second cherishing her touch.

She pulls back. "I have to go now."

"You're still not telling me who is coming to get you, are you?"

Smiling, she shakes her head. "No. But I think you should probably lay in the bed. No matter what you hear, don't come out, okay?"

"Mamá..."

She takes out a spray and sprays the air between us. The smell from the spray is sharp, and I sneeze against the harsh scent. "What's that?"

"Oh, you know. Just something to make sure no one can blame you for this."

"What?" I try to look at her but my head is starting to feel fuzzy. The air around me shimmers, like it's having a hard time staying... real.

I go to move my lips, and they don't seem to do it.

"If this man of yours, the father of your children, is anything like your father, he's going to come here for you," she whispers. It almost sounds like I'm in a dream, and my eyelids feel heavy and they start to droop. My mom gently tugs on my hand, pulling me toward the bed in her room. I follow her and flop onto it.

The covers smell like her. Patchouli and Dior.

"You're going to have to make some tough choices, Marisol. Just make sure they're choices for you, and you don't make them for anyone else."

Choices? "Ma..."

I can't even finish the word.

I'm asleep before I can, and the last thing I remember is my mother laughing quietly, and the press of her lips on my forehead.

Someone is yelling.

I know that I need to wake up to figure out what's going on, but I just... I can't seem to. My head feels heavy, like it's stuffed with cotton, and my eyes won't open.

I have to get up.

Portuguese. Words flying around. Suddenly someone is banging on a door, and I manage to blink my eyes open.

I'm in my room. Not that the small space that is behind a false wall could be called much of a room, but it's where I've been designated to stay when I'm here. The last thing I remember, I was in my mom's room, so to get here...

The spray.

"Oh my God," I whisper out loud. "She drugged me."

Leave it to my mom to drug me and put me in my own room, then disappear.

Swearing, I swing my legs out of bed. The persistent fist slamming on my door continues. "I'm here," I murmur, my voice not quite back online yet.

I swing the door open. It's Paulo, one of my father's head goons. "What?" I say, trying to play up my sleepiness as much as possible.

"Where the fuck is your mother?" he hisses.

I narrow my eyes at him. "How should I know?"

"You were with her! You made that bargain with your father for her safety. You two were planning something," he snarls.

"If I was planning something, why would I know where she is now?"

"Because you didn't want us to stop her!" he barks.

His words confirm that my father was not, in fact, going to honor his word with me.

Ice creeps over my features. "Go away, Paulo."

One of his meaty hands slams onto the doorframe, and I wince.

"I'm warning you, bitch, that if you..."

There's a strange, juicy noise. Like someone cutting into a steak.

Paulo's face, inches from mine, contorts into a grimace and he looks up.

There's a knife sticking out from the center of his hand, grown in the middle of it like some kind of sick mushroom.

I gasp and step back. Paulo goes to remove it, but a flash of metal reveals another knife, this one as his throat.

"I would not do that if I were you," a cold voice slithers over his shoulder.

Paulo's eyes widen. "Moretti... you fucking..." he grunts, but the knife, and the elegant hand that holds it, press deeper into his neck.

"I would not do that if I were you," Andrei repeats softly.

I shiver. The threat in his words is palpable. It's no wonder that he doesn't talk all that often.

Andrei Moretti's voice is as violent as any part of him, and it's scary as hell.

Paulo is sweating. He tugs, yelping as the knife pinning his hand shifts slightly. "If I fucking can't use my hand..."

"You can. I made sure to only hit muscle, not a tendon. But if you keep bothering Marisol, I'm going to not only sever all the tendons in your hand, I will take this knife right here—" Paulo yelps and a thin trickle of blood starts to cascade down his throat "—and I will use it to peel the skin off your body. I will make you watch as I take your muscles apart, one by one, and you'll have to hold them while I do. I don't hear screams, Paulo, so no matter how much you yell, I will still keep going."

"Fucking monster," Paulo spits.

I can barely see Andrei's face from where I'm standing, but as Paulo spits the words at him, I see a flicker of something surprising.

Disgust.

At Paulo?

I'm not sure, but Moretti's lip curls in a sneer as he continues. "I am a fucking monster, Paulo. And I'm the monster who will rip you apart if you dare to bother her again. So will you fucking leave, or do I need to begin?"

Paulo swears in Portuguese. "You're fucked up."

"Marisol is my problem," Andrei says.

The hair on my arms raises as he says it.

Because even though he called me a problem, it doesn't sound like that's what he's saying.

It sounds like he's saying *Marisol is mine.*

And I'm really not sure how to feel about that.

"Deal with your problem then," Paulo hisses.

In a swift movement, Andrei steps back. He plucks the knife from Paulo's hand, earning a fresh cry from Paulo. Paulo cradles his bleeding palm, giving both of us a dark look before he hastily scoots into the hallway.

My heart skips as I look at Andrei.

We haven't been alone together since he brought me back. Since I found my dad and my mom at dinner.

Since I counted him in, and made him my... what? Keeper? Babysitter?

Guard dog?

Andrei is staring at me. Not for the first time, I notice that he's handsome. However, it feels distant. He looks handsome like a sculpture or a painting, something beautiful to look at, but cold and distant.

He certainly doesn't make my heart race like Dino does.

I take a deep breath. Between the adrenaline from Paulo trying to force his way into my room and the drug that my mom used, my system is panicking, and I have no idea what to do to get it to calm down.

Andrei tilts his head. "Are you hurt?"

"No. What happened?" I might as well start there.

"About ten minutes ago, your father went to your mother's room and discovered that she was gone. Security footage shows you in her room last, but you were not in there. You were in here," he says, gesturing to my room.

Unlike Paulo, he doesn't try to enter.

"Yes. I was... asleep," I say.

His eyes narrow slightly, and I know that he picked up on the hesitation in my words.

"I was really tired. The journey was hard, you know. And... the trauma. It's just a lot."

"I see," he says. One of his weirdly well-groomed eyebrows raises. "The trauma."

"Yeah. The trauma."

"So you do not know where your mother went?"

"No," I shake my head. I'm not even lying about that. I have no idea where my mother went, or who she went with. I know that she's heading back to the States, of course, but beyond that?

Nothing.

"Interesting. I also found this, when I was looking through her room," Andrei says.

I look at the small perfume bottle in his hand, and recognize the spray that my mom used on me to knock me out.

"She loves that perfume," I sigh, like I'm missing her.

Andrei looks at me, studying me for another minute. He holds it out. "You should keep it then."

I freeze.

It's clear to me that he absolutely knows what's in the bottle. It's also clear to me that, despite that, he's offering it to me anyway.

I look at the bottle in his hand, then look back up at him.

"You'd give this to me?" I whisper.

He nods. "Everyone should be able to use the gifts their mother left behind for them."

His voice is so quiet, I almost don't hear it. However, his answer confirms what I suspected.

Slowly, I take the bottle. Andrei nods, turning to head back to where my father is still yelling somewhere in the house.

"Moretti," I say to his back.

He freezes and turns. "Yes?"

"Thank you. For this. And Paulo," I whisper.

His eyes glitter, ever so slightly. "It was nothing, Marisol. I am your guard, after all."

Then, he slips away.

I stare at the space he occupied for a minute. My mother's words creep back into my mind. *That boy wants to be more than just your father's guard dog.*

Suddenly, I have a terrible feeling that I know exactly what that means.

Even more terrible, I realize that at some point, I'll have to address it. Because right now, if I use this weakness to my advantage, I'll be manipulating Andrei Moretti.

Men like him do not take kindly to manipulation. And honestly, I'm not very good at it.

But if I tell him that I don't feel that way about him...

I shudder.

He's dangerous. Too dangerous. And who knows, maybe this could be a good thing.

Dino isn't coming for me. I have to let that go.

Moretti, however, he's here. He's already kept me safe once.

Perhaps he would do it again. Maybe I could…

I shut my eyes. My heart feels heavy. No matter what, I'm in a position I don't like. Nothing is as it should be.

I just want to get back to my girls. I need to figure out the fastest path to do that. Many women before me have pretended to be a happy wife for their own safety.

Maybe I need to do that as well.

10

MARISOL

It takes a few days, but once everyone settles down after the disappearance of my mom, life seems almost... normal.

In the sense that I'm nearly completely invisible to my father.

My dad is spending so much time preparing for the arrival of the cast of felons that he's trying to marry me off to, he literally doesn't have time to talk to me.

And honestly, I am truly not complaining. It gives me time to just... sit. Be thoughtful. Meander around the house.

I sleep a lot. I think that's a very important thing, because I've heard that when you sleep, your mind essentially runs a protocol where it gets rid of things it doesn't need.

Maybe my brain just needs to do a lot of deleting in order to feel better.

Paulo, and his goons, are the biggest threat. They follow me around the house, lurking where they shouldn't. Three days after my mother's disappearance, they're making me feel uneasy.

A feeling that keeps growing through the day.

I'm in the shower, thinking about Dino, when I hear the doorknob to my shower rattle. I've long learned to lock doors in my father's home, so at first I don't worry about it. Someone might have come into my bedroom, because the bathroom is connected to it, but I didn't lock that door.

I think.

Either way, locking the bathroom door definitely happened, so I manage to keep my shower going.

Then, I hear something else.

A key.

Sliding into a lock.

I freeze, not sure what to do. The water beats on my shoulders, and I'm still covered in soap.

The key sound clicks. Then, there's quiet, just for a minute. The doorknob turns...

Oh God.

Someone's coming in.

I look around the shower, grabbing the razor I use to shave my legs like it's going to be some kind of weapon. Maybe I can slice sideways with it? Or I guess if I just press hard enough, I can rip someone's skin apart with it. I'm still contemplating how to best use it as a weapon when I see the door creak open, just slightly.

Shit.

I hold the razor up, ready to slash whoever is coming through that door...

Then, it stops, and I hear a muffled sound. Several of them, actually, including some pretty hefty noises that could be someone falling down.

Or someone being pushed down.

Either way, I need to figure out what the hell it is that I'm working with.

Quickly, I rinse myself off and grab a towel. I pull my long hair up into it, and then step into the fluffy robe that's on the back of the door. Gripping the razor, I cautiously pad over to the door.

It's quiet out in my room.

Too quiet.

My heart is slamming in my throat. I'm not sure if I want to open the door and see what's going on out there at all. The best-case scenario is that one of Paulo's people came into my room to get me, and he just... got lost.

The worst-case scenario is...

Worse.

"It's safe, Marisol," I hear a soft, dangerous voice say.

I know that voice.

I open the bathroom door. Andrei is there, standing over a body.

A very suspiciously still body.

Andrei's eyes widen as he looks at me. "I... Please go back," he says. "You don't need to see this."

"Is he dead?"

Andrei doesn't say anything.

I sigh. "Is there a lot of blood?"

"Would that bother you?"

Normally I'd lie and say no, but... I wrinkle my nose. "Yes."

I don't particularly want a ton of blood in my bedroom, if I'm being honest.

"Si. Well. Give me about fifteen minutes and it will be done. You can finish your..." he doesn't say it.

I don't miss, however, how his eyes glide down to my bare legs.

Shit.

Just like my mom said, it's clear that Andrei Moretti is not just interested in me professionally.

You could do worse than a man who kills people for you.

Unfortunately, I don't want a man who kills people at all.

"Okay," I say quietly.

Then I sneak back into the bathroom.

I don't get into the shower. After locking the door, I take the chance to brush my teeth and do some other grooming. I have some clothes in the bathroom, just the soft lounge pants and a shirt that I was wearing before my shower, so I quickly put those on.

A soft tap on the door comes eventually. I don't have a clock on me, but I have a feeling it's exactly fifteen minutes later.

Cautiously, I open the door.

It smells heavily like cleaner. Hydrogen peroxide, actually.

I look down at the tile, and I don't see a single speck of blood there.

My eyes shoot up to Andrei. "You cleaned it?"

He doesn't say anything.

I shuffle, vaguely uncomfortable. "Thank you," I say finally.

He tips his head.

God.

What is wrong with me? He's handsome. He's already assigned to be around me all the time. Dino is out of the realm of possibility. I need to marry someone that my dad is going to approve of, in this stupid competition.

Moretti can't enter.

But he can keep me safe.

I know what I need to do. I need to keep him interested, keep this going. Make him think that he has a chance with me, so that he can protect me when…

You need to lead him on. You need to keep him close.

You're a terrible human if you do that.

I suck in a deep breath.

"Listen, Andrei…"

"Would you like to go for a walk?"

I blink, looking at him.

To my surprise, Andrei looks… nervous. His big, elegant hands, that normally are completely controlled, fidget on the zippers of his jacket. He looks like he's waiting for my response, and he's afraid of what he's going to hear.

"Is my dad going to be mad about that?"

He gives me a look, and just the very corner of his lips tips up. "He won't complain."

"Okay," I whisper. "Let me put on my tennis shoes."

I quickly do so. Andrei is waiting for me by the door, which I close with a soft click.

He follows me into the hall.

Andrei always follows me about two steps behind. I thought, previously, that it was like... a guard thing. He would fall behind so that I could walk in front of him.

I didn't consider that it was anything other than his work.

Until now.

Quickly and quietly, I take the fastest route to the garden. The estate is on top of a massive plot of land, and my father does employ someone to maintain a huge garden space. It's not as big as the compound that El Chapo had, supposedly, and we don't have a zoo on the premises or anything like that.

But I think that, given the chance, my dad would definitely try to import some zoo animals here.

We start through the garden, following a gravel path. My feet crunch on it, the sound almost too loud. We pass a couple of guards, who take one look at Andrei before looking quickly away.

Finally, toward the further part of the garden, I turn. "Do you notice that anymore?"

Andrei pauses. "Notice what?"

"That," I say, my eyes drifting to the place that we passed the last guard.

Andrei's face hardens. "I don't notice anymore."

However, based on the darkness there, I think he very much does notice.

"Hmm." I sigh. I look around. This part of the garden has a little green hedge, which my father employs multiple gardeners to keep looking crisp. I guess he must have let the gardening team go, though, because the hedge looks unruly and overgrown. Banana trees loom overhead, and there are other fruits as well. Mangoes, my mother's favorite fruit, as well as some figs. Guava, which is what I love.

Huh.

I never noticed before.

The hedge arches around a large circle, and there's a fountain at the center. The water moves quickly and smells slightly chemical, which is probably because of all the mosquito stuff that's tossed in it to make sure we all don't come down with malaria or something. There's a small bench in front of the fountain, a cement thing that is slightly covered in moss.

"Here," I say, gesturing to the bench. "Sit with me."

I sit, and my heart beats a little faster.

I've never invited anyone to sit with me. Any man, that is. The only man I've ever really even tried to get close to is Dino.

And he's not coming for me. Not here. Not when he has so much at risk...

And he better be looking after the girls until I can come back.

There's a long moment where I'm alone on the bench. The fountain jingles, the water cascading over the sides in a clear, bell-like tone. It's peaceful out here. I remember my dad saying that he built it so he and my mother could wander it together, before my mother told him she didn't much like gardens.

Especially gardens in Brazil.

There's a soft crunch of gravel, and Andrei joins me on the bench.

We don't say anything. I don't know what to say. I'm nervous, but not in the same way that I was nervous with Dino.

I'm just plain nervous here. I'm playing a game that I don't know the rules to.

And I don't know how to win.

"Why are you protecting me?" I finally manage to say.

Next to me, Andrei shifts. "I have to."

"Not like this," I clarify.

He huffs out a small breath. "No. Not like this."

"So why, then?"

He opens his mouth. Shuts it. Opens it again. "Do you know why I work for your father?"

I shake my head.

He continues, each word halting as though it's coming from somewhere deep within him. "My mother was... a businesswoman. She moved here from Italy when she was a teenager, and had me after."

Usually, that's code for a sex worker. I nod, showing him I understand.

"She was killed when another gang raided our... establishment. I was alone. Your father found me and took me in, and taught me how to be... me. How to get revenge on the people who hurt her."

"He does that," I say bitterly.

"I owe him for it," Andrei says softly.

I turn to look at him.

He nods. "I owe him for that," he continues, "but I also think maybe that the things I owe Benicio Souza are.. ending."

His words are so heavily accented that it takes me a minute. I turn to look at him. "You don't want to work for him anymore?"

He shakes his head. "No."

"So the plan is what? To marry me and run everything?" I snort. "He'd never allow that."

"I know," Andrei whispers.

Ice skates down my spine. "Andrei..."

"If no one wins the competition, Marisol, he will still need an heir."

I shut my eyes.

"I am not so bad," he says. "I would make... I would make a suitable husband. I would not be cruel. To you," he clarifies. "I would treat you well. I am not so bad to look at, no?"

I don't laugh at his joke.

He sighs, leaning back. "You are not so bad yourself."

"I'll pretend that's a compliment."

"It is," he says quickly. "It is. You are beautiful. And there is so much more."

He's right.

There's so much more to me. There's my father's organization. His debts. His failures.

Everything he has access to through me.

"Why not just enter the competition?"

"I can't. No... I am not an heir," he says with a frown in his voice.

"That's a stupid rule," I murmur.

Andrei doesn't respond.

I don't either. I stare at the fountain, aware of the dangerous Italian next to me. Andrei Moretti's right. He wouldn't be so bad, and I would be well taken care of with him. I think that I also would even be able to get the girls and bring them to live with me.

He's not bad. It's true.

But my heart holds on to one truth that it refuses to let go of.

He's not bad.

But he's not Dino.

Another three days, and it's time.

VIVY SKYS

My father is in the best mood. I haven't responded to Andrei's question, and he hasn't pushed me on it. I'm grateful for that, because I don't have an answer.

It's an arrangement that makes sense.

But my mother's voice keeps ringing in my head.

Decide with your heart.

My heart, unfortunately, is definitely not on board with the Andrei proposal.

I need to let that go. My future is about to walk into our courtyard. The whole thing feels absolutely archaic.

I'm dressed in an evening dress, like some kind of medieval princess. Inside, my father has prepared a welcome dinner. My role is to stand to the side, look pretty, and wave each of the men inside.

There are five, if the information I've overheard is accurate.

Five potential suitors. Five wealthy heirs to mafias across the world.

Five people who want to marry me for my father's empire.

Zero who want to marry me for... me.

I shuffle. I hate wearing dresses like this, and I feel kind of naked standing here. Behind me, Moretti tenses, and I give him a little wave with my fingertips.

I'm fine.

He doesn't move again.

Benicio opens the door to the house and the sound of the door slamming against the frame makes me jump. "Let them in!" he shouts to Paulo. My father turns to me, his grin turning sour as he does. "There will be no funny business from you, girl."

I toss my hair back and set my shoulders. "I know what I've done."

"You're here willingly because if not, I will kill your mother."

He's clearly posturing. We both know that my mother has her ways with him, and he's never quite been able to master them. All the same, I nod, showing him that I'm not going to fight. "I'm here willingly, father," I say.

He stares at me for a minute before nodding. "Good. You're not going anywhere. This is... if you do, I will come for more than just your mother," he says darkly.

My eyes snap up to his.

This is the first time that he's threatened the twins.

Ever.

My heart feels hard, but my father turns, waving me away. "Open the gate, Paulo."

Paulo, whose hand is still in a bandage, shoots me a glare before snapping an order into a radio. Minutes later, we hear the sound of tires and an engine, and a car pulls into the courtyard.

Out steps a tall, pale man with a shock of white blond hair. His blue eyes run up and down, and I want to hide.

"Alexei Volkov. Russian," Andrei whispers behind me.

"Thank you," I murmur back.

The Russian shakes hands with my father before heading inside.

Another car appears. Then another. I listen to each of their names, muttered softly behind me, while I evaluate all of them.

Vuk Pavlovic.

Luca Costa.

Bastien Deloitte.

Johnny Spinoli.

Five men. Five people that I need to be on guard around, constantly. Five sets of hungry eyes...

My eyes widen as I hear another car drive up. My father, who was about to head inside, pauses. He mutters something to Paulo, who shrugs.

The guards lower their automatic rifles, pointing them at the car.

There's a long moment before the door opens. Everyone is staring. There were only supposed to be five men here.

This sixth one?

Clearly, someone messed up.

Behind me, Andrei steps forward so he's right at my shoulder. He's staring into the car, his gaze as focused as a panther on the door.

The hair on the back of my neck raises.

Finally, the door to the car clicks open.

My heart is in my throat, and the sound of safety's being clicked off of each gun only makes my nerves worse.

One leg, well clothed in a suit, emerges from the car. My eyes trace the line of the man's body up, until they get to his face.

When I see who it is, my heart stops. I lose the ability to breathe.

Completely.

I make an effort to bring oxygen back into my lungs and I blink.

It can't be.

I take another look. The tattoos covering his neck, I know. His eyes are the eyes I see in my children every day.

And they're completely focused on me.

"Who the fuck are you?" Benicio snarls behind me.

Dino's gaze never leaves mine.

"Bernadino Drakos," he says. The name makes a murmur go around the courtyard.

"What the fuck are you doing here?" Benicio barks.

The smallest hint of a smile tugs at the corner of Dino's mouth.

"I'm here to enter the competition."

11

DINO

Inside the house, I do not eat anything.

Neither do the five other men around me.

There are plates in front of us, sure. But none of us are stupid enough to consume the food that Benicio Souza has in front of us.

Not tonight.

Besides, my eyes haven't left Marisol. Not fucking once.

I can't, for one thing. She's fucking stunning.

It feels like some kind of cheap charade that he made her dress up in a long, sparkling dress. She looks like she's going to the fuckin' Oscars, not in the middle of a jungle in the home of a drug dealer and thug known the world over.

Her long, dark hair cascades over her shoulder in a wave of warmth. Her eyes are huge, the makeup around them accentuating their softness. Between that and her delicate features, she looks like some kind of fairy princess.

She looks like someone who inspires a man to beat his chest and go to war.

That's what you're fuckin' doin, asshole.

I grit my teeth, my fingers clenching around the napkin in my lap.

I recognize some of the men around me. The Russian is one of the horde of bastards that stand to inherit some of the Russian organization, now that there's been a power gap. I'll have to tell Marco to get in touch with Stassi, who probably knows more about this white-haired douchebag than I do. There's a Serbian, Pavlovic, and some guy I don't know. Some guy who looks distinctly French, which sets my nerves on edge.

The French have a tendency to fight fuckin' dirty.

I recognize the last man. Johnny Spinoli, a Long Island boy. His whole family was arrested in the big RICO purges of the 80's and 90's, and he and his cousin Vito have done some contract work for us before.

He gives me a wink.

Idly, I wonder what he's doing here. He really doesn't bring anything to the table, in terms of financials, so unless he has something up his sleeve...

He's faking it.

Same as I am, I guess.

"Drakos," the word booms out of Benicio Souza, who is sitting on a dais somewhat above us like a king holding court.

My eyes snap up to his.

He's studying me. Benicio Souza looks weathered, but I'm not buying that he's old or feeble, by any stretch of the imagination. He reminds me of a gorilla, one of the ones that's covered in silver hair. He might sit up there away from us, but there's no doubt in my mind that the second he needs to, he'll be able to jump into action.

Hardened. He might be thick, but it hasn't made him any less slow.

Or any less dangerous.

"It's been a long time since I heard the name Drakos," he continues.

I don't say anything. I just stare.

"Who was your father?" he asks.

This is where I have to play it close to the chest. While Marco suspected that it is the Drakos family whose blood runs through my veins, he doesn't have confirmation.

And we don't have a name, either.

"Do you care about my father that fuckin' much?" I respond.

Marisol's eyes widen slightly, and Benicio's gaze gets hard. "You speak like an American."

"Grew up in New York."

"Hmm," Benicio says, his head tilting as he looks at me like I'm fuckin' steak on a plate. "That is interesting, isn't it?"

"Didn't come here to be entertainment," I snarl.

The other contestants are watching with interest now. Volkov, the Russian, is frowning at me.

Johnny turns to the guy next to him. "You Luca Costa?"

"Si," Luca says in Italian.

"I think I fucked your sister once. When she was here on her study abroad," Johnny says with a wink.

In a heartbeat, Costa's face goes beet red.

He stands and curses in Italian. He takes a swing at Johnny, who ducks it neatly. The chairs screech on the tile in the dining hall as all of us rise, and I go to Johnny's back.

"Enough!" Benicio's voice thunders in the hall.

We all freeze.

From wherever he's been hiding, I see Andrei Moretti slink forward. He's dressed like fucking James Bond, all black, with a gun belt and multiple holsters banding across his body.

I have no doubt that each one of them holds a knife, or something even more sinister.

"No speaking. No fighting. You are not here to settle old feuds or discuss sisters," Benicio glares at Johnny.

Johnny grins.

What the fuck is he doing here?

"You are here because of one thing and one thing only. You are to compete for my daughter's hand in marriage," he says, sinking back into his chair.

Slowly, we all follow suit. Costa and Spinoli switch so they're no longer sitting next to each other, and Johnny joins my right hand side.

"Stupid move," I mutter out of the corner of my mouth.

"Marco says hi," he murmurs back.

Oh for the love of the fucking baby Jesus. "I don't need a babysitter," I hiss.

"I'm not a babysitter. I'm backup," he sighs.

Fucking Marco.

"Shut up," Benicio snaps.

Johnny goes still.

Stewing, Benicio glares at us. "I have been blessed with many things in life. But I have never been blessed with a son and heir," he finally says.

That is a load of shit. Benicio has plenty of bastard sons.

For reasons that none of us can fathom, he won't pick one of them to inherit his crumbling empire.

Well.

I suppose that's the answer. He's flat broke, so instead of offering his cartel to one of them, he needs money. A cash infusion that he's going to get by auctioning Marisol off to the highest bidder. A man that's sitting in this room. A man that, he assumes, will come with the financials of their own organization.

That makes me fuckin' nervous.

If Benicio digs too deep, he'll not only realize that my connection to the Drakos family is tenuous at best, but that there's no financial reward there. Any resources that they might have had are not going to go to me.

I'm a bastard, in their eyes.

And I'm no one for the De Lucas either.

I swallow the bitterness on my throat. None of that matters now.

Right now, the only thing that matters is Marisol.

If I can get her out of here, then nothing else will fucking matter.

There's two ways that this ends. First, I steal her from under their noses. Given the rather impressive security along the way, which has increased by about a hundred percent since the last time I was here, I'm not so sure I can do that anymore.

The second option?

Win.

And she's fucking mine, fair and square. There won't be shit that Souza can do about it.

But, it also means that I have to *win*.

Benicio looks around the room. "You are all here because you represent organizations that need my connections. I am here because my precious daughter, who is my only heir, means more to me than life itself. I will not allow her to just go with anyone. The man who marries my daughter must be worthy. He must prove himself to me and her, and there will be a series of trials. Each one is designed to show off how well you will do as my son, and how effectively you can assume my business."

Great.

This is so fucking weird. Benicio must really be off his fucking rocker, because to think that he thinks himself so important that he needs someone to like... audition to be his son-in-law?

Utterly ridiculous.

Not to mention that, as near as I can tell, running this shit is essentially just a crapshoot. Either you try to make the business somewhat legitimate, like Elio has, or you go to fucking jail before you're fifty.

There are very few old men in this game.

Most of them are dead.

I guess that I have to give Benicio that, though. He lived long enough to run his cartel into the ground and come up with absolutely fucking nothing to show for his life.

Love that.

"The next few weeks will be challenging. I expect some of you may die. If you wish to spend tonight making amends with your families, you should do so. The competition begins tomorrow," Benicio says.

His chair screeches as he stands.

Noiselessly, he and his closest bodyguards leave the room. Marisol and Andrei Moretti remain, sitting at a table up to the far right corner of the room. The six of us stare at each other.

The Russian and the Serbian start muttering to each other. Luca Costa and the French guy bow their heads together.

Leaving Johnny and me alone.

I turn. "Seriously? Marco sent you to watch me?"

"Marco sent me as a scion of my family," Johnny winks at me. "But I'm always down for a fuckin' adventure, so I thought to myself, *Hey. Why the fuck not?*"

"You could die, you fucking idiot."

Johnny shrugs. "It will be pretty fuckin' noble to die helpin' a friend get the love of his life back though, right?"

My jaw drops. "Friend?"

"Yeah man. We're friends. Remember when you helped me get out of that thing with the Nostras?"

I blink. "We were like... eleven."

"And I ain't fuckin' forgot about it once."

I'm not sure how to respond to that. Johnny Spinoli isn't someone that I would have counted as a friend. Hell, I wouldn't have even said he was an acquaintance.

"You don't owe me shit for somethin' I did when I was a kid, man."

"Never said I owed ya, Dino. I said I was willing to help out a friend. That's all," he puts his hands up.

Jesus H. Christ. This fuckin' guy.

"So that's the gal, huh?"

I turn to look at Marisol, who is staring at me from her spot in the corner. "Yeah. That's my Marisol."

"I can see it," Johnny says.

I snap my face back to his. "You see fuckin' nothin', Spinoli."

He laughs. "Listen, you think I'd try to swipe you? Not in a fuckin' lifetime, man. I'd have to be one crazy motherfucker to get between you and her."

My eyes glide over Marisol, to where Moretti is standing behind her.

He's glaring at me. Pacing, slightly, from side to side.

"Yeah. Crazy motherfucker," I murmur.

Moretti leans forward and whispers in Marisol's ear. She nods, and rises from her seat, following him into the house.

I don't like that. Why did she follow him so quickly? Why...

"You want me to go after them?" Johnny asks.

"Andrei Moretti will wipe the fucking floor with you, man."

"Fair enough. So what's the plan?"

I watch them go.

I have to talk to her. I know that. She's... shocked. Probably confused. If I were her, I'd have a ton of questions.

But right now?

I have to wait. There's too much at risk, and I have no doubt that the second I get close, Moretti's going to push me the fuck away.

I sigh and look back. "The plan, motherfucker, is to win."

Spinoli grins. "Hell of a plan, Dino."

It's not a plan.

It's the only option.

Marisol is mine.

Anyone who stands between us is going to get laid the fuck out.

Crazy motherfucker, indeed.

12

MARISOL

Bernadino Drakos.

I still can't believe it.

Is he under some kind of assumed name?

How did he get here?

Has that always been his name, and I just didn't know it?

What is he supposed to be an heir to? He can't say that he's here for the De Lucas. He also can't be here as a Rossi.

Drakos...

It sounds Greek. Is it Greek?

I'm sitting on my bed, staring at my hands. I'm still wearing the stupid evening dress. I have no idea where all of the... candidates are sleeping.

Or if they're even here.

I don't know what my father has planned for them. Knowing

him, I'm very sure that it's something brutal and unspeakable, but I can't imagine that he's going to kill them all right away.

Potentially.

The dress is beginning to dig into my sides. I shift, but I still don't move to take it off.

Dino. Bernadino.

Drakos.

Do I even know him?

There's a slight sound at my door. I freeze, then notice a small piece of paper shoved underneath.

This could be...

Well. Honestly, I have no idea what it could be.

I creep over to it and retrieve it.

Unfolding the paper, I blink twice reading the message.

Meet me in the garden.

There's no additional information. Nothing that would signify who sent the note. I don't know how to explain it, but the handwriting doesn't look Slavic, so that rules out Pavlovic and Volkov. Costa's English isn't very good, and neither is the Frenchman's, if Andretti's information is accurate.

Leaving me with Johnny... or Dino.

I've never even seen his handwriting.

In a normal world, I'd know what his handwriting looks like. It would be on school forms for our girls. It would be all over everything that we do together, as a couple. Maybe he would have even written me a card or a note, something for our anniversary.

This is not normal.

I squeeze my eyes shut.

The note doesn't say when I should meet this mysterious person in the garden. Only that I should.

How the hell do any of them even know about a garden anyway?

My father's estate is... well. Closely guarded, to say the least. It's not something that he advertises, especially because it would also advertise his weaknesses.

But someone knows he has a garden.

And someone wants me to meet them in it.

I would.

If I could get around my guard dog.

Cautiously, I open the door to my room and peer into the hallway. Andrei is nowhere to be seen, which feels...

Well.

Even if I can't see him, I have no doubt that he's there.

He might not be watching right outside of the door, but he wouldn't be Andrei Moretti if he simply walked away from guarding me.

Shit.

Quickly, I duck back into my room. My heart is pounding in my chest.

If Dino is here, that means....

It means nothing.

I put a hand over my heart, trying to calm it down. There's something in the jumping rhythm that's making me feel almost sick.

I know why.

The strange fluttering in my chest, the way that I feel kind of... like I'm waiting on something.

I'm hopeful.

Dino came here, and now I'm hopeful.

Tears press against the edges of my eyes, and I put my head into my hands.

I feel so stupid for feeling hopeful like this.

Hope is a worthless emotion. Feeling it right now is just my traitorous body, or something like that. Dino and I don't have a connection. We aren't lovers, and we aren't dating. We're not married. There's no rational reason why Dino would come, because there's nothing for him to come after me for.

I need to stop hoping.

I need to address the realities.

Biting my lip, I sigh. "Okay Marisol. Let's look at this from the beginning," I whisper to myself.

The reality of the situation is that there are too many unknowns. I don't know why Dino is here. It's stupid of me to think that he might be here for me. That he might have come here to save me.

Given that I clearly don't know him after all.

Bernadino Drakos.

His name, the one he gave, makes my stomach roll again.

If he is the heir to some long-lost mafia family, a Greek one at that, then...

There it is. Sure as a punch to the gut, the air puffs out of my lips softly at the realization.

Of course there's no reason to be hopeful. I know exactly what is happening.

Dino didn't come here for me.

He did come here for something. I'm part of that something, but I have no doubt he wants the same thing from me that all of these other men do.

He wants a piece of my father's empire.

It makes sense. Dino's a second son. He's been his family's black sheep, or so I understand, for quite some time. Dino never intended to come after me.

He's coming after an empire.

The tears fall from my eyes. It *was* silly to think that Dino would try to come for me. Clearly, I told him everything that he needed to know about this competition, about my father.

About what was at stake for him.

He knows exactly why my father needs a new heir. He knows about the debt, and he knows my father's greatest weakness.

He might even be trying to use me, and our connection, as a way to get a leg up on the competition.

I look down at the note.

Hope.

What a stupid thing to feel right now.

I crumple it, and toss it aside. Instead of giving in to hope, I harden myself.

I need to do what's best for me. I need to choose a life that I can give my daughters. What I need to do is not entertain thoughts of some random person in the garden.

I need a strategy. Moretti is the closest thing that I have to one.

So that's what I'm going to do.

I'm not sure what happens to the little note. I turn, leaving it behind without looking back.

I definitely do not go to the gardens. I'm not going to go tonight, nor any other night.

When I climb into bed, I don't think of the note.

Not once.

Or at least, that's what I tell myself.

Without any more information from my father, I assume that my days should function as normal.

The following morning, I get dressed. I walk out to have breakfast like normal, and Andrei follows me into the small breakfast nook next to the kitchen.

Just like normal.

I sit down. There's no one in here. No staff, no security. Nothing and no one, except Andrei and myself.

I turn to him. "Are we supposed to be somewhere?"

He shrugs.

Turning back to the empty table, I sigh, frustrated. "It would be helpful if my father wanted to clue us in to what's happening today."

"His choices don't change what we are doing."

I glance at Andrei after he says that. "What?"

Andrei looks down, an uncharacteristically nervous gesture. "I had thought that we might go to the beach while the... festivities begin."

"The beach?" it's not impossible. The beach is probably somewhere around an hour drive, less if we take the helicopter.

"The beach," he confirms.

I...

I can't leave Dino.

The thought is buoyed up by that stupid, asinine feeling of hope. Again.

How many times do I have to remind myself that there's nothing there for me? That Dino isn't here for anything other than the empire that I possess.

The empire that he wants.

The empire I gave him the keys to.

Except one, I guess.

Andrei is the safer choice. He will definitely be able to get me out of here, and he won't mistreat me.

He's already said so.

Dino hasn't promised me any of that.

I open my mouth to say *yes of course, I'd love to go to the beach with you*, but there's a moment's worth of hesitation.

And it's just long enough that the door to the small room next to the kitchen slams open.

"Marisol!" my father yells.

I cringe. "I'm right here."

"Come," he commands.

Both Andrei and I watch him go. I turn to Andrei with a rueful smile. "Rain check?"

He looks confused.

"It's an English phrase. It means that we'll have to reschedule our... beach day to another time."

The word *date* had been on the tip of my tongue.

But this is not a date. It absolutely can't be a date.

I don't want to date him.

I can't 'date' him, not in the conventional sense. I need him to protect me.

And that fact alone makes me so angry that I have to take a minute to breathe before I get up to follow my father.

I hate this.

I follow my father out the door that leads to the garden. The irony of this isn't lost on me. For a split second, I wonder if whoever it is that sent the note knew about this... whatever's going on.

It's not possible. I didn't even know what was happening in the garden until now.

However, there's not really much time to think.

All six competitors are in the garden. There's kind of a big space, marked with crushed stone and benches, that marks the entry into the winding pathways that the garden contains. In this space, they're all gathered.

My father gives me a glare, and I walk over to him. He's seated in a patio chair next to a small iron table, and gestures for me to have a seat. I do, but not before Andrei takes out the chair so that I can sit as well.

Once I scoot in, I can see Dino's eyes are glued on Andrei.

The violence promised in them makes my skin pebble.

"Well, it is probably no secret that the... six of you," my father sends a nasty glare toward Dino, "are here to show me that you are strong enough to have a place in my organization. Part of that, of course, is that you must actually be strong enough."

Oh no.

I know where this is going.

I cast a look back at Andrei, whose face is completely impassive.

Turning back to the gathered contestants, I pick at the edges of my sundress.

This is not going to be good.

"One time, I was in the middle of the Venezuelan jungle. I had just been betrayed by my business partner, who attempted to expose me to the United States DEA. Instead of being arrested, I ran into the forest, convinced that I would be able to survive."

Despite myself, I'm kind of interested. My father has not once told me anything about himself, and certainly nothing about his past.

He smirks. "In order to find my way home, I entered into a... fight club? I think that's the word you would use. I knew that the only way to get back to my business and destroy my former business partner was to fight."

Benicio pauses, and for one second his eyes linger on me. "I did have some help," he murmurs. Then, his eyes shift back to the group, and he booms, "But that is not the point. You will not always have help."

Interesting. Why did he look at me? I don't have long to wonder, because he stands, raising his arms like he's some kind of Cesar. "The first of three trials will be this. You will fight each other. There are no rules, except there are no weapons. The last man conscious will be the victor," my father booms.

The contestants all shuffle. None of them seem to be intimidated or confused, but they do seem like they're... ready

Or like they're getting ready, anyway.

My father gives a broad, scathing grin. He turns to the group and says one word.

"Begin."

13

DINO

As soon as Benicio calls for the competition to begin, I have approximately three seconds before everything around me explodes.

Literally, in the case of a fist to my head.

Despite the ricochet of pain exploding across my face, I grin.

One thing I can do is fuckin' *fight*.

I don't know if it's rage or blood that turns my gaze red, but it doesn't fuckin' matter.

I'm here to fight.

Fast as I can, I round on the person who hit me. When my fist connects with his body, it sends a thrill of something wild and animalistic through me.

I don't have time to feel. I don't have time to do anything except *move*.

So that's what I do.

I don't know what is happening. Not consciously, really. I move like I'm programmed, like every movement is flowing through me, channeled by something that I'm not in control of.

It's like a bar fight, but so much better.

Everything around me is chaos. Fists. Feet. The crunch of bone and cartilage under my fingers.

At some point, someone is manically laughing. It takes me a second to realize that it's me.

Then, I keep going.

"Dino!" I hear Johhny yell.

I look over at him.

The Russian, Volkov, is towering over him. Johnny isn't a huge guy, maybe somewhere around six foot, with a fairly lean build.

Volkov is built like a fuckin' polar bear.

I snarl, dodging someone's fist before I duck and roll over to Johnny and Volkov. With a swift kick, I hit Volkov in his ankles.

Big men have ankles as weak as anyone. Weaker.

Volkov howls, and goes down. Johnny dodges his body as it dips, and ducks towards me.

"Behind you!" he yells.

I spin just in time to move away from the Frenchman's fist. I come back, knocking him down. I know it's a good hit because the sound it makes is like pounding into a steak.

I know it's a great hit when he doesn't get up.

"Dino!"

I turn to Johnny. Volkov is definitely reeling, but he's rebounding quickly.

He, Johnny, and I are the only ones still standing.

Johnny looks at me, giving me a wink. "I'd rather it was you, man."

Shit.

Instead of punching him, I walk up behind and grab his neck, pressing my hand against his windpipe. Volkov watches me, his eyes narrow, with all the patience of a wolf.

Gently, I lay Johnny down, and Volkov and I circle each other.

I don't have any formal training. I'm just fuckin' winging this.

But I can tell that Volkov is not going down easily.

We feint a couple of times, each of us dodging in the other direction. He's big but he's fast, and while I took his ankle down earlier, he's recovering well.

Still. If it's bruised, he has a weakness there.

Let's see where else you're hurt, motherfucker.

I duck in, landing a hit on his side. He winces, grunting. *Ribs.*

I spin away from him as one meaty fist moves.

Shoulder. He's slow on his right side.

Dancing behind him, I put a punch in his kidneys, and he groans.

That's the spot.

Enough pain from a kidney and liver shot will be more than just debilitating.

If I hit him hard enough, he'll pass out.

I grin.

Volkov grunts and dashes for me. I spin, but not fast enough. The pain in my shoulder is intense, to the point where I stumble for a second.

It's enough of a pause that Volkov swoops in, roaring like a wounded boar.

He hammers in another shot to my collarbone, and I hear something crunch.

That's not good.

There's a gasp that has to be Marisol. I turn, instinctively, toward the sound.

Her scream makes me turn back to Volkov.

I just manage to move fast enough to get out of his way. I'm on the defensive though, and that's not somewhere I want to be.

I run across the garden spot, my feet crunching on gravel. I need something. I can't use a weapon, but I could use...

There's a bench.

That I could use.

I turn back to Volkov, edging backward toward the bench. "Hey motherfucker!" I yell at him. "You think I'd go down that fuckin' fast?"

Volkov snarls something in Russian, a language that honestly, I never fucking bothered with, and stomps toward me.

Good.

He's dragging his back leg ever so slightly. I know that if I can get him to put weight on it, he'll collapse.

And then I can knock him the fuck out.

"Yeah, that's right, you giant fucking Russian piece of shit," I yell. The more that I talk, the angrier he gets.

It's a predictable reaction. Men like Volkov think they're powerful.

They're sensitive enough, though, to let words goad them into action.

"Yeah, that's right, you ugly fuckin' son of a..."

"Shut up!" He roars.

He's one foot from me when I hop up backwards onto the bench. Using the height, I fly forward, connecting with Volkov's shoulders.

Volkov roars, and I twist so that I'm behind him. One of my arms wraps around his neck while he tries to tear me off.

But he's not very flexible.

Can't forget to stretch after you work those pretty muscles, asshole.

I drive my knee into his kidney, and Volkov howls. I do it again and he staggers down. I push back, coming off of his back, and then stand over him as he falls to his hands and knees.

He looks up at me. He's panting, and blood is pouring from his mouth. Split lip or internal bleeding?

I don't give a fuck.

I bring my foot up, stomping him hard in the back again. He makes a sad, small noise, unusual for such a big man.

From this angle, I could stomp him in his jaw. Shatter the lower part of his face. I could...

"It's over," I hear a cold voice near my shoulder, and the sound of a safety being clicked off.

My chest heaves, but I look to the side.

Moretti is there, pointing one of his fucking big-ass pistols at my head.

I sneer at him, and he looks at me with flat, reptilian eyes. I'm not a fuckin' biologist or nothin, but I can tell that this guy isn't human.

Those are the eyes of someone dead inside.

I hold up my hands, wincing at the pain in my shoulder. "I think I won, asshole."

"Maybe," he says in response.

I give him a grin. I can taste the iron of blood in my mouth, but despite that, I smile so that he can see my teeth through the gore.

So he knows I am not fuckin' scared of him.

And if this gun wasn't between us, I'd fucking stomp his ass too.

Clapping sounds from where Benicio is sitting. He takes a step down, his polished boots crunching on the gravel.

He comes within about ten feet of me before he stops. "Bravo, Drakos."

I don't miss how his voice makes the word *Drakos* sound like a sneer.

"You did well. But I am curious, why did you merely choke this one," he gestures to Johnny. "Why not take him down completely?"

"I prioritized," I grunt.

Benicio stares at me for a minute. He makes a noise, nodding. "I think it would have been better to not reveal your weaknesses.... Drakos."

His eyes shoot to Marisol, who is standing. She's staring at me, her chest heaving. It makes her breasts press against the edge of the dress she's wearing.

That, in turn, makes my vision go red all over again.

But for a very different reason.

I take a deep breath through my nose, trying to control myself. I can fucking do this.

"Did I win or not?" I manage to grit.

Benicio frowns. "You did not lose," he concedes.

Good enough for me.

"Fine," I spit. "That's just fuckin' fine."

Benicio moves closer. "Do not think that this gives you the advantage. Even though I am holding this as a competition, I will not allow my daughter to marry someone I do not like," he says.

The words are cold.

Quiet.

For a second, I understand completely the type of killer that Benicio Souza is. Before now, he's been a somewhat arrogant, weird guy, who seems to be making us all dance at his whim.

Now, though, I see him.

The Benicio in front of me is a fucking threat.

And I would do well to remember it.

I nod sharply. "Noted," I say, not willing to give him anything other than that.

I don't want to give Benicio Souza a single thing that he could use against me.

He grunts. "Clean up. We will have dinner once the others regain consciousness."

It's approximately nine in the morning.

Clearly, he's building out some time for recovery.

Aware that Marisol is watching me, I limp away, back to the spot in the barracks that Souza gave us.

I need to get my shit together. I need to figure out if my collarbone is broken.

But most of all, I need to figure out how the fuck I'm going to win this shit.

Johnny, unsurprisingly, is one of the first to recover.

I didn't knock him out that badly. Choking out is an easy one to recover from.

"Bro," he says, a big grin on his face. "That was fucking epic."

"I need you to set my collarbone," I tell him.

Johnny blinks. "Bro?"

"Here," I gesture to him. After spending the better part of an hour poking at it, I figure that it at least has a hairline fracture.

I'm going to need to set it. I have a makeshift sling, made from a pillowcase, and I think that if I can just get it fuckin' straight, I'll be able to keep it semi-immobile unless I'm out jumping through Benicio's hoops.

Johnny blinks at me. "You want me to set your collarbone."

"Yeah. Didn't you spend like six months as a medic?"

He shakes his head. "Yeah but like that was a fuckin' minute ago, and I was dishonorably discharged bro."

"For setting collarbones?"

Johnny shuffles. "Nah man, for smoking weed."

I sigh and gesture him closer. "Set my fucking collarbone," I growl at him.

Blinking, Johnny steps back. "Jesus Christ. Okay. Let me just..."

I whip off my shirt, and he winces as he looks at the bruises covering me. "I think a broken collarbone might be the least of your problems," he says, eying the spot where my ribs are bruised so badly you can't see the tattoos on my skin anymore.

"Not broken. Collarbone," I point to it.

"Are you sure you need me to set it? Normally that stuff kinda just heals on its own with immobility."

"There's a piece of it that's not in the right spot," I grit. The feeling of your bones being in an incorrect place is not pleasant, and talking about it is making the whole situation even worse. "Set. My fucking. Bone."

"Jesus okay. Hold on…" Johnny presses his thumbs on either side of the broken bone.

The pain is blinding. I grit my teeth so hard that I hear one of them crack. Johnny's hands move, and with a little bit of a snap, I feel a dizzying wave.

It's in pace.

Panting, I wave my good hand at the pillowcase I made into a sling. Johnny eases me into it. Once I have it on, I collapse on my bed.

I'm in so much fuckin' pain, I feel like I'm going to throw up.

The nausea overwhelms me and I break out into a sweat. The only thing I can focus on is the rise and fall of my breath.

I let everything else fade.

In.

Out.

In.

Eventually, the urge to throw up diminishes. I'm left with the shaky after-effects of adrenaline.

Shock.

I need to get warm.

I sit up. Johnny's still here. "I need a blanket," I say, from between my chattering teeth.

Johnny leans forward and wraps something around my shoulders. "Already got you, boss."

"Not your fuckin' boss."

He sighs. "Yeah but. For now."

We sit in silence for another minute. He looks over at me. "You know, you could leave."

"No."

"The French guy and Costa left after they came to."

"Good," I mutter.

It is good. That's less competition. Volkov, Johnny, and the Armenian are the only ones left.

And me.

Johnny looks at me, his eyebrows pinching together. "You really want this chance at Souza's empire, don't you?"

I shake my head. "Don't give a shit about that."

"So why... oh," Johnny's eyes widen. "The girl. You really are just here for the girl."

I nod.

"I really am."

14

MARISOL

There's another note.

Meet me in the garden. Afternoon.

At least this one is more specific.

Ish.

It's been two days since the melee fight. I haven't seen any of the contestants since. I do know both Luca Costa and the French man have left.

Apparently my father is being merciful, and allowing contestants to leave rather than just die here.

It's unusual of him, but I think he likes that. He wants to keep everyone on their toes.

Myself included, I guess.

Which is why when the note appears, another awful, terrible thought enters my mind.

What if it's my father, trying to trick me into something?

Shit.

I pace again, staring at the note on my bed. At this point I don't know that it's Dino, but I also don't think it could be anyone else...

Or at least, I hope it couldn't.

There's a rap on my door. Quickly, I snatch the note up and fold it in my hands. "Come in," I say to the person on the other side.

The door creaks open, and Andrei's head pops in. "Your father would like you to come to the kitchen for brunch," he says.

Quietly.

My stomach sinks. "Why?"

"Why does he do anything, Marisol?"

Fuck.

"Okay. Just. Give me a second," I say.

I don't want Andrei to know about the note. If it is Dino, then I need to make sure Andrei doesn't see it.

The scene at the melee a few days prior is still fresh in my mind.

I think Dino would have smashed Volkov's head in. If he'd had the option. The way he stood over Volkov's body, the way Dino's leg was tensed... I'll never forget that.

He was... unhinged. Violent. Brutal. They didn't know, but my dad was commenting on every single one of the fighters.

And for Dino?

Even Benicio Souza said that Dino was 'aggressive'.

I'm not certain why my dad gave Andrei the command to stop him. Clearly, he'd been enjoying the show so far, so for him to just... call it off like that was wild.

I did, however, catch the way that Andrei looked at Dino. The coldness in his face. I've seen that look before. Andrei hates Dino, with something more than just the average amount of dislike.

Whatever he feels towards Dino, it's... deeper than that.

For his part, Dino also seems to hate Andrei. The smile he gave wasn't joyful in the slightest. It was a baring of teeth, and the flash of white through the blood dripping in his mouth had been nothing short of savage.

I shuddered.

Quickly I duck into the bathroom and put the note in my makeup case. I grab a lip gloss and step out, holding it to my lips to apply it as I walk toward Andrei.

He raises an eyebrow.

"Can't leave the room looking disheveled," I comment. "My mom always said that your appearance is like armor. Putting it on right can help you stay safe during the battle."

My mother did say this often. She also said that beauty was a weapon that could take out a man's heart as sure as a bomb, and to be sure to use it with that intent.

I didn't tell him that, though.

Andrei quietly falls in behind me as I walk down the hallway. When I get to the kitchen, my father is sitting in the small breakfast nook, which is unusual.

He is also alone, which is even more unusual.

I sit and he nods at Andrei. "You can take the door," he commands.

Andrei's eyes linger on me for just a second. I look away, hoping my father doesn't notice.

When Andrei leaves, Benicio sighs. "Your mother has the same effect on people."

"What effect?"

"Draws their attention like a flame."

I duck, my cheeks red. "I don't want to," I say quietly.

"You never have, have you?"

Curious at my father's calm tone, I look up at him.

His eyes study me. I definitely favor my mother in terms of looks, but I can see how my father and I are related. The high, proud cheekbones, for one. I have his nose, arching and patrician.

Have I noticed the gray in his hair before?

Or the scars that feather out from one side of his head?

"You are quiet."

"I have nothing to say," I murmur.

"Nothing to say, or nothing to say to me?"

I don't answer that question.

My father sighs and looks over the table. "You know, I would let you have a choice, if you wanted it."

That makes me bite back an acidic laugh. "Excuse me?"

"In the suitors. You could tell me who you prefer."

Absolutely not.

I look at my father. "Do you remember when I was six, you kidnapped Mamá and me, and you kept us in your house that was on the plains?"

He grins. "Ah yes. I loved that time."

Of course he did. "You told me you would buy me a horse."

"Anything for my princess."

"It was a nice horse. I think they call the color palomino."

"Gold," he grins. "For my golden girl."

"Then, when Mamá and I escaped, you sent its hide to us."

His face falls.

I stand. "I would not tell you my choice, even if I made one. I will choose whatever you want. There will be no horse hides on my conscience. I will agree to this marriage. I will participate in your farce. But do not think that for one second, you can pretend to be a father."

"Marisol, I..."

I hold up my hand. "You have done nothing but hurt me. This is no different. I will not be manipulated by you, Benicio."

I can tell the use of his given name instead of "father" or "Papao" irks him, because his eyes flash. "You are my child. I am free to do with you as I wish."

Anger, bright and hot, flares in me.

I'm lucky that I had my mother. She taught me that children

are not clones of their parents, but their own people. I am not a tool to be used by Benicio.

I choose how and when I will be part of his plans.

I'm only here now because I had no other option.

I lean forward so that our faces are close. "I am not a child, Benicio. I am my mother's daughter. I will play your game now so you can get what you want, but I will also get what I want."

"That is what I am trying to tell you. You could tell me which of these..."

"And have you kill them? No," I sneer. "You'll have to make those decisions all on your own. I'm just the prize. But when you're finally flush with the cash you need and you have your precious son-in-law to hand everything over to, remember that you will just be their father-in-law. I will be their *wife.*"

I grin at him, as some kind of understanding flashes. "You are not the only one who can manipulate others, father," I hiss.

Then I gather myself.

And I leave.

I stalk toward the pool.

While there is an outdoor lagoon, which my father maintains for reasons I can't fathom, the indoor pool is where you could swim laps. Built for a politician and his family, this estate has many such amenities.

I want to take advantage of it.

Andrei follows me, a shadow that's always three paces behind. I turn to look at him. "I want to be alone," I say, right outside of the changing room where I keep a couple of swimsuits.

"Marisol…"

His accent makes my name musical.

But it's not the raspy growl that makes my blood run hot.

"Please," I whisper. "There's only one entrance. You can sit outside of it. Please just leave me alone."

Actually, it's not true. There are two ways to enter the pool. One of them happens to be connected to the pool maintenance room. It's a mess of pipes and chemicals, and if someone did enter through that way, they'd have to navigate a terrible crawl space filled with whatever nasty insects the jungle wants to produce that day.

Technically, there's another entrance, but I've never seen anyone actually use it. They'd have to know the compound really well, and they'd have to be very okay with being bitten by something that would likely take their life.

Or worse.

Andrei looks at me. His eyes, which normally are so impassive, become rounded with concern. "Marisol…"

I look away.

He sighs, but relents. I hear the door to the pool room close, the sound echoing around the space.

I'm grateful that he is willing to leave me alone.

God knows my own father would be less willing to do that. Clearly.

Remembering the horse has dredged up a thousand more memories of my father. I'm struggling under the weight of them, and I think a quick swim might be helpful.

I braid my hair into a long rope before I change quickly into the unassuming one-piece that I keep down here. I've definitely grown a little since I last put this on, so it stretches tight against my breasts and comes up higher on my ass, but it's fine.

I'm alone, after all.

Silently, I play a game that I used to play when I was little. *How quietly can you swim?*

I think my mom taught me this one with the vision that one day, I would likely need it to escape.

One day.

I silently glide into the water. I take a few tentative strokes, noting how smooth it feels against my skin, before I drop the routine of silence and shut my eyes.

I start to swim, eyes closed, and see how long I can go without breathing. How long it takes me to reach one side and push away, gliding back.

How long it takes me to stuff the memories down of my father, and remember the ones I love instead.

The girls.

My mother.

Unbidden, Dino's face springs into my mind. I pull up, gasping, wiping water out of my eyes.

I can't count him among the things I love.

I don't even *know* him.

The brutal man from several days ago. The bloodthirsty fighter. The man who entered, uncalled for, and stood before my father.

Drakos.

I tread water, trying to shake my head as I rid myself of thoughts of Dino.

There's a sound. It's so small I might miss it, but in the pool room, every sound is magnified. I can hear the water sloshing, and my own breath, sawing in and out of my lungs.

And something else.

The back of my neck prickles. I spin, looking around.

It feels like there are eyes lingering on me.

"Andrei?"

The word echoes. The door to the pool room snaps open, and Andrei comes in, his pistols out.

"Marisol. Are you okay?"

I frown. I look around again. There's no sign of anyone else, and the room echoes with the last of Andrei's concerned footsteps, accompanied by the light slap of water against the tiles.

"I'm fine," I whisper. "I just..."

I pause.

I just thought someone was watching me.

15

DINO

A week.

That's how long we've been waiting for the motherfucker to pose his next goddamn challenge.

One.

Fucking.

Week.

In that time, I'm going absolutely crazy. My collarbone hurts. My whole body feels like shit. I might be going crazy.

I have to find a way to see Marisol again.

Johnny, surprisingly, is somewhat helpful in that regard. Since no one feels like he's a serious contender for the role, he's able to joke around with some of the guards. Get some insight into where Benicio keeps Marisol, and for how long.

From what I can tell, Marisol has free reign of her own home. My concerns about her being a fuckin' captive are unfounded.

Except that she has the Italian bastard following her everywhere.

Moretti hates me. That's clear as fuckin' day. Every time he sees me, his eyes turn into some kind of hateful, disgusting glare. He looks at me like I'm fuckin' scum.

Which is fine.

It's nothing new.

What I can't figure out, though, is why. Sure, everyone hates me, but I don't know specifically why Moretti does.

Prior to this, we haven't ever met. I ain't seen his ugly fuckin' face one day in my life, even if I did know of him.

And knowin' of him is all that we had, before this.

Moretti's reputation as Souza's hound, guard dog, and executioner is somewhat legendary. I wasn't shocked when he showed up looking for Marisol.

But I am shocked to see how much he doesn't like me.

The door to my little barracks room opens, and Johnny saunters in. "I think I know how to find you some time with your girl."

That gets my attention. "What?"

He flops on the bed, and eyes my arm in the sling. "You think you can make that thing work?"

"For Marisol?" always.

He sighs. "Marco didn't really say you were here because of a girl."

"He sent you here without any context?"

Johnny shakes his head. "Only that you wanted to win this fuckin' thing."

"Why else would I want to win it?"

That earns me a scathing glare. "Because whoever wins gets the keys to the fuckin' kingdom, man."

I tilt my head. "Do you want this kingdom, Spinoli?"

Johnny sighs, leaning against the wall. "I mean it's not like I've got another one to walk into."

Johnny's not a second son, like me. He's the scion of his family, and in theory, he could definitely be in the running for his family.

But instead of that, his whole family has been nailed on so many charges, they have a whole section of prison dedicated just to the Spinolis.

Or at least, that's what I've heard.

"You don't want what Benicio Souza has to offer," I say darkly. Benicio has built his empire on blood. It's not necessarily surprising that he drove this thing into the ground, financially, but at the same time it is kind of surprising that he allowed himself to get in this position.

That he didn't just kill everyone in order to cover it up. That he has enough people coming after him that he needs a financial infusion.

"You know why he's trying to sell Marisol off to the highest bidder, right?"

"Man, I don't know how you think of sellin' someone, but I'm sure this ain't it," Johnny grins and points at my collarbone, then at the black eye he's still sporting."

"Doesn't matter how he's hiding it. Benicio only wants people with families that he can tap into because he needs the money."

"How so?"

"Marisol told me."

He shrugs. "Man, I know that. But still. The chance to take over one of the greatest cartels in history? You gotta admit, that sounds pretty fuckin' good."

I don't care about the cartel.

All I want is Marisol.

When I don't answer, Johnny sighs. "Well. Guess I better tell you about what I have."

"Please."

"She swims at the pool. Once a day. Around three."

"The outside pool?"

"Inside lap pool."

Fuck. I narrow my eyes, and Johnny continues. "There's a door. It's a maintenance door on the outside of the building. Guard change is around two, then again at four. In theory if you snuck in, crawled past all the spiders and shit, then you'd be in there with her."

My heart kicks against my ribs.

I frown, looking at him. "How the fuck do you know?"

"I braved the spiders."

Which means he saw Marisol in her swimsuit.

My eyes glaze over. Johnny's talking, but I don't hear him.

In a heartbeat I fling off the sling and grab him by the throat. "Don't you ever fuckin' look at her again."

He coughs, squirming under my grip. "Fuck off!" he rasps.

"Never. Fuckin. Look at her," I snarl.

"Okay! I won't!"

I drop him. Johnny coughs, wrapping his hand around his throat. "Fuck, man. I'm just tryin' to help."

I don't answer.

Johnny mutters, giving me a glare. I know that I should apologize. Say something.

I don't want to.

"I'm not after your girl, asshole," he says finally. "You can calm the fuck down."

I don't have anything to say.

"Jesus. Look. Do you want to get in to see her or not?"

I nod.

"Tomorrow. Meet me and we'll go."

With that, Johnny leaves.

I can't help myself. The hope I have is...

Terrifying.

The next day, in the afternoon, Johnny and I set out like we're going for a run. We don't go together, because being seen as an alliance is going to get us fuckin' killed.

But I follow him, slowly, as he jogs around the compound.

When he gets to a sheer wall, without any windows, he runs over and slaps a sweaty hand on it.

Gross.

I hesitate, then a few minutes later, I follow.

The wall doesn't have any discernible places where it's clear that I can get into it. For a second, I think that Johnny has been fucking with me.

Then my fingers find the slightest dent.

I follow it, outlining a square on the side of the building. Cautiously, I push, and to my surprise the door clicks open.

Huh.

It's not big. It looks like the door to a crawl space, maybe four foot square. Still, it's exactly as Johnny said, and the guards are changing as we speak.

Time to crawl.

I get on my hands and knees and push. Inside, there's a mess of dripping, chlorine-scented wires. Once or twice, I feel the brush of spiderwebs over my skin, or the feeling of too many legs on my arm.

Being bitten by something in the Brazilian jungle is not how I want to die.

But it's worth it to get to Marisol.

Eventually the crawl space opens up slightly, making room for bigger pool maintenance items. I'm not a fuckin' pool boy, so I don't know exactly what all of this shit is.

I do, however, know that Marisol is worth wading through this garbage for.

When I can stand, I see another door. This one has a handle and everything, which is a good sign. I press against it, listening to the room beyond.

There's nothing. Silence. I look down at my watch, noting the time.

Johnny said that she swims at three. It's two fifteen.

Fuck.

I have forty five minutes to wait it out.

I slide down, putting my back to the door. Idly, I wonder if there's any kind of locker room out there. I could do with a shower, and if no one is going to be in here for a while...

Cautiously, I crack the door, just slightly.

There's no one in the room.

It's huge, containing what must be at least an Olympic-sized pool. There's sunlight coming in from bright windows up overhead, and it plays on the still water. You can hear a light sound, the pumps running probably, but nothing that would give any indication that there are other human beings nearby.

I spy a door that looks like it might be a restroom. There's two of 'em.

Forty-five minutes.

I can make that work.

Quickly, I move. I slip into one of the rooms and lock the door. If someone is gonna bust in on me, I'll at least be able to hear 'em comin.

I turn the shower on.

My clothes are kind of fucked. They're covered in mud and some spider shit, but at least I'll be able to smell like I didn't just wade through some mud.

That gives me plenty of comfort.

Showered, clean, I slip my clothes back on and peek out again. Still no one. I slip back across the space, my feet padding softly on the tile, and into the pool room again.

Then, I put my back against the door and I wait.

Eventually, I'm beginning to be very sure that Marisol isn't even coming. After all, why would she? She's not held to a schedule or required to be here or nothin' like that. I'm certain that I should just leave when I hear something.

Despite the fact that I'm behind a closed door, I still, my heart in my throat.

I hear Marisol's voice.

"Thank you," she says, muffled through the door. I tilt my head so my ear is flat against the door, listening in. "You can leave."

"Marisol. Every day, you ask me to leave."

"I know."

There's a man in there with her.

My whole body goes rigid, and a growl forms in my throat.

Who the fuck is in there with her?

"Are you certain you don't want..."

"I am. I just... it's my time. To be alone," she says.

I think whoever this is, he's making her fucking uncomfortable.

"Have you thought of my offer?"

That voice is heavily accented. Italian, if I'm not mistaken. Since Luca Costa went home, and Johnny doesn't have that type of an accent, there's only one person who could be in there with her.

Ice covers my heart, but my body builds rage like a furnace.

I know who that is.

I know exactly who that fuckin' is.

Moretti is in there with her. He's her fuckin' personal guard, and this also explains why he was such a fuckin' dick to me that day.

He wants her for himself.

Jesus Christ. Everything in me is telling me to get in there. Storm in, knock his fuckin' lights out, and take her. Run away from this place, crawl through all the goddamn spiders and somewhere that they can't find her.

That he can't find her.

"Andrei..."

The use of his name, his first fuckin' name, is like a bomb in my ears.

A horrible thought occurs to me.

What if she likes him being around? What if she's choosing to keep this... whatever it is going with him?

What if she feels the same way about him that he feels about her?

Rage, hot and clean, burns through me.

"I haven't thought any more about it, Andrei."

"Marisol..."

No one gets to use her fuckin' name but me.

"Please. I just want to be alone right now. Can you do that, Andrei?"

There's silence.

If he doesn't leave her alone, I don't give a shit about the consequences. I don't give a shit if he shoots me so full of holes I look like Swiss cheese.

I can get to him before that. I can do enough damage before I die that...

"As you will," he says.

There's another silent heartbeat. I hear footsteps echo.

Then, there's just the sound of splashing.

I open the door.

16

MARISOL

The feeling of being watched is much stronger this time.

I've been coming every day to swim around the same time as the first day. At first, it was just convenient, but as the week wore on it's more than that.

If someone was watching me that first day, they'll probably come back. The notes came back. Once a day. *Meet me in the garden.*

Meet me in the garden near the mango tree.

Meet me in the garden under the banana leaves.

Meet me in the garden at two-thirty, on the bench near the fountains.

Each one is more and more specific, like whoever sends them is insistent on meeting with me, and they're getting more frustrated by the day.

So this has to be the same thing.

Right?

But every day, I don't see anyone. It's just me, swimming laps in the pool, and Andrei guarding the door.

Andrei is getting impatient with me. I can practically feel it in my bones. I know that he wants an answer from me.

Today's conversation confirmed it.

I set off on another lap, unwilling to look up from the pool. There's no one in here except me. Andrei doesn't watch me while I swim, which is a relief.

My hands slice through the water. I'm almost to the edge of the pool. I reach forward, expecting to connect with smooth tile...

Instead, I feel something else.

A body.

A very, very firm body.

Startled, I rear back. My eyes snag on a man's chest, covered in tattoos...

And bruises.

I look up.

Standing in front of me, in the shallow end of the pool, is a familiar face.

Too familiar.

Dino... Drakos, I guess, is staring at me from the pool.

For a minute, I don't know what I should do.

Then, I realize what I should *definitely* do.

I open my mouth to scream.

Quick as lightning, Dino's arm snakes out and he pulls me close, covering my mouth with his hand. I struggle, making noises, and they echo in the hall.

"Stop," he rumbles in my ear. "I'm not going to hurt you. I just want to talk."

I must be insane. That's the only explanation.

Because when he takes his hand off of my mouth, I don't scream.

I just nod.

Dino takes a breath, but I shake my head. My eyes dart to the door, where Andrei is definitely standing outside.

If he finds Dino in here...

Fear makes my chest ache.

Dino nods. He gets up and looks around, poking into the little baskets around the edge of the pool. Eventually he comes back...

With a wind-up toy.

I have no idea why there's a toy down here. I've never played with it, even though it looks to be a little old. Dino winds it up, then sets the little boat in the water.

It makes a sound...

But most importantly, it creates a rhythmic wave that slaps against the sides of the pool.

Just like someone swimming.

In the space, the noise of the toy sounds just like me doing my laps.

Dino jerks his head toward one of the changing rooms, and I nod.

As quietly as I can, I follow him out of the pool. I do my best to not make any sound as my fingers press against the hard tile, aware of every single drip of my swimsuit on the smooth surface.

Dino pulls me into the changing space, his hand like a brand of fire around my wrist.

He leaves the door slightly cracked, and we move in.

The changing room is small. There's a small space to wash your hands, and a teak bench to aid in putting swimsuits on and off. There's a shower back in the corner, and judging from the droplets of water clustered on it, Dino's been in here somewhat recently.

"What are you doing here?" I hiss.

Dino glares at me.

"If Andrei finds you, he's going to…"

"Andrei?" he rumbles.

God, his *voice*. The rasp of it, the way it sounds so hoarse and harsh, skates over me like a hand.

My nipples pebble, and Dino's eyes drift down to my chest before snapping back up again.

"That's his name," I say, not willing to give him an inch.

"But why are you calling him that," he snarls.

"Because I…"

I don't have time to react.

Dino leans in, crushing me against him in an earth shattering kiss.

For a second, I don't have any thoughts. I am nothing but feeling. Nothing but the sensation of his lips on mine.

Nothing but the fire that's burning through me.

It's not like being numb. Not really.

It's like...

Coming home.

The safe, calm sensation quickly dissipates though, when Dino slants his mouth over mine. His fingers glide up my back, threading into my hair, which he pulls roughly, tugging my head to deepen the kiss.

Then, I'm more than just sensation.

I'm detonating.

Just like our first kiss, this one makes me feel like I'm perilously close to melting. His hands are hot as they roam me, tugging and kneading at my wet skin under my swimsuit. When he slips one of my straps off of my shoulder, I let him.

When his fingers find my taut nipple, I let him do that too, gasping against him at the sensation of him tugging at me there.

Hard.

Dino moves down to my neck, kissing me as he goes. "There are no more men's names in your mouth except mine," he snarls against my breast.

I'm about to protest when he sucks my nipple into his mouth.

Then, I don't protest.

I arch against him.

I want to moan. I want to scream his name. *Dino....*

Drakos.

"Stop," I whisper.

Dino snarls against my skin. It feels so good, but I...

I don't know him.

"Stop," I repeat, louder.

Dino's head snaps up and he stares at me. "What?"

"I said stop."

It's clear that he's not exactly okay with this. His eyes flare with darkness, and he looks at me like he's considering doing exactly the opposite.

"Please," I whisper. "We need to talk."

Dino visibly makes an effort to pull himself back. I slide my shoulder strap back into place, staring at him as he paces the small space.

The door is cracked. He listens intently, then looks back at me. "Nothing," he whispers.

I nod.

"You wanted to talk. What do you want to say?"

"Who are you?"

The question seems to make Dino unbalanced. "What?"

"I said who are you?"

"I am Dino De Luca. The father of your children. I am..." he stops.

I stare at him. "And how much of that is a lie?"

"None of it," he says fiercely.

I arch my eyebrows at him. "Dino Drakos?"

"A technicality."

"How?"

"A technicality I exploited so I could come to this fucking place and save you, Marisol!" he barks.

It's loud.

And we both know it.

Dino cautiously pokes his head out of the door again. The only noise I can hear is the gentle slapping of water against the pool, and the thunder of my own heart.

He turns back. "It's nothing. I just want to get you the hell out of here."

I blink at him. "You can't."

"The hell I can't," he snarls.

"Dino. Seriously. Think about it," I whisper.

He stops, looking at me.

"If you try to pull me out of here right now, my dad is going to know exactly who it is. And your little pseudonym isn't going to do anything to hide you. He's going to know that it was Dino De Luca who pretended to be Dino Drakos. It's going to be obvious. Then, he's going to scour the globe with whoever he decides wins this competition, and he's going to find you. He's going to find me," my lip trembles.

Dino's eyes widen, watching the wobble in my lip.

I take a breath. "And he's going to find the girls. He doesn't care about his grandchildren, for reasons that I can't figure out. But this might be the time that he finally does, Dino."

"He wouldn't hurt them. He can't..."

"My dad once killed an entire village because they wouldn't let him store his supplies there," I whisper. Tears are gathering in my eyes now as I remember the untold number of atrocities I've seen my dad commit.

And I'm sure I haven't even scraped the surface.

"He would hurt the girls. He would kill all of the Rossi family. He would hunt down everyone related to you until he found us."

"Marisol..."

"He would kill my children, Dino," I whisper.

He looks at me.

"Our children," he says.

The word *our* sounds painful. Full of longing.

Full of something I can't quite put my finger on.

"He would hurt them, Dino. I can't let that happen."

"I can protect you."

"For what? So that we can live on the run for our entire lives? SO that the girls will never know peace?"

"What peace are they gonna' fuckin' have here? You think that if that fuckin' Russian wins, he'll let you live with the girls?"

"No. Of course not. I'm not betting on the Russian."

"Then who..."

His eyes narrow to slits when he figures it out. "Moretti."

"He promised that I could have the girls with me. That he would protect me."

"That fucking rat bastard is not going to have my fucking family," he snarls.

"He's not, Dino, but I'm not your family."

Dino freezes.

I take a deep breath. "We don't know each other. I don't even know you, Bernadino Drakos," I say in a whisper so small, it's barely audible.

Dino looks like he's going to explode.

"We aren't anything to each other, Dino. We had sex. One time. Years ago…"

"You're wrong," he mutters.

I look at him.

"You're wrong, Marisol. If you don't want me, that's fine. If you truly don't fuckin' want me and you want to choose him, I won't beg you. I won't fuckin' beg someone to be with me," he mutters.

It sounds like he's reassuring himself more than making a statement to me.

"But you're wrong. You ain't meant to be with Moretti. You, and the girls, are mine. You're meant to be with me," he says.

The ferocity in his voice makes the little bubble of hope in my chest, that I've done such a good job of squishing down, feel like it's expanding.

"Dino…"

"Drakos is a Greek name. Apparently, my mom had a little vacation right after she and my dad got married. She came back and I was born too soon for comfort, so they just... yeah," he mutters.

My jaw drops. "You aren't your father's son?"

"No," he says.

It looks like it pains him to say.

"Dino..."

"Drakos is the name Marco gave me. He fuckin' apparently knows the whole thing. Read my mom's fuckin' diary after she died."

"And he kept that information from you?" If I remember right, the patriarch and matriarch of the De Luca family died several years ago, after Caterina's engagement to Elio was formalized. The whole underworld was buzzing, speculating on who it was. Many people blamed my father, but he had a good alibi at the time.

And, he didn't have any issue with the De Lucas.

Then.

Dino's jaw clenches, and I know that Marco's lies of omission hurt him more than he's willing to say.

"Look. I ain't askin' you to love me. But I am..." Dino looks down at me.

He takes a huge breath.

"I've lived a shit life, Marisol. Shit in a lot of ways. But you are the only thing that's kept me going. You and the girls," he adds.

"I don't know what to say…"

"Don't,'" he says. "Just don't. I know. You don't know me. But I… I'd like to change that," he mutters.

"I'd like that too," I whisper.

Dino studies me. "You swim here every day?"

I nod.

"I'll be back tomorrow," he grunts.

Then, on feet so soft and quiet I'm surprised that they belong to him at all, he opens the door and pads away.

I watch him go. He slips into the pool maintenance room before disappearing.

Staring, I almost forget that I need to be in the pool.

By the time Andrei opens the door again, I'm back to swimming. The toy is hidden, back safely where Andrei can't see it.

Tomorrow.

I don't know if Dino will be here tomorrow.

But I will be.

17

DINO

I dream of Marisol.

It's so fresh in my mind now, all the things that I used to think I had imagined. The way she tastes. The sweet smell of her. The little moans that she makes when she's kissing. The feel of her thick hair wrapped around my fist. Half of these things I thought that I fuckin' made up, because there's no way that they could be real.

There's no way that they could have been as good as I remembered them.

Except now, it's clear that they are that good. I kissed Marisol yesterday, and now my mind keeps running through the sensations that aren't forgotten anymore.

They're fresh.

Marisol is real. The spark I thought I might have imagined between us is still a fuckin' five-alarm fire.

And I still gotta win this fuckin' thing to get her home.

Johnny raps on the door frame. "Hey boss,' he grins, looking me up and down. "I see you didn't die from some kind of freak spider incident."

"Nope. Did not."

"Did you get to see your--"

I cut him off, pulling him into the room and shutting the door. "Damn, Johnny," I hiss. "Shut the fuck up where people can hear you."

"No one's here, man. The Russian and his fuckin' lackey are out running laps in the garden."

I raise an eyebrow. "Why?"

"Probably because your girl is out there and they think that they have some kind of chance with her if she sees them without their shirts on."

I snort. Marisol isn't someone that's impressed by shit like that.

We don't really know each other.

Her words from yesterday echo in my mind. I sit up on my bed, looking over at Johnny. "You have shoes you can run in?"

"Man, I can run in basically anything. Come on, Dino. You know better than to ask that," he grins.

"Good. Let's go."

Johnny trails me out into the barracks hallway, and then to the main house and garden area. I say the garden, but it's really so much more than that. There's a terrace that backs up to the house, which is where the fight took place, and is the only place that I've currently seen Benicio sit out on. It's also the only place that I've seen Marisol outside of the house, so I assume it's a somewhat integral part of this whole place.

The garden is much bigger. It extends for about an acre, maybe an acre and a half, to the north of the house away from the terrace. The house's main entrance is on the South side, with the pool wall, and secret maintenance tunnel, arching to the west.

The day is hot. It feels oppressively humid, like the clouds above us are heavy, and they're sinking down to ground level.

"Fuck this," Johnny pants as we make our way to the garden terrace. "It's so humid out here, I think that I'm going to just turn into a damn frog or something."

"You're from New Jersey. You can handle a little humidity," I call back at him.

Johnny, however, clearly doesn't agree. As we run, he continues to mutter and gripe, but I tune it out.

When we get to the terrace, I can see the Russian and his creepy friend doing what I can only think are some kind of fucked-up Soviet calisthenics. Johnny runs up behind me and stares at the sight.

"Bro. Are they like training to be the bad guys in Top Gun?"

"I think they're trying to be impressive," I say with a look up at where Marisol is sitting under an umbrella.

God, she looks so fuckin' good. Her hair is curling in the humidity, a riot of curls that I want to run my fingers through, just to feel them.

"Your girl clearly doesn't give a shit if they're halfway through the Russian gymnastic training program. But you know who does?"

I look over at where he's staring.

"Fuck me," I mutter.

Moretti has his eyes glued to us like a goddamn bird dog.

"Any particular reason why the scariest assassin in the world is looking at you like you're in the sights of his scope?"

I don't answer.

There's no way Moretti knows about me and Marisol in the pool yesterday. For one, if he did, she wouldn't be out here on this patio.

For another thing, if he knew, I'd already be dead.

Still, he clearly heavily suspects somethinhg, and he's watching me with those weird, flat eyes.

I fuckin' hate that guy.

"Heads up. Big guy on deck," Johnny whispers.

We walk closer, trying to look casual. Benicio Souza enters the terrace, his pug-faced security chief behind him. Moretti's eyes flick to the security chief, and when the injured man sees him, he adjusts his hand, which looks damn uncomfortable wrapped in a mummy bandage.

Interesting.

Clearly, I'm not the only person that Moretti has dark thoughts about. However, given that mine are because of Marisol, I'm curious what beef he has with the security chief.

And whether or not I can use it to my advantage.

"Well. How appropriate that we are all gathered here today," Souza beams like we're all his fuckin' children. "I was just going to call for you, because I have your next challenge.

Please, come, join me," he smiles, gesturing to some chairs that the staff are bringing out to the terrace.

Exchanging a look with Johnny, we walk over. The Russian puts his shirt back on, which is a fuckin' blessing for all of us.

Nobody wants to see that shit.

"Sit, sit," Benicio croons. It's fuckin' creepy how he's acting right now. He's got it into his head that he's like... some kind of benevolent grandfather.

Not a sadistic, murder-minded cartel leader.

We sit in the chairs. I'm on the end, then Johnny, then the Russian, then the Romanian. The other contestants, it seems, have backed the fuck out.

Good.

From where I'm sitting, I can see Marisol and Moretti out of the corner of my eye. Marisol continues to read her book, which makes my heart sing. She's clearly doing her best to make it seem like she's stayin' out of all this, and like she doesn't care who is here, what the outcome is, or just generally what the fuck is going on.

Keep 'em guessin', baby girl.

Benicio claps his hands. "Wonderful. Now that we're assembled, Paulo will go get the appropriate and necessary elements of this challenge."

The fuck?

Marisol pauses, her fingers lingering on one of the pages of her book. Moretti shifts on his feet, looking over at her.

No, baby. You need to make sure he doesn't think there's anythin' happenin'.

She starts to read again, and the tension in my shoulders dissipates.

Slightly.

"This test will be one of practicality. You see, as the person who will find themselves at the center of my universe, and the one who will handle my business while I enjoy a blissful retirement, you will need to demonstrate an appropriate level of intuition. The last test showed me who was the most bloodthirsty–" his eyes drift over to me "--And this test will show me who can take that level of blood and turn it into a productive element."

A shiver of unease skates up my spine.

"The leader of my organization will need to understand who to trust, you see. They will need to know who they can rely on to accomplish the needs of the business, and who they will not be able to trust. In the event, of course, that there is a breach in trust, they will need to know who to punish."

There's movement off to the right, where the barracks and the garages and all that shit are. I look, turning away from staring at Marisol.

My knuckles go white as I clench my fists against themselves.

Six heavily armed guards are pushing five men forward. The men look like they're in rough shape; each one has a bag over their head, and their clothes are covered in what looks like blood, with varying states of tears and rips over each one. Some of the clothing is really closer to rags, which makes me wonder how long these men have been imprisoned.

"This is not fuckin' good," Johnny says.

Yeah.

He can say that again.

The men are frog-marched forward, then dropped to their knees in front of us. I'd look over at Marisol, but right now, the best thing that I can do is figure out what the fuck kind of fresh hell this is.

If I don't get out of here, neither does Marisol.

So I need to get my shit together and get the lay of the fuckin' land.

"In front of you, you see five men. These men are among my staff, men that I had trusted. Men that I thought were on my side, who had passed all my tests. One of them is stealing from me. It is your job to figure out who, and what they stole. You will each receive twenty-four hours with them. Volkov, you will have the first attempt. In an hour you will be escorted to where I am holding them. The rest of you will be fetched as it is your turn. In four days, you will each take your turn to announce who you believe the traitor to be, and what you belive they stole. Now leave," he barks.

Johnny and I stand. Robotically, we walk toward the barracks, coming close to the prisoners that are being forced to kneel on the ground, their hands tied, guns pointed at the backs of their necks.

It's chilling.

I've seen Elio do some shit. Hell, I've seen Marco do some shit. I've seen my dad punish someone, and I've been in a fight more than once that ended with some pretty brutal fuckin' shit.

This is different.

It feels like I'm watching something that's supposed to happen in a world I know nothing about. Our world is brutal, but there are rules. There's a way that you deal with people who have betrayed you, and it's not usually like this. It's cleaner. You fuckin' hurt them back and then they're either dead or you move on with your life, point blank, period.

This?

This is violence.

I feel uneasy about the whole thing. I don't know how to interrogate people. That's Sal's job. My job is just to beat the shit out of them.

My throat itches where Elio cut it with a knife, once.

I know what it feels like to be tortured, and that's for damn sure.

When we make it back to the barracks room, I grab Johnny and slam him into my room. "Do you know how to contact Marco?" I hiss.

Johnny's eyes are wide. "Man, I was just thinkin' the same thing."

"No the fuck you weren't. I want you to get in contact with him, and I'm going to need to talk to Sal."

"Sal?" Johnny's eyes go wide. "Dude. I want to get the fuck outta here. I was never meant for this shit. Do you understand? This is some bullshit that I don't fuckin' know..."

"That's fine," I interrupt. "I don't fuckin' need you."

Johnny's face falls. It feels like I just kicked a goddamn puppy.

I clench my fist and pull back from the wall. Johnny's not

built for shit like this. His family has been out of the thick of things for so long, he's good at support or recon, but this?

"I don't want you to get hurt," I say, clarifying my earlier statement. The sight of Johnny's usually happy-go-lucky face, crushed by my words, haunts me for some reason.

"I mean, I know what I signed up for…"

"You fuckin' don't!" I yell at him.

Johnny's face locks onto mine.

"You have no fuckin' clue. What you saw out there? That's who Benicio Souza is. It's who he's always been. He doesn't fuck around with shit, Johnny. I know you're a second son and all that, and that you thought maybe, just maybe, you'd have some kind of pull out here, but you fuckin' don't. Do you understand? This is not a world that you can just fool around in. Your dad and uncles were connected. They were in. But the world that they were connected in doesn't fuckin' exist anymore. And, above all that, Benicio Souza is fuckin' insane," I hiss, close to his face.

Johnny looks like he's going to cry.

I shut my eyes. *Fuck me.*

Opening them, I look Johnny up and down. "If you don't want to be here, then fuckin' don't. You wanted to help me, and Marco asked you to. Whatever that is, it's a fuckin' favor. You don't have to be here, Spinoli. You fuckin' don't. But if you want Marco to extract you, have him send me Sal instead."

I don't know when it will be my turn to interrogate the potential traitors. I have no fuckin' clue.

But I can't get Johnny into this further if he doesn't want to be here.

Johnny sighs, looking away. "I want to work for whoever is coming out of this. Either you, or Marco, or whoever the fuck it is. Hell, I'd win this myself if I didn't think you'd kill me for bein' with your girl."

"I would," I say.

I'm dead fuckin' serious.

Shaking his head, Johnny looks away. "That shit that we saw in the courtyard... that's fuckin' scary, man."

I know. "That level of violence is how Benicio Souza will always operate. He's always going to be one mean motherfucker, man. If you work for him, you have to constantly be looking for those guns to be aimed at your head."

"And you're willing to go through all that for this girl?"

"Yes."

There's no hesitation. There's no doubt. I will always come for Marisol. It doesn't matter if she's on the other side of the fuckin' world.

I will always come for her. No matter where she is or who has her.

The only thing that could make me stop is if she clearly, beyond a shadow of a doubt, told me she didn't want me.

Doubt skates through me again. Marisol made it clear that she didn't think we knew each other enough for it to matter.

You need to change that.

My eyes snap to him. "What time is it?"

"One-fifteen. Why?"

I nod, pushing off from the wall. "I'll be here this evening. Whatever you decide, Johnny, I support you. If you talk to Marco, then tell him I fuckin' need Sal."

I don't wait to see what Johnny says. I turn, opening my door and slamming it behind me.

None of this will matter if I don't convince Marisol that she's meant to be with me. She wants to get to know me?

She's gonna get to know me just fine.

The pool is quiet.

Really quiet.

I'm in there for so long, I know it's past the time Marisol usually arrives. I chose to hide in the bathroom again, reasoning that Marisol knew I was in there before.

Maybe she would come back again.

I'm about to fuckin' leave when i hear noise. Freezing, I tuck myself into the side against the door.

It's Marisol.

And Moretti.

"Thanks, Andrei. I'll be good now."

"I do not think I will leave today," Moretti's heavily accented fuckin' voice filters through the room.

My hands squeeze into balls at my side, and I breathe out through my nose, trying to keep myself from exploding with rage.

Calm the fuck down, calm the fuck down...

If I go get to Marisol now, I'm going to fuck it up.

"Oh," Marisol breathes, her shock clear. "Oh. Did you... is there something wrong?"

"I don't think you are safe here alone."

"Why's that?" her voice holds the tiniest note of panic, and I swear to fuckin' God, if Moretti picks up on it...

"There's a security breach I was just made aware of."

Fuck.

For a split second, I wonder if Johnny sold me out. It's possible, but I guess that it's improbable.

It makes no sense for someone as... well. As *Johnny* as Johnny to sell me out like that. Marco would fucking kill him.

If I didn't do it first.

It has to be one of the guards, or someone else who knows the property. Someone that could easily tip Moretti off, and who might stand to benefit...

I bite back the growl in my throat.

Fucking Volkov.

Motherfucker definitely knows, and he's trying to get Moretti to take me out.

Mentally, I make a note to strangle Volkov the next chance I see him.

For actual reasons this time.

Well. Other than he's Volkov.

"It isn't safe for you to remain here," he grunts. "Not alone, because someone might be hiding."

Fuck.

If he comes for this door, I'm just going to fucking lay him out. That's the plan. It's the only plan, and I'm going to stick to it if I have to.

Marisol sighs. "Okay. Stay," she murmurs.

Then, there's the sound of clothes rustling.

Rage explodes through me. Hot. persistent. Rage that I can't hide or stop.

She's getting undressed in front of him. She probably has her suit on, but...

I hear splashing.

She's in the pool now.

Moretti doesn't approach my hiding spot. Instead, I'm just driven insane thinking about Marisol in the pool. Her elegance. The way she glides through the water. The way her hair streams behind her.

I'm tortured.

For fucking *ever*.

Finally, Marisol stops. She hops out, and I imagine her grabbing a towel.

She speaks to Moretti.

"See? Nothing. No one came to get us. I'm at far more risk in the garden," she says.

Loudly.

Very, very loudly.

"The garden is protected by the patrols," Moretti growls.

"I know. It's true. Since I'm much safer there, I think I might take a walk."

"When?"

A pause. "Tonight. Maybe after dinner."

"Marisol, I..."

"My father's guards will be there. It won't be a problem. I need the time alone, Andrei. I do. I know it's nice of you to be here with me, but it's not the same. I wish to think about my mother, and see the trees he planted for her."

There's a pause. A hesitation.

Finally, he sighs. "Fine. You may go after dinner."

"Wonderful," she murmurs.

There are footsteps.

Then, silence.

I would be disappointed. However, I can't be.

Marisol, my clever, wonderful Marisol, figured out a solution.

The garden.

After dinner.

I'll be there.

18

MARISOL

It's raining.

In itself, that shouldn't be unusual. Rain happens often in Brazil, especially in the area around our compound.

But somehow, it feels... different.

This rain is heavy. it's persistent, coming down from the sky at a steady pace that sounds like a heartbeat echoing all around the house.

Or, maybe that's the thundering of my own heart as I pace my room.

Andrei's inability to leave me alone earlier felt terrifying. It was a reminder that I'm playing a game that's out of my league.

Not for the first time, I shut my eyes and take a deep, steadying breath.

All I want is to be with the girls.

I miss them with a ferocity that rips at my gut. For the first time since arriving here, I sit on my bed, letting my panic consume me.

I'm absolutely terrified that I'm never going to see them again.

The terror is something that I can keep at bay, normally. I don't know if it's the rain, exactly, or something else.

But right now, I can't keep it from consuming me.

I can't even cry.

There's too much fear. Too much that could go wrong. Too much that is at risk.

What if I never see them again?

I've told myself, over and over, that I'd be fine with it if I never see the girls again. If they're safe and happy, that's all that matters to me.

Or at least, that's what I told myself.

Right now?

It's not true.

I want to see them again. I want to hold onto them. I want to kiss their faces and hear them say my name.

I want, more than anything, to see my babies again.

You have to choose the option that gets you back to them.

The thought echoes through me with all the strength of a scream. It's true; I have to choose whatever gets me back to them.

If I die without seeing the girls...

Don't think of that, Marisol.

That can't be an option.

One way or another, I'm going to make sure that I see them again.

I have to.

The rain keeps drumming on the roof, but I ignore it.

I need to go meet Dino.

Dinner passes without any incident. After, Andrei is coming to follow me, and I'm certain that he's not going to let me walk in the garden alone.

My heart thumps in time with the rain.

Then, my father grabs his elbow. He murmurs something in Portuguese. Andrei looks at me for a long minute before he nods, and lets my father lead him away.

This is my chance.

I don't bother with a jacket. I know that I should, and that I might attract attention if I walk out into the garden with nothing on, but I don't care.

I need to get out of this house.

I need to meet with Dino. He's the only person in the world, interestingly, that reminds me of my girls, and I miss them so desperately that I'm just dying to be closer to them.

He's the only one who can fulfill that for me, and it's extremely confusing, but I need him.

I need...

The realization that I need Dino confuses me. I don't want to need him, that's for sure.

We don't know each other. Nothing has changed.

Except for the fact that every cell in my body is craving him right now.

My feet slide around in my sandals as I steal out into the garden. I mentioned the mango trees to Andrei earlier, when Dino was there in the pool room.

Or, at least I think that Dino was there.

The panic claws at me again. There are too many things that I'm leaving up to the world, and that are currently just... chance.

I don't even know if Dino was listening earlier. I tried to see if I could look inside the changing room for his feet, but I couldn't do that without getting Andrei's attention.

I have no idea if he heard me or not.

So, I'm still charging out into the garden with nothing concrete to go on whatsoever.

I guess if nothing else, I'll be able to look at the mango trees and think of my mother.

It takes one minute for me to realize that coming out here was a mistake, without a raincoat of some kind on. My dress is clinging to me within seconds, because the rain isn't just coming down.

It's flowing like a waterfall.

Slowly, so that I don't slip in my shoes, I walk toward the back.

The mango trees are in the furthest part of the garden. There's a little bench underneath them, and I find that if I sit on it, I'm sheltered from the worst of the rain under the thick branches of the trees.

I can even tuck myself further back into them so that someone coming up the path won't be able to see me.

The privacy hits me.

I haven't been alone like this in...

Forever.

I look up at the branches, wishing that my mother was here. She would know how to get me out of this.

And what to do next.

I hear a rustle, and I turn, my heart pumping.

"It's me," Dino rasps.

The sound of his voice doesn't necessarily make me relax. Instead, it makes me feel...

Hot.

"I..."

He tugs on my wrist from where he's hidden in the bushes behind me. "Come here," he murmurs.

God help me.

I go with him.

"I can't be seen out of the garden," I whisper. The sound of water falling from the sky more than covers our voices.

Dino nods, but keeps leading me up the path.

Not more than ten feet back from where the mango trees hang heavily over the bench, there's something else.

Something I didn't know existed.

A little gazebo.

Dino tugs me underneath it. The rain has plastered his white t-shirt to him, making it transparent. I can see every tattoo, every scar, underneath the thin cotton that's covering him.

I want to touch them with my tongue.

"Are you good?" he grunts.

That voice.

My eyes look at the thick scar across his throat.

I nod. "I'm fine."

"You look cold," Dino murmurs. His big hands come to rest on my shoulders.

They radiate heat, each one a furnace against my skin.

"I'm fine. Really. I am," I whisper.

His hands move up my shoulders.

I want to lean into his touch. I want him to hold me.

I want this to be something it's not.

I want Dino to... want me.

"Red," Dino grunts.

I blink up at him.

"It's my favorite color. Red."

"I'm sorry, I'm not following."

Sighing, he takes his hands off of me.

I shiver.

"You said we didn't know anything about each other. That we

didn't have any connection. Well I'm fuckin' connectin'," he says, throwing his hands up in the air.

Aww.

"So you want to tell me your favorite color?" I smile.

"If that makes you feel connected to me then fuck yeah," Dino grumbles.

I can't help it. The smile that twitches across my lips is genuine. "I like purple."

"That makes sense to me," Dino grunts.

"Okay. Favorite movie?"

"Don't watch movies," Dino shakes his head.

I deflate a little.

"I don't watch movies because I ain't got much time, but when I was a kid, uh..." he scratches the back of his head.

The movement makes his biceps pop, and my eyes follow the motion.

"I really liked the uh... the movie with the dogs."

I frown. "Movie with the dogs?"

"Yeah, you know. The fuckin' cartoon. There's a whole bunch of dogs and a mean lady tries to make goddamn coats out of 'em..."

"One hundred and one dalmatians?" I smile at him.

"Yeah. That's the one."

I can't stop myself.

I laugh.

Dino looks away. "Look, it's a stupid movie, that's why I don't watch movies—"

"Dino. I'm not laughing at you. I think it's adorable that you like that movie."

He looks down at me, his forest green eyes serious. "Adorable?"

"Yes. I can just picture little Dino, begging to watch it again," I smile.

He looks away. "Well, if I did, I don't think anyone would listen."

Oh.

I gently put my hand on his shoulder. "Because of the whole... dad thing?"

"Yeah. The dad thing."

Biting my lip, I slide my hand down his arm. His muscles feel like they're carved out of stone, and I really want to just wrap them around me, because I feel like in Dino's arms it wouldn't rain on me.

Like nothing bad would happen to me ever again, honestly.

I wish that were true.

"Do you want to talk about it?" I whisper.

He tilts his head.

"The dad thing," I clarify.

Dino huffs out a breath. "I don't know."

"Okay. I understand. It's a lot..."

"I don't know because I don't know what to say," Dino amends.

I still, my fingers halfway down his forearm.

Dino takes a deep breath.

"Out of my family, I'm not the one who does... who says shit. My brothers are good at talking. Marco's smoother than a snake and Sal is smart as hell. Caterina never got in trouble, so she never needed to learn how to get herself out of trouble. But I'm the one who is always in trouble," he murmurs.

I slide my hand the rest of the way into his hand, and I squeeze slightly.

Dino looks at where our fingers are twined, and his big palm wraps around mine.

It sends a surge of heat through me that makes me bite my lip.

"I fucked everything up, all the time. I couldn't do shit right. Not a goddamn thing. After a while, I stopped tryin'. I did what the fuck I wanted, when the fuck I wanted, and I never took no for an answer, unless it was Marco and he goddamn begged me."

"That sounds lonely," I murmur.

Dino's eyes are wide with surprise. "Yeah. It was lonely. It is lonely."

"I'm sorry."

He shrugs. "Nothin to be sorry for. You didn't do it to me."

"I can feel how much it hurt you anyway," I say with a squeeze of his hand.

Dino nods, seemingly encouraged by my words. "I never felt like I belonged in my family, Marisol. Hearin' that I... don't..." he hesitates. "It's actually kinda... normal."

"You belong wherever you belong, Dino. You belong where you feel belonging."

The laugh that rattles out of him is bitter. "Then I don't think I've ever belonged anywhere."

Oh God.

I squeeze his hand. "I'm so sorry. That sounds awful."

"It is."

For a second we sit there, the rain humming around us.

Then, Dino says, in a voice that's so hoarse I can barely hear it, "Actually, that's not right."

"What?" I blink, looking up at him.

Dino's eyes are dark. He slides the hand that I"m not holding against my face, and leans down ever so slightly.

If he moves forward again, he's going to kiss me.

I want him to kiss me.

"I can think of one place that I have felt belonging."

"Oh?" I whisper.

His lips are almost touching mine.

He leans closer again, and I have to strain to hear the words.

"I belong with you."

19

DINO

I've never been this honest.

I'm not a fuckin' liar, by any stretch, but right now is the first time ever that I've actually told the entirety of the truth that's been sitting in my chest.

Marisol makes me want to pull my heart out, so she can hold it. I think it might be safer with her.

That's a fuckin' terrifying fact. But with Marisol, I want to be so much more than who I am. I want to be good. I want to be someone that she can see herself with. She's mine, whether she knows it or not.

But if she loved me? I couldn't hope for something as good.

I am, however, trying to get to a place where she at least tolerates me. Where she can see a future together.

Where she won't fuckin' leave me.

So I'm doing something new. I'm giving her a little bit of myself, which I wouldn't normally even think about.

But for Marisol?

I want to be better than I am.

She's so close. If I lean forward any more, I can take her lips.

The thought sends blood straight to my cock.

The rain on my skin is fucking icy cold, but I think I might be radiating it off of me in steam, because right now Marisol is making me feel like I'm on fucking fire.

I want to kiss her.

If I was just being myself, I'd fucking kiss her and never think a fucking thing about it.

But I want her to want *this*.

I'm fucking desperate for her to want me, and it makes me feel...

Scared.

She breathes, her eyes wide, her breath sweet. "Dino..."

"I know," I growl. "I want us to fuckin' get to know each other. Like you asked."

"It's sweet," she murmurs.

I fuckin' hope it is.

"You're being very sweet," she whispers. One of her hands skates up and slowly tunnels into my hair.

"God damn it, Marisol," I groan, letting her nails scratch against my scalp. I arch backwards, trying to get her to do it harder.

When she does, I can't help the moan that escapes me.

It feels so fucking good.

"It's nice when you're sweet," she murmurs.

Good. This is fuckin' hard.

"But I like it even more when you're not, I think."

Her nails dig in just a little harder.

Hard enough for me to look down at her.

She's biting her lip, but I can't mistake the lust in her eyes.

It sets me on fire.

I dive down, my lips catching hers in a fierce kiss. She tastes like rain and Marisol, and it sends a shuddering gasp through me. Running my fingers up into her hair, I tug her head back, drinking in the moan that she gives me like it's the last ounce of water in a desert.

She tastes so fucking good. I can't believe that she's here.

That she's *mine*.

Her fingers tug at the hem of my shirt, and I pull it up.

Marisol's nails skate over my torso, and I flex against her fingers. Her fingertips linger against the tattoos there…

And the scars.

Suddenly, I'm weirdly self-conscious of them. I'm not a fuckin' baby. I have scars, and I haven't given them one fuckin' thought since I got 'em.

I just need them to be sewn up. Healed. Then I don't give a shit about them.

Or, I didn't… until now.

Does Marisol think that I'm some kind of fuckin' weirdo? Or that I'm weak because I've been hurt so many times? Or...

All of my thoughts come to a screaming halt when she presses her lips against the long scar from a knife fight that cuts diagonally across my torso. It runs from the bottom of my left pec to my right hip. I have it covered with an array of tattoos, but you can still see it underneath.

Her tongue traces the line of it, and when she descends to have her face at my hips, I think I might fuckin' explode.

She bites at my hip bone.

"Fuck me," I bite out. I lean down and scoop her up, because if she gets any closer to my cock, I'm going to come like a fuckin' teenager. Dragging Marisol up to meet my mouth, I pull her lips to mine and crush her into a kiss.

Her legs wrap around me.

I want to fuck her so badly, it's taking every ounce of my self-control to not.

"Dino," she whispers when she breaks the kiss and pulls back. "I need you."

Fuck.

Fuck.

"I... we..."

I can't fuck her here.

We're in the middle of her father's garden. Someone could walk up on us at any time. We wouldn't hear it because of the fucking rain.

But I can give her something.

I turn and gently set her down on the bench that's slightly covered by the wooden structure. I kneel in front of her, staring up at her as I do.

Marisol's eyes are wild and frantic. Her chest heaves, and the rain has glued her dress to her breasts.

I bite back another curse, because I want nothing more than to play with her pretty nipples where they're poking through the fabric.

But, I have something else in mind.

"I want to taste you," I manage to grunt. My hands push her dress up, until it's at her waist.

Marisol's eyes widen. "Dino..."

"You're the only person I'll ever fucking kneel for, Marisol," I say through clenched teeth. "The only person I'll get on my knees for. If I have to fucking beg you for this, I fucking will. Let me taste you, so you can come apart and I can remember what you taste like when you come."

She pants, and opens her legs.

"Good girl," I breathe. My hands come back down her hips, dragging her cotton panties down with my fingertips as I go.

She parts her legs wider, and I put them over my shoulders.

My first taste of her is like heaven. She tastes like sweet rain water and Marisol, and I can't fucking believe that I'm lucky enough to call her mine.

She's fucking mine, no matter what.

After tonight?

She better fucking know it.

Marisol's moans drive me fucking insane. I lap at her, using my tongue to move the bud of her pleasure around, and she writhes against my face.

I want her to come.

Hard.

Now.

I slowly press two fingers inside of her, the squeeze of her making my cock twitch. I want to be inside her more than anything but...

More than that, I want her to come. I pull back, my fingers still pumping in and out of her. "When you come, you can't scream, Marisol."

Dazed, she looks down at me.

"You have to be quiet. Can you do that for me, baby?"

Slowly, she nods.

"Good."

I return to her, another finger joining my other two, and bite at her clit.

Hard.

Come for me, baby.

I don't have to say it out loud.

Marisol lets out a moan, and I feel her squeeze around my fingers. She shudders, her legs kicking into my back, and I grin as moisture that tastes like Marisol and nothing like rain hits my tongue.

God damn. She's a fucking drug.

I don't want to let her go.

"Dino?"

Her voice catches my attention. I look up at her, my eyes tracing slowly up her body.

She's looking down at me, her eyebrows pinched together.

"I... Can I touch you?"

Fuck me.

I pull my fingers from her slowly, pocketing her panties. Gently, I tug the dress down her hips, and I come to sit on the cement bench next to her.

Marisol bites her lip and looks at my lap, where my erection is obviously tenting my pants.

"Marisol..." I start.

I should tell her no. That I don't need her to touch me. That I don't want her to.

But that would be a fucking lie.

And I'm not a fucking liar.

So when she presses her fingers gently to the outside of my pants, I don't do anything other than groan.

"Let me make you feel good," Marisol murmurs. Her eyes flick up to mine, and she gives me a small smile.

"I want to touch you," she repeats.

I never said I was a good man. Never fuckin' once.

So instead of telling her no, that I was fine with letting her come apart for me, I let her fingers tug at my button. I let her unzip me.

And I just groan when Marisol takes my cock out and holds it in her beautiful fuckin' fingers.

20

MARISOL

I don't know what's gotten into me.

Maybe it's the rain. Maybe it's just the strangely addicting way that Dino presents himself, or the sight of his tattoos and scars, covered in rain.

Maybe it's the fact that he told me his favorite color.

Maybe it's the fact that he's the closest thing to my kids that I can have right now.

Maybe it's all of those things, plus the fact that I think he's the most handsome man that I've ever seen.

Whatever it is, I feel wild. There's a need pulsing through me that makes me feel like I'm possessed. There's some other entity powering me right now, making my hands clench around Dino's smooth, beautiful cock. There's some other woman driving me, because I couldn't possibly be the one who fits my lips around the thick head of him and slowly sucks him into my mouth.

When he moans, though, I realize that I'm the one making these decisions.

Because I want to be the one that makes Dino make that sound.

Always.

A weird possessive feeling creeps over me. The thought of Dino doing this with another woman makes my skin crawl.

And, it makes me want to... make an impression on him.

Something that he'll never forget.

Dino grunts, his hands like claws on the stone bench as he grips it. "Fuck, Marisol," he groans. "That feels so fucking good."

Pleasure flushes through me, and I moan around the feel of him in my mouth.

One of his hands touches the back of my head. The hesitation there makes my heart ache, and I look up at him through my lashes. Slowly, I pull him out of my mouth, a sight that both of us are watching.

It looks sexy.

"Tell me what to do," I whisper.

His eyes squeeze shut, and the little muscle at the side of his jaw works like he's trying to figure out what to say. "Marisol... I... You..."

"I want to make you feel good, Dino. Like you made me feel good. Tell me what to do."

"Fuck me. Whatever you were doing. Just fucking... do that," he manages to get out.

It's not specific. It's literally anything but specific.

But somehow, I know exactly what he means.

With his eyes glued on me, I take him back into my mouth. Dino grunts again, and his hips pump once.

I gag, slightly, as he presses further into my mouth.

Instantly, Dino freezes. "Fuck. Sorry. Marisol. Fuck. I can…"

I stop him by wrapping my hand around the base of him and pushing him in deeper again.

I'm not experienced at this. Far from it. So yeah, I'm gagging a little. It's a lot, and he's so big, and again, I'm not in the practice of relaxing my throat or anything.

But I try.

Slowly I'm able to take more of him, gag and all. Dino groans and his hand comes to the back of my head again. "Yes, Marisol," he seems to chant from between clenched teeth, his words resonating in time with my head as I bob up and down on him. "Fuck. Yes. Marisol."

I love this.

It makes me feel so powerful to have him in my body like this. To have every little movement of his be a direct result of me.

Of the way I hold him. Of the way I use my mouth and tongue on him.

It's addicting.

Dino gasps and grips a fistful of my hair. "I'm going to come, Marisol."

Good.

The thought of him spilling in my mouth, like I did in his, makes me wet all over again.

He grunts, and one of his big hands comes and grips the base of him, taking him out of my mouth.

I feel lost. Why did he...

"Not today," Dino gasps. "Just watch."

The way he says 'today' kind of feels like there's a promise for tomorrow.

It makes me... happy.

The strange, precious happiness is washed away in an instant, though, when he starts to explode.

I can't look away.

"Marisol," he growls as he twitches. "Look at me."

My eyes shoot up to his...

I shiver.

The look he's giving me is the most intense that I've ever received in my entire life.

It makes me feel stripped down in a way that even him touching me didn't.

That weird little possessive urge rises in me again as he finishes, and gently uses his shirt to clean himself up.

I know that Dino keeps saying that I'm his but...

Is Dino mine?

I don't know. The only people I've ever really trusted enough to *belong* to are my mom and my kids.

Men, in my experience, don't want me to be part of a family with them. They want to own me. Use me. I'm just a pawn in the games that they play with each other.

I know that I want Dino to be different but...

He might not be.

Dino tucks his shirt into the back of his pants and leans forward. Gently, he tugs me up so that I'm sitting on the bench next to him.

The rain splatters against the roof of the little shelter, and I feel suddenly a little awkward. I don't know what to say.

What is there to say, after that?

"You should get back," Dino says in a hushed voice.

Oh.

Okay.

I guess we aren't going to talk about this at all, then.

Rising from the bench, I turn to study him. "That's it?"

"What's it?"

"You're just going to dismiss me after..."

I don't get to finish the sentence, because before I do, Dino's arms are wrapping around me and he pulls me close to his chest.

"Marisol. I'm not dismissing you. I'm not sending you away. There's a fuckin' countdown clock in my head right now and we've been out here too damn long."

I sigh and lean into his body. He's so warm, and it feels so good. The chill from the rain is finally getting to me, and I don't want to be cold anymore.

I want to have him around to keep me warm.

"If I had all the time in the world, I'd fuckin' spend it with you," he rasps.

My heart melts, just a little bit, and I wrap my hands around him too.

Dino's chest feels red hot under my hands, like he's run a marathon instead of sitting on a bench for a while. I gently rake my nails over his back muscles, and he groans.

"Don't fuckin' do that, Marisol. We don't have the fuckin' time."

I know he's right, but I can't help that it feels a little bit like rejection.

Or, I guess, the longing for us to have more time.

"I know. I should get back," I murmur. I pull back from where my arms are tucked around him, and the loss is almost palpable.

I don't want to leave him.

The realization is somewhat shocking.

Dino bends down, tipping my lips up to his with one finger. He kisses me, and I wait for it to become heated.

It never does.

"I'm going to get you out of here, Marisol," he whispers when he ends the kiss.

I blink up at him.

His green eyes are serious. "I mean it. I want to get to know you. But I don't want to do it here. We need time. I need time to fuckin' make you mine, and time for you to choose me."

I laugh softly. "You think I will?"

"I know you will, Marisol. Because you're fuckin' mine."

I laugh again. "You're something else, Dino."

"I ain't nothin' but yours, Marisol," he says softly.

The words send a chill down my spine.

"I should go," I murmur again. One of these times I'm going to say it and it's going to be true.

The rain intensifies. I could stay out here forever, rain and all. I don't want to go back in there, to my father.

To Andrei.

"When can I see you again?" I ask Dino.

"Swimming."

I nod. "I'll go every day."

"I'll be there," he whispers.

With one last soft kiss, I step away. Walking out into the garden again, I look up at the fruit trees.

I wonder how Dino's been getting me the notes. I should probably ask him before I go. Quickly, I turn, dashing back under the shelter. "You could send me another note," I say softly.

Dino looks at me, a frown pulling at his lips.

Ice skates over my spine as he straightens. "What are you talking about?"

My stomach clenches. "The notes. From the garden. The ones telling me to meet you out here?"

It feels like I'm grasping at straws. Like I did something wrong, even though I know I didn't.

He rises slowly. His face darkens, and I see the hint of danger creep back into his eyes.

"I haven't sent you any notes, Marisol."

21

MARISOL

I haven't sent you any notes, Marisol.

The words still send a chill down my spine. As I walk down the path back toward the main house, I feel cold, colder than I should, even with the volume of water pouring down from the sky.

The notes were kind of cute when I thought that they were from Dino.

Now though?

I feel... dirty. Like someone's been keeping tabs on me in a way that I not only wouldn't want them to, but didn't ask for.

Like someone is watching me, and I don't know who.

I'm going to get rid of all of them when I get back to my room. I never want to see them again, and if any more notes appear, I'm not even going to open them.

I'm going to put them straight into the toilet and flush them away, so that no one ever sees them.

Including me.

I'm halfway back to the house, but still in the garden, when I hear my name. "Marisol?"

It's Andrei, his heavily accented voice ringing through even the rain.

"I'm here," I say, looking at him through the water that's still sluicing down from the heavens.

Catching sight of me, Andrei curses. He whips off his leather jacket, wrapping it around my shoulders. He swears in Italian and puts his hands on my shoulders, hustling me toward the house.

"The hell are you thinking? You could catch your death out here."

I laugh, somewhat bitterly. "You're turning into a grandmother, Andrei. I'm fine. I'm Brazilian, a little rain never hurt me."

"This isn't a little rain, Marisol. This is some kind of plague sent down from above," he spits.

I don't acknowledge that.

I let Andrei hustle me inside. His jacket is warm and I do appreciate it, but it feels chilly in comparison to when I was in Dino's arms.

He tugs me down the hallway, taking me to my room. I don't protest.

"Clean yourself up. Shower and then I'm calling the doctor," Andrei hisses.

The doctor is one of my least preferred members of my father's staff. He's a blustery old man who likes to touch my legs way too much. "I'm fine, Andrei. I'm definitely going to take a hot bath but then I'm going to bed."

"No. You might be sick. I won't let you…"

That rubs me exactly the wrong way.

I turn, glaring at him. "You don't control my body, Andrei. If I say I'm feeling fine, there's no one in the world who knows how I'm feeling better than I do. If I say I'm feeling sick, I will ask for the doctor, but you don't get to act like you know better than I do what is happening in my own body," I snap.

Andrei's face turns harsh. For a minute, my heart rate skyrockets, and the hair on my neck stands up.

This is the killer that everyone's afraid of. This is the man that my father hired to keep everyone at bay.

This is Andrei in his truest form.

And he's staring at me.

I step back, my eyes wide. "Andrei. I'm fine," I reassert gently.

I hate myself for taking some of the heat out of my words, but I've lived around dangerous men for long enough to recognize when I need to play into their egos.

Right now?

I need to pretend.

Andrei shakes himself, and the killer gaze fades. He steps forward, reaching for me.

I flinch.

Emotions flicker across his gaze before his expression goes carefully blank again. "If you feel even a tiny bit unwell, you will call the doctor," he mutters.

I hate that it's yet another command, but I swallow my pride and nod. "I will."

He studies me for a minute longer. I remember that I'm wearing his coat and slide it off of my arms, holding it out for him.

He takes it, but his eyes linger on me.

"There's dirt on your dress," he says, his eyes sticking around my knees.

Oh.

Oh dear.

I must have gotten it dirty when I was kneeling in front of Dino, taking him in...

Do not blush.

"I fell," I say cooly, trying to lie as evenly as possible. I am a practiced liar, especially when it comes to the men I need to keep at a distance.

Andrei's eyebrows raise. "You fell?"

"The rain made some of the rocks slippery," I explain. "I slipped and fell."

"On your knees?"

"And my hands, as is pretty normal with a fall," I say softly. I see Andrei's eyes slide to my hands, and I resist the urge to clench my fists so he can't examine my palms for cuts.

"Next time, take me with you. You would not have fallen if I was there to protect you," he finally says.

But the words aren't even remotely warm. Andrei isn't exactly a warm and fluffy guy, but I've come to recognize what counts as affection from him.

And what doesn't.

My spine tingling with unease, I nod. "I know. It was just clumsy of me, especially with all the rain. But I'm fine. I'm going to go to bed. I'll see you in the morning," I say softly.

I turn to leave. I can feel Andrei's eyes on me as I open the door to my room, but I don't turn back to look at him.

Once inside, the door safely locked behind me, I step into the bathroom. I turn on the tap for the bath, and that's when I finally let myself sink, sliding onto the tile floor.

I put my head in my hands.

You're a fool, Marisol.

I underestimated Andrei. I believed him when he said he wouldn't hurt me. The man that I just saw in the hallway? He's the type of man who would hurt me.

The type of man who absolutely would want to hurt me, if he didn't get his way.

I can't keep him at arms length for too much longer. I need to either bring him in closer, or...

There is no other plan.

I can't show Dino any type of favoritism. I can't do anything to show my hand, because if I do, my father will kill Dino.

And Andrei will be more than happy to do it.

I also need to make sure that there's enough distance between Dino and I. After tonight, Andrei is not going to just let me swim by myself. He thinks something is up. After seeing the marks on my knees, it's little wonder that he does.

It looks like I was kneeling on the cold, hard ground.

Which I was.

Andrei isn't safe. I let myself trust that he did have my best interests at heart, but it's clear to me now that I shouldn't have done that.

He is not a sheep in wolf's clothing. He's a wolf. Through and through.

And a predator will always try to go for the kill.

The roar of the bathwater fills my ears as shame pulses through me. How could I be so stupid?

How have I put myself into this place again?

There's no denying that I like Dino. I like being around him. There's some kind of animal attraction between us that I can't keep myself from participating in.

I can't stay away from him, honestly.

But I have to.

Andrei suspects something. He's going to look at Dino first.

I can't be the reason Dino dies.

You have to stop seeing him.

The pain of that realization lances through me, a little crack in a heart that I didn't think could break anymore. With the bath running, I tuck my head onto my knees, pulling them close.

I start to cry.

I don't want to live like this. I don't want to be forced to choose between the options that are least favorable to me.

I want to live my own life.

For me.

Sobs rock me, and I clutch myself, holding my knees closer.

I want Dino. I know that I do. But I don't think that Dino is the path to the life I want, either. He said that he wants us to get to know each other, so that I would choose him.

But he said it like it was inevitable.

I misjudged Andrei.

Maybe I've misjudged Dino too.

I wake the next morning feeling drained. My heart aches and I want to talk to my kids, and I want to talk to my mom.

And the rain is still coming down.

The compound is somewhat up on a hill, but there is still even more hillside above it, covered in jungle. I'm sure that the jungle can absorb a lot of water, so I shouldn't be too concerned but…

It feels like a lot of rain.

More than that, I feel doomed. Like there's something hanging over me, and a pervasive feeling of something bad happening.

And happening soon.

It's just the challenge, I tell myself as I glide out of my room, wearing more practical jeans and sneakers today. I know that my father is going to have a meltdown that I'm not wearing a dress, but I want to be comfortable and warm today.

Sneakers it is.

My father's challenge, to interrogate the traitors in his ranks, is brutal. It's just like him. Last night I know that Volkov had his turn with them, and this coming day it will be someone else.

I don't want to see what happens to them. I don't want to know.

And I don't want to see what happens when Dino gets to them.

If I do...

It would ruin the image that I have of him in my mind even more.

I don't want Dino to be as brutal as my father. I don't want him to be as cold and reptilian as Andrei can be.

I want him to be different.

He isn't, Marisol. Stop being a silly little girl and grow up.

"Marisol," Andrei says, greeting me with a chilly tone.

I steel myself.

Andrei is a crucial piece in my happiness right now. I need to keep him happy in order to keep him away from Dino.

So I smile at him, pretending to soften. "Good morning, Andrei," I say, intentionally lowering my voice. "I slept so well," I purr.

His eyes flash, and I see lust in their dark depths.

Good.

He's also incredibly easy to set off if just the mere mention of me sleeping has this reaction. Andrei must be tense right now, a caged tiger that's been kept here for too long.

That could work in my favor...

Or be incredibly dangerous.

I smile at him again, hoping to keep the flirtation going. "Are you here to walk me to breakfast?"

"As I am every day," he says softly.

I stare at him. "Well, are you going to offer me your arm?"

"Do you want it?"

It's a question.

Underneath his tone, I can feel his trepidation. My chest aches because even in that question— even seeing him, the stone-cold assassin, standing in front of me— I can sense that it's not just the adult Andrei asking.

It's a little boy, desperate to be accepted.

I could answer him. I have the words to.

But it's going to be a lie.

And I do not like to lie... at least not so directly.

"I would like to be taken to breakfast," I respond instead.

Andrei studies me for a little longer, then offers me his arm. I tuck my hand into the crook of his elbow, moving forward as I do.

"I wonder what fresh hell my father has for them today," I chirp softly.

Andrei whistles. "A wet one, Marisol."

I laugh, but it sounds too bright.

Everything about this feels wrong, and my dread increases.

I don't know what to do. But I have to get out of here alive.

And I have no clue how to do that.

22

DINO

The dream of Marisol gives a lightness to my step that I have to get under control. I don't want Andrei to get suspicious, or for Benicio to notice

Having her body twist against mine in the rain was...

Well.

Pretty fuckin' incredible.

It's still raining the next morning, which is a sweet reminder of the way she tasted with raindrops against her skin.

It's enough to make a growl rasp through my broken vocal cords.

Marisol is fuckin' *mine*.

And anyone who stands between us is going to get wrecked.

My hand is on the knob of my shitty barracks room when I hear a rap from the other side. Cautiously, I open it, peering out.

Johnny's on the other side.

I tense; the look on his face is enough to make my chest tighten. "What."

"It's your turn, bro," he whispers.

Fuck.

Marisol and I had such a fuckin' good night together, I forgot about the next task from her father.

"How did yours go?"

Johnny's face, already drawn and pale, gets even whiter. "Man... I just... I don't..."

I clap him on the shoulder. "You did what you needed to, Johnny. That's all you need to remind yourself."

He gulps.

I know that feeling.

Humans only have a certain capacity for violence. We aren't born that way. I know there's all kinds of shit out there claiming that humans are like violent, hateful creatures or whatever, but few of us pop out into the world screaming for blood.

Some of us learn to have a higher capacity than others, though, when it comes to giving the world as good as we get. If the world was a cruel place full of harsh shit to us then, well...

Some of us learn to be even more cruel.

From the look on his face, though, I can tell Johnny isn't one of those people. I don't have time to baby him through this but...

Fuck.

The guy's been good to me. I owe it to him to at least check and see if he's alright.

"You good?" I ask, a little reluctant to open this fuckin' can of worms.

Johnny shakes his head. "No. I... As soon as you give me the word, man, I'm fuckin' tellin' Marco to pull me."

Jesus. Way to layer on the fuckin' guilt as well. "You can leave whenever you need. Marco doesn't know shit about me or what I've done, and I don't fuckin' need his charity."

This gets Johnny's attention. "So you knew about how to get into the pool all by yourself? And that your girl went for a swim? That was all you?"

Fuck me. "Man, I didn't mean—"

He holds up a hand, cutting me off. "Look. You have a big-ass chip on your shoulder, and I get it. I really do. I've watched the De Luca boys for a long time, man, and I know exactly how your family fucking functions. But shit. You keep throwing help back in my fucking face, and in other people's fucking faces, and you're going to not get it. Ever. Fucking. Again."

I blink.

This is the most aggressive that I've ever heard Johnny be.

Like.

Ever.

"Johnny..."

He shrugs me off and walks away.

I need to get my ass to the main house to figure out what the fuck Benicio wants me to do with his goddamn prisoners, but for a second, I watch Johnny's receding back as he walks down the long hallway to his room in the barracks.

I've been an outsider in my own home for so long, it doesn't even occur to me that people in my family want to help without any other motive.

Johnny doesn't know me. Not really. He hasn't watched Marco and Sal get every ounce of love from the man who I thought was my father, with nothing left for me. He didn't see both of our parents dote on fucking Caterina like she hung the fucking moon. He didn't see everyone else get time and attention…

Except me.

He doesn't fucking know.

When I was a kid, Marco would help, but it came at a cost. Namely, my fucking freedom.

There's a cost now. I know there is.

I just don't know what that cost is right now.

What if there isn't?

I push the thought aside, burying it deep in my mind.

Of course there's a fucking cost.

Things don't work in that fucking rainbows-and-sunshine way. Marco might be my brother, but our family doesn't work like that. We don't do shit for each other. We don't expect things to just be given to us.

Well.

Caterina does, I guess.

But Sal and Marco and I have had to fucking fight our way into the good graces of this fuckin' family. Literally, if you're me. I've had to take on so much shit just to even be considered fuckin' part of the goddamn picture.

All because you weren't really his son.

And he knew it.

The wound that I've never had a name for, buried deep in my chest, aches again.

I slam the door to my barracks room shut.

Marco isn't looking out for me. He wants something from me. I make a mental note to ensure Johnny gets the hell out of here after this.

He's not built for this shit.

Not like I am.

I crack my neck as I prowl down the hallway toward the main house. Benicio Souza wants me to torture some fucking pissant to see if he's stealing?

Fuck it.

He'll have that information from me. Ten fucking minutes, flat.

The scar on my neck tingles, and a grimace crosses my features.

Yeah.

I can torture information out of this poor fuck. I'll have no fucking problem with it.

I learned from the best, after all.

My brother-in-law, my brothers... they taught me all I need to know about how to cause pain.

This motherfucker is about to learn every lesson I've learned...

The hard way.

Standing in front of Benicio, my hands at some form of parade rest behind my back, I truly can't believe that this fucker is related to Marisol.

I don't see it.

Marisol is... soft. Sunshine. She's the sweetness that I've never experienced, and she's all things good.

Benicio Souza is hard.

Life has really chewed him the fuck up and spit him out, because he looks every inch of his age as he surveys me as well.

Yeah.

He looks nothing like my Marisol.

If her mom had a different father for Marisol, she's hid that well, because for whatever reason Benicio seems to accept Marisol as his child without question.

Ironic, that he could do that and my own fucking dad couldn't.

He opens his mouth and some fucking language that I don't know spills out.

I don't respond, choosing instead to just glare at him.

Benicio's eyes narrow. "It's Greek."

My jaw stays clenched the fuck shut.

"You'd think that if you were a Drakos, you'd know how to speak Greek."

Interesting.

He seemed pretty fluent when he vomited out the Greek phrase just now. I'm not an expert, and I sure as fuck don't speak Greek, but I wonder if this is a way that they might be connected.

Marisol also seems to have a gift with languages too.

For a fleeting second, I think about my own kids. I don't know them. Not in the fucking slightest. Genetically, they're obviously mine, as they do look like me.

But beyond that...

Would anyone say that it's clear that they're mine?

More than that, what are they like?

Are they good with languages? Are they... like me?

Or are they soft and sweet like Marisol?

My fucking knuckles crack as I think of my girls. *My girls.*

I might not have been much of a fuckin' father, but I can protect them the best I know how.

If they've been hurt, ever, if this man has ever tried to fucking do anything to them...

No matter what, they're this man's grandchildren.

Fucking hell.

"Don't talk much, do you, Drakos?"

I tilt my head. "Only when it matters."

"You sound American."

I don't say anything to him.

Benicio sighs, leaning back in his chair. We're somewhere in the barracks, in a basement that's somehow buried underneath them. The walls around me are cement, the ceiling is cement, and the floor is a wreck of disjointed cement and cinder blocks. It looks like a drunk mole came down here to lay the whole thing, and it doesn't make me feel super confident about the whole fucking structure.

Likely, Benicio had his men build it, and not one of them seems to have a lick of fuckin' sense, or even two goddamn brain cells to rub together between them.

Let alone any knowledge of building or code.

The glimpses of bare walls that I see, though, make me think that they somehow drilled into bedrock to be down here, but it looks like limestone, which is about as sturdy as a fucking house of cards.

This whole thing is probably as sturdy, and it makes me nervous. If I get trapped down here, how will Marisol...

Shut the fuck up. Do what you need to do. And get her the hell out of here.

I did made a note of the labyrinth of stairs and fucking curves that took us down here, but even I would have a hard time finding my way out of here.

It's a fucking mess, but if I need to get myself the fuck out of here, I will.

The fucking rain isn't helping. It's been coming down for another day, still at the same strength as last night. At this point, it's seeping into the rocks around us, and the whole basement of this fucking place has all the ambiance of a medieval dungeon. I can hear dripping sounds, and there are small puddles of water beneath

So much for a fuckin' rainforest.

"Well. If you won't talk, I doubt you'll do well with this," Benicio sneers.

I raise an eyebrow. "I'm not the one who fuckin' needs to talk, right?"

His eyes narrow, glaring at me. "I don't like you."

"Good," I say.

The word seems to piss him off, but then he laughs. "You're a hell of a contender, though. When you punched the Russian in his face? I haven't seen a move like that since the eighties."

I nod.

Benicio sighs and waves at one of his fucking henchmen. I hear a door clang, and the sound of shuffling feet throws me off.

A man, dragged by the goon that Benicio indicated, appears in the room.

The goon tugs his head back, and my heart kicks up a beat.

I know this man.

How the fuck do I know this guy?

"This man isn't one of mine. However, I did find him sniffing around the building a while back. He's been here for a while, he's eating my food like a rat, and I need to figure out who he is and why he's here," Benicio says softly.

The man's eyes widen when they look at me.

He knows me too. How...

"I will give you thirty minutes. Figure out who he is. Kill him if he's a threat," Benicio sneers.

With all the grace of a bloated corpse, Benicio rises from his chair and leaves the room. The henchmen do too, with the exception of one who positions himself at the door, presumably to report back that I'm not a soft fucking baby.

I do a quick assessment.

The man's hands are bound, and there's a gag in his mouth. He looks skinny as fuck, and I know that he probably is weak too.

There's no way he's going to hurt me.

I stride forward, my hands going to the gag. I rip it off and get down in his face. "Who the fuck are you?" I snarl.

The man blinks, looking up at me. "Luca," he breathes.

I lean back on my heels.

Holy fuck.

I do know this man.

He works at our shipping business. For my brother. He's an enforcer, and a goddamn good one at that. Got married a couple of years back.

I was at his fucking wedding.

"Luca?" I say, my mind racing. "How..."

"I was helping Marco," he breathes. "Keep tabs, so Ben... he didn't hurt the girls."

The words are like a slap in the face. Fuck me.

If he was helping Marco monitor Benicio, to make sure that Souza didn't do anything to hurt my kids, he was helping *me*.

Which means Luca had to leave his pretty wife...

For me.

"Fuck," I mutter.

Luca heaves a breath. "I know... what you need to do..." he rasps. He shuts his eyes and collapses, turning into a puddle on the floor.

"Just make it quick. And tell her... tell her I love her," he whispers.

I shut my eyes.

Fucking hell.

I'm not good at this part. The strategy stuff isn't for me. It's for Marco and Sal, who are fucking smart and shit.

I'm just Dino. The bruiser. The fuckin' muscle to send in when you don't want to solve the fuckin' problem.

This isn't something that I know how to handle.

I need time.

"Listen. I'm not going to kill you. But I'm... I don't know if I can get you out of here," I say honestly.

Luca nods. "I know."

"Fucking hell. And I... man. I don't know what else to say except this is gonna hurt," I whisper.

Luca looks up at me. "Do it."

Fuck.

This is bad. I'm good at fighting, but I can't just... hurt someone who is sitting on the ground, staring at me.

You have to.

You fucking have to.

I let the thought spur me into action, and I slam my fist into his nose.

Luca doesn't do *shit*.

I do it again. Again. His back. His shoulders. By the time I'm done, he's a bloody fucking mess, but he's still breathing.

That, I know.

I open the door, motioning for the goon. "Done," I grunt.

The goon stares at me.

"He's not fuckin' dead," I snarl. "I know who he is and I know Benicio wants him alive."

It's a lie.

But I don't know what else to do.

The goon stares at me again.

"Take. Him. And. I'm. Going. To. Benicio," I repeat slowly.

That seems to get some traction. The goon hauls Luca up, and I walk to the edge of the hallway...

Then I turn.

I mark the door that the guard slams Luca into before quickly pivoting and dashing up the stairs.

I have no fucking clue what I'm doing. I need to tell Benicio some bullshit, but first...

I need to find Johnny.

Luca doesn't deserve this shit. I'm not going to tell his wife that he fucking died in a basement in Brazil.

And, if Johnny wants out...

I think I might be able to get the both of them gone before Benicio can fuck with them any more.

23

MARISOL

The rain feels incessant at this point.

It is, actually. According to the news station, which I briefly overhear on the radio as I walk the halls of my father's home like a ghost, this level of rain is starting to cause problems in the flood plains along the river.

I sigh.

I wish it would cause problems here.

Nothing short of an act of God will help me now.

My footsteps echo on the stone floors as I meander through the compound.

This is what I've been reduced to.

Pacing.

Pacing the halls. Pacing my room. I spent a restless night last night just... turning, until I finally got out of bed and decided to pace around instead.

I can't do this anymore.

Something has to change. But I can't change anything.

I'm just...

Stuck.

The door to the house creaks open, and my father comes in. I freeze; I'm not sure that I want to talk to him.

Well.

I definitely don't.

But unfortunately, he's already seen me. His face seems to... soften. Slightly. "Marisol," he rumbles. He collapses onto the living room couch, dismissing Paolo as he does. "Come sit with me."

Cautiously, with all the awareness of a mouse creeping in front of a cat, I pad into the room.

"How are you?" he says after a minute.

I blink.

I don't remember the last time that my father asked how I was.

"Andrei tells me that you have been enjoying the pool," he continues.

If I could glare at Andrei, I would, but that would give too much away. "I like to swim."

"I know. Why do you think the house has a pool?"

I blink.

"The house has always had a pool."

"Well of course. Your mother told me when you were a baby that you enjoyed water. It was your birth month, or something like that," he huffs. "Honestly, I didn't know, or care. She said to build you a pool and so I built you a pool."

I raise an eyebrow. "I thought this house used to belong to Ricario Pinto?"

"He did not have a pool, Marisol."

I'm confused.

It feels like my father is trying to say that he made modifications to the house... for me?

It's not just the house. The whole place is a compound, literally built to hide criminals and allow them to engage in activities that the central government can do nothing about. It comes with a *barracks,* for the love of everything holy.

There's no way that my father tried to make it family-friendly for...

Me.

"You had a lot of children, father," I say quietly. "Any one of them could have enjoyed the pool."

He stiffens.

The mention of my long-dead (and probably murdered) half-siblings makes his face go hard. He rises from the couch, coming closer to me.

I refuse to cower.

Benicio Souza and I stare at each other. My jaw sets in a hard line, and while I'm fearful of standing my ground in front of my maniac of a father, I instinctively know that giving in to him would be worse.

Benicio hates a coward.

Finally, he sighs. He turns, stepping back toward Paolo. I'm ready to leave as well, but my father's voice echoes through the room.

"You and your mother almost made me think something... different."

I freeze.

"I am not a kind man, Marisol. I do not think I ever have been. I have fought for everything, and I will continue to fight for it. The world is mine," he says fiercely, aggressively, "and I will eliminate anything and everyone who stands in the way of what I want."

That's more like the Benicio Souza I know.

"But..." his voice lingers.

"For you and your mother? I thought maybe, for a minute, I was more than just the monster."

With that, my father leaves the room.

I do turn to look at him, then. But it's too late.

He's gone.

My heart twists.

My father is a nightmare, one that I've been afraid of for a long time. I've never seen him as human; just a monster, like he said. I've certainly seen him be capable of monstrous things. I've seen him destroy everyone: family, friends, without so much as blinking as the blood splatters on his face.

But why hasn't he ever come for you?

I used to think it was because of my mother.

But I'm here. Trapped, sure. A prisoner, definitely. I'm here against my will, and while I'm trying to protect my mother and my children by staying here...

It never really occurred to me that my father might genuinely have something other than cold-hearted calculation about us.

I frown as Andrei approaches me.

He looks me up and down. "You do inspire something in people, you know."

"What?"

"I know what your father means. You make a man think of something other than the terrible ways of the world. I can see why he wishes to protect you," he murmurs.

I know it's meant to be a compliment, but I resist the urge to wince.

Is that the reason?

Am I so soft, so utterly helpless, that I inspire men to protect me like some kind of fairy tale princess?

The thought... disgusts me.

I am not soft.

My shoulders tense, and I look at Andrei. "I do not need to be protected."

His eyes cloud with confusion. "Marisol..."

"I have carried and given birth to not one, but two children. I have navigated the swamp that is my father's influence. I am the product of both my father and my mother, and they are both fearsome people. You look at me like I'm some kind of... doll," I spit.

Andrei is visibly confused now, but I'm on a roll.

"I'm not fragile. I'm not broken. I've survived in ways that you couldn't think of, because they don't involve violence or harm. I chose to be here, Andrei, to protect people I love. I don't need you... infantilizing me," I finish.

I don't let him say anything.

Turning on my heel, I march toward the pool.

Andrei, as always, follows.

When we get there however, I pause at the door.

The pool is... flooded.

There's no other way to explain it.

The beautiful marble floor around it is covered in an inch of grimy, smelly water. I can hear the sound of a pump running somewhere, but clearly, it's not working. The pool itself is a dark brown, stained with mud that's slowly seeping in from somewhere near the bathroom.

The rain.

"Let me take you out of here, Marisol," Andrei says gently. "We can get someone to fix it, but it's not safe right now."

He's not wrong. Flood waters contain more than just mud.

But something about the scene makes my heart beat with apprehension.

I turn to look at Andrei. "Has my father ever had a flood risk assessment done on this house?"

"No, miss. We're halfway up a mountain. There's no reason. Any water runs downhill, and the river might flood, but I doubt we would be in any danger here."

Noting that I've been downgraded from "Marisol" to "miss," I nod. "I see. Well. In that case... I guess my room will do."

Another time to be locked in my room. With nothing to do.

That's just great.

I sigh.

I'll put on some athleisure clothes and pretend that I'm going somewhere. Then, I'll stare at the wall and contemplate why every man in my life considers me to be incapable.

I'm so tired of it.

But there's nothing I can do about it.

Yet.

24

DINO

The incessant rain is beginning to grate on my nerves.

I reported my findings (which were total fucking bullshit) to Benicio. He seemed unwilling to accept that Luca, who looks very obviously Italian, was a member of the Irish mob, but he didn't disagree. I had the impression that he was distracted by something, because he seemed to be less than attentive when I told him who Luca was.

Still, I'm not dead.

I passed this test.

That task done, I head back to my barracks room. I knock on Johnny's door, and when he comes into my room, I sit him down on the bed.

"I need you to leave," I growl.

Johnny glares at me. "Oh. You do? Is that what you need, Dino? Fuck—"

"Shut the fuck up," I snap. "One of Marco's guys that I used to work with, an enforcer, is down in the fucking dungeon. I beat the shit out of him and pretended he was Irish. You're going to get him the fuck out of here."

Johnny's eyes widen. "Who?"

"Luca. Don't remember his last name."

"Didn't he recently get married? Couple of years back?"

I nod.

"Fuck, man. Marco must have sent him down here..."

"How Marco pulled that off when he was fucking hiding in Ireland I'll never fucking know," I grunt. "But we gotta get him out of here."

Johnny surveys me. "What about your girl?"

"Let me worry about Marisol."

"Dino..."

"Look," I say. "You've been great. You really have. I fucking needed you here. But I'm going to get Marisol out of here, and I don't need help. What I do need," I say in a firm voice that's definitely not gentle, but it's not fuckin' mean, "is for you to get out of here, and to get Luca the hell out of here and back to Elio and Marco."

Johnny blinks.

Good. He's paying attention. "We gotta get two of our fuckin' people out of here, man. You get Luca back home. I'll get Marisol. You understand?"

"I... yeah," Johnny says.

I grin. "Good. Now this is how we're gonna get him the fuck out of here."

It's not a good plan.

I ain't no fuckin' planner, that's for sure.

But it's gonna fuckin' work.

We creep down into the barracks dungeon. God, I would hate to be a poor soul trapped in here. The water is ankle-deep now, and the rocks around us are making noises.

That isn't fucking good.

Rocks should not make noises.

"Hey, I didn't pass science past the seventh grade," Johnny whispers as we hear something particularly fucking shady, "but should that wall that looks like it's made out of solid fucking rock be making that sound?"

"Absolutely fucking not," I murmur.

The guards are easy to dodge, because none of them are fucking down here.

I have no clue where they are, but I'm hoping that it's just a stroke of luck and not some kind of disaster waiting to happen.

Better not count on that, fucking idiot.

Eventually we get to the door that's keeping Luca's cell closed.

Johnny blinks at me. "You got keys?"

"You don't know how to pick a lock?" I fire back.

Johnny sighs. "No, I didn't learn that either."

Fucking hell.

Digging the pins in my pocket that I stashed just in case, I kneel down. I can barely hear the lock over the noise from the cells around us, but eventually it clicks.

I move quickly up and tug at the door handle. It opens.

"Jesus fuck," Johnny breathes.

Luca looks fucking bad.

He's curled into a ball on the floor, which is not even remotely dry. Water laps dangerously close to his mouth, which looks like it's open so he can breathe.

I think he can breathe, anyway.

"This motherfucker is not going to be able to get out of here," Johnny murmurs.

"Help me get him up," I snap.

But, I'm thinking the same fuckin' thing.

Slowly, we help Luca up. The groan he releases is a good thing, as it tells me that he's alive.

Until now, I wasn't fucking sure.

"Luca," I say, listening to the rattling breath rasping in and out of his lungs with concern. "You fuckin' good, man?"

"I... Just..."

"He's in no condition to travel even if we had a fuckin' five-star service to get us out of here," Johnny hisses. "How the fuck are we going to.."

"Luca," I say, ignoring Johnny. "Johhny here is in contact with Marco. He's going to get you to whatever drop point he has, and then you two are getting the fuck out of here."

Luca's eyes flutter. "What..."

"Can you do it?" I demand.

I know I'm not being nice. I know that I'm being intense.

But fuck.

Luca has to be able to walk out of here. Johnny can't carry him.

He has to be able to do it all on his fuckin' own.

Johnny grunts as Luca's knees go a little weak.

Fuck. "Luca," I bark. "Do you want to get back to see your wife and kid or do you not?"

Luca's eyes snap open at that.

"If you want to fucking die in this rathole that's on you. I ain't gonna make you go. But shit, if you want to get the fuck out of this fucking piece of shit place..."

"I'll go," he says.

His voice is surprisingly steady.

"Back up," I bark at Johnny. "Let's see if he can fucking stand."

We slowly back away.

Luca wobbles, once, and I'm worried that it's all for nothing because there isn't any way that he can fucking make it...

Then, he takes a deep breath, gets both feet underneath him, and pulls himself up to his full height.

My chest constricts, because damn.

Luca is a big guy. But right now? He looks... gaunt. Clearly the last few weeks or however long he's been down here haven't been kind, because he looks like the shell of who he once was.

I look at Johnny, who shrugs. "We'll make it work."

"Let's get out of here," I mutter.

We head back out.

My feet are fucking cold at this point, and I hate to think of what kind of germs and nasty shit are in the water that's at my ankles by now. The other cells seem empty, or their occupants are too far gone to care that the water seems to slowly be creeping in.

I can't think about that.

Benicio Souza is a fucking monster. He really is. Elio and Marco are both hard fuckin' guys, but they don't have people rotting in cells, slowly dying as water creeps up on them.

Well.

I guess Elio does.

Having been one of the people who rotted in one of his cells, once.

Bile rises in my throat.

This whole fuckin' business is dirty as shit. And I've never really thought about it until now.

Until seeing one of my friends, my guys, that's been harmed.

We make it out with no guards again. Johnny leads Luca about a hundred yards away from the barracks, near to the main house. The rain is coming down in fuckin' buckets, but with a quick nod, Johnny and Luca disappear into the forest.

Fucking hell.

I don't know where his contact point is with Marco, but I know that he better fuckin' make it there.

I want Luca to make it home.

I'm trudging back to the barracks, my shoes squelching, when a dark shape crosses my vision. It's almost night, and the square of someone's shoulders cuts a clear silhouette against the fading sky.

Fuck.

The Russian.

He looks at me, arms folded, eyes narrowed. I glare back at him. "The fuck is your problem?" I hiss.

He gives me one more second before he waves his hand...

And Benicio's men, armed to the fucking gills, sprout out of the forest around me.

25

DINO

I LET them march me to the house.

It's my only fuckin' choice. I need to make sure their eyes are on me, and not on Johnny and Luca, who haven't been frog-marched out of the jungle yet. I hope that they somehow managed to escape the guards, but it seems unlikely.

Who knows.

Maybe they got fuckin' lucky.

Like you did?

Fuck.

Outside, in the courtyard, Benicio is waiting.

"What the fuck did you do?" he says, looking at the Russian.

Volkov sneers. "I found him. Walking outside. Alone. After going into the dungeon."

Aha.

This dumb motherfucker doesn't know what I did.

Souza sighs. "If you brought me out here because you have a suspicion that is unconfirmed, spare me, Russian. And somehow, you convinced my men to follow you? I do not appreciate that move," he growls. "You should have consulted me first, without the use of my own men against me. Fucking Russians," he sneers. "You, just like your father and uncle, are not thoughtful."

Heh.

Good to know neither one of us is gonna give him the respect of his name.

And, that he thinks Volkov is dumb as a rock too.

Time to cause some chaos.

"You brought me here because I was fuckin' *walking?*" I sneer at the Russian. "You're stupider than a fuckin' chicken with its head cut off, shit-for-brains."

"Silence!" the Russian roars at me.

I laugh. It's a rasping, halting sound, and I know it sounds fuckin' inhuman.

Remind me to thank Elio for making me sound like one scary asshole.

"You're so fucking dumb, Russian, I bet you couldn't pour water out of a boot if the instructions were on the fuckin' heel."

Benicio's eyebrows raise.

Volkov's English is not quite as good as he thinks, and he definitely takes a minute to process that one.

If I can get him to hit me, then I can start the kind of fight that's a good distraction. With a good enough distraction…

Hope flickers in my chest.

With a good enough distraction, I might be able to get Marisol out of here too.

"Oh, you didn't understand that shit? I'd give you a penny for your thoughts, but I'd probably get some change back."

Volkov growls. "Shut the fuck up."

"No way, motherfucker. You're gonna have to make me shut up. Unless you need a fuckin' minute to figure out how?" I taunt.

I don't miss the ghost of a smile crossing Benicio's face...

Or the thunder in Volkov's.

"You. Be. Quiet," he rumbles. He takes another step toward me...

Almost.

I'm not restrained or anything. But if I can get him to throw the first punch, then I can start a fuckin' riot with his big dumb body.

And that's the fuckin' vision.

"Yeah, I'll bet you want me to be fuckin' quiet. Because it's hard to listen to words, isn't it, big guy? Yeah, giving you brains was about as useful as puttin' a fuckin' screen door on a submarine..."

That does it.

Volkov howls, coming at me with a punch. I dodge, rolling under him, the mud coating my back as I move toward the circle of guards.

Volkov is big. I wasn't fuckin' kidding about that. But big means slow. Big means inertia.

And in mud like this?

Big is a wide fuckin' door for an accident.

Volkov manages to pivot and comes in after me. The mud squelches under his feet. Directly behind me, I can practically feel Benicio's apprehension.

Which is exactly the fuckin' point.

Bearing down on me, the Russian snorts like a pissed-off bear. I see him raise his fist in almost slow motion. *Wait. Wait. Wait....*

Now.

I dodge to the side.

The punch that he had for me sails forward, though, and goes straight for Benicio.

I hear the guards yell.

Rolling to my feet, I grin.

The guard nearest Benicio jumped in front of him. He might have been talked into this shit by Volkov, somehow, but right now, his primary priority is the man who pays his fuckin' bills.

The Russian's meaty fist lands on the guard.

Which prompts another guard to move forward, swinging his fists.

Which brings another guard in...

I grin.

Yeah.

Complete fuckin' chaos.

As the guards go after Benicio, the rain pelting us all, I quickly move backward. If I can sneak around to the side entrance, provided it's not underwater, then I can get in through the pool door, and get Marisol...

"What the hell is going on?" I hear a clear voice ring out.

My heart sinks.

The scene in front of us seems to pause. Benicio, from his safe position behind the melee in front of him, stands.

"What are you doing out here, Marisol?"

We all turn to look at her.

My heart stutters.

She's so fucking beautiful.

Even just wearing sweatpants and a long-sleeve sweater, she's fucking stunning.

Mine.

I want to rip everyone's eyes out just for looking at her.

Moretti's ugly fucking face, however, ruins everything. He steps in front of her, glaring at the crowd.

Benicio moves to the steps, standing next to his daughter. "This is not for you to see," he says.

Marisol holds her chin up. "I think I want to see who is causing all of this chaos, if it's someone that I'm going to chain myself to for life," she says in a clear voice.

It strikes me then, that even though I have this urge to protect her and I want to take her away from all this...

Marisol is kind of a badass.

All five-foot-two of her is glaring at the lot of us like she's a fucking queen. Her head is held high, twin braids containing her riot of curly hair, and she glares down her nose, making her dad's men visibly cringe.

I quickly squash the grin that's forming at the corner of my lips.

My girl.

She's so fucking brave.

I don't think I've given her credit for that before, but now…

I will.

"Marisol," Benicio says, exasperated. "Go back inside. You'll catch your death in the rain…"

Huh.

His tone seems genuinely concerned.

I blink.

Does Benicio Souza actually… care about his daughter?

The whole situation is bizarre. The Russian and the guards are frozen, mid-fight. Moretti has wandered over to them, his feet squelching in the mud of the courtyard like the rest of us.

And Marisol, standing on the patio, a queen surveying her kingdom.

"Father, I…"

Marisol pauses.

The hair on the back of my neck stands straight up as a rumbling sound reaches me. It sounds like… thunder. Except it's a lot louder. And the ground under my feet is starting to shake, ever so slightly.

What the fuck is this?

Everyone turns, looking around, but I'm the only one looking at the house when I hear the creak of trees screaming as they're being moved.

Then, I fucking know exactly what's going on.

Mudslide.

"Marisol!" I yell. I take a step toward her. She's less than ten feet from me, and I know that I could get to her if I just...

Before I know it, I'm punched in the ribs by something solid, and my world turns dark.

I'm tumbling.

Over and over, the world rotates around me. I tuck myself into a ball, just trying to keep the rocks that I can feel pelting me from hitting something important.

My mind offers helpful images of being stuck through by a tree branch.

I'm in a mudslide.

I never in my life thought I would be in a fucking mudslide. Not once.

And here I fucking am.

I have to get out of here before I'm buried.

I have no idea how to do that. I don't know what's up. I have no idea if I'm pointing down.

I just fuckin' pray, and start moving.

The air is burning in my lungs by the time my fingers hit something that feels like air.

I pull myself up, coughing the dirt out of my mouth as I come up to the top of the river of mud that's cascading around me.

Fuck.

The world is still moving. I sip air before taking another huge pull with my arms. I need something to hold onto. I need…

A tree appears next to me, and I grab it, hauling myself up on the trunk.

The mud, at least, appears to be slowing down. It's solidifying around me, and while that's not a good sign, at least I can crawl out around it.

I think.

The tree feels solid underneath me, which is fucking good. I pull myself up, trying to survey the surroundings.

The rain, and the darkness, make me completely lose sight of everything, and my heart squeezes with terror.

Marisol.

I have to find her.

I have no fucking clue where I am or how far away from the house I am. The mud must have exploded over the house, and I don't know if it's buried or swept away or…

Fuck it.

"Marisol!" I scream.

Silence greets me.

"Marisol!" I scream again.

I have no fucking clue which way to even go. The house should still have some electricity... it's not on a grid, but a generator, and that's housed in a building pretty far away. In theory, I should be able to see lights.

Peering into the darkness, I look around, calling Marisol's name. I don't see shit, and I don't want to cross the river of mud...

I hear something.

Any concern that I have about the shifting mud underneath me is gone as I scramble, hand over foot, toward the source of the sound. "Marisol," I rasp, hoping against everything that she's fucking there, in front of me.

The rain makes it so hard to see. So fucking hard. But scouring the mud in front of me, my eyes catch movement.

I wade over to it.

A hand is sticking above the mud.

I fall to my knees, digging around it. I pull, hopeful that it's her...

The ugly face of Benicio Souza fills my view.

He gasps, the rain leaving rivers down the mud on his face.

I lean back.

Marisol was right in front of him. If he's here, then...

"Boy," he says, coughing up mud. "Drakos."

I look at him.

Benicio's lungs are heaving, and I know instinctively that something's wrong.

He's dying.

I don't know from what, but I can tell from the look in his eyes that he knows it too.

"Benicio..."

He shuts his eyes. "You're the father. Of my grandchildren," he wheezes.

Fuck me.

I'm not about to lie to a dying man. "I am."

"You're not a Drakos."

"I am, actually. They just don't know it," I say.

His eyes flutter open at that, and I have the brief satisfaction of knowing that I managed to surprise Benicio Souza. "Interesting," he manages.

I don't say anything.

I'm not really interested in what Benicio has to say. But when he coughs, I turn my attention back from scouring the mud.

"She's... by house..."

I lean in.

"I pushed her under the eave of the house," he wheezes. "Should be okay. The mud... took me. Not her."

Hope flutters in my chest.

I stand, ready to wade through the rapidly solidifying mud and find the house, when he grabs my ankle.

I look down at Benicio.

He blinks. "Save her," he whispers.

Then, his face goes slack, the rain gathering in his open mouth as he rasps.

I'm not sure what to do. This feels like… an anticlimactic way for him to end.

But I have to find her.

Turning to where I think the source of the mud came from, I wade forward. I fight every step of the way, thick pools of it sucking at my feet, threatening to drag me under. There are trees and rocks and what look suspiciously like bodies in the muck, but I don't give a single fuck about them.

Marisol is the only thing that matters to me.

Finally, I see something. In the darkness, something starts to look suspiciously like a light.

The house.

I stride forward.

As I get closer, the mud dragging at my legs, I hear something that makes me move a whole lot faster.

A woman, panting and struggling.

And the growl of a man.

Fucking hell.

I fight forward.

The house is demolished. The light that I'm seeing is a flickering porch light, halfway sunk into the mud.

But the roof, a corner of it, and part of the space that overlooks the courtyard where we were just standing, remains strangely untouched.

And underneath it, I see two shapes.

One is undoubtedly Marisol.

And the other...

Has his fucking hands on her.

After that, I don't think.. Rage, pure and clean, powers me through the mud. My body feels like it's possessed by something that I can't quite name as I race toward her.

I'm going to kill him.

I reach her just as she falls.

The man is just one of her father's goons. I don't know who. Don't give a fuck. Because as soon as I lift up one of the large rocks that the mud brought forward, it's all over for him.

I crack it across the back of his head, blood mixing with the mud that's soaking us, and he tumbles down.

Right across Marisol.

She screams, and I grunt, pulling him off of her. The mud is thinner here, clearly at the edge of the lava-like mud flow, and the man gets to his feet quickly.

His eyes narrow at me. "You," he hisses.

I heft the rock again, and I come after him with a ferocity that I never have had before.

The fight doesn't last long. He's down quickly, and when I smash the rock into his face, the assorted blood and gore assures me that he's dead.

I stand up.

Marisol is staring at the body.

Quickly, I move in front of it. "Marisol, don't look."

"No," she murmurs.

She moves forward, pushing me to the side, and grabs the knife off of his belt. To my surprise, she takes it, raises it over her head...

And stabs the body.

Straight through his heart.

I blink.

Slowly, Marisol stands. Her eyes are practically glowing in the dark, and her chest is heaving.

"Dino," she pants.

"Yes?"

"Get me fucking back to my children."

26

MARISOL

My mind refuses to acknowledge what just happened.

One minute I was standing on the porch, trying to figure out what on earth was happening after I listened to what sounded like a major battle happening from my room. I walked outside to see Dino, taunting my father's guards and the Russian, and starting a riot.

Or what looked like a riot, anyway.

Then, the ground under my feet rumbled. The house seemed to shake. And when I turned, I saw a wall of earth coming straight for me.

I waited for it to hit me. I did.

But the only thing I felt was my father's hands on my waist, shoving me to the side, under the roof of the house that was just out of reach of the wall of mud.

I watched the mud sweep my house, and Dino, and the full courtyard of men, down the hillside, taking chunks of the jungle with it.

For a second, I had an outrageous thought, because the forest in front of me was basically clear cut.

If it was a clear night, you could see the stars.

But it isn't a clear night.

The stars aren't out.

And I just watched the mountain swallow nearly a dozen men.

Including my own father, who might have just saved me...

And the father of my children.

I was standing, completely frozen, when Paolo found me.

And apparently, he saw that as his opportunity to do something he'd always wanted to do.

Covered in mud and broken, men, apparently, will still be men.

I almost had a grip on the knife at his belt by the time Dino hit him with the rock.

But stabbing him through the heart?

I needed that.

I'm looking at his body when Dino touches my arm. "We need to go," he murmurs. "The mountain might give out, and I don't know where the rest of the men are."

Volkov.

The rest of the guards.

All of them will be a problem right now, and after coming within inches of being swallowed alive in a river of mud...

All I want is to get back to my girls.

I nod.

Dino looks at Paolo, then back at me. He kneels, taking the knife out of his chest. I try not to flinch at the ugly noise it makes, but I can't help it.

It's not a good sound, and even over the rain I can hear it squelching.

"You had good aim," he murmurs as he wipes the blade off on Paolo's shirt. "Try not to stab straight on. Easier to glance off a rib that way. And definitely don't stab in the middle of the chest."

"I know where the sternum is," I say calmly.

It's remarkable how clear some details are right now. The slow pump of blood out of Paolo's heart. The knife. The rain making little rivers down his face. I don't feel anything, not heat or cold, but I just…

I don't know what to do with myself.

"Here," Dino says, offering me the knife. I put my hand forward, my motion jerky as my fingers close around the handle.

We both watch as I take the knife and hold it at my side, shaking.

"If you need to, use that," Dino murmurs. "Side. Kidney. Leg. Stab someone in the groin and you'll hit an artery. The neck would be best though. The force you put into that last blow? That's what you need," he says.

I blink, looking at him. "Aren't you going to tell me to leave it to you? That I'm delicate? That you should protect me?"

I'm still bitter, apparently, about being treated like I'm made of tissue paper, which is absolutely the stupidest thing to be upset about right now.

My father was just swept away in a mudslide.

I shouldn't be worried about being *protected*.

"No," Dino says softly.

That catches my attention.

He looks at me. "I want you to be able to protect yourself. I will always be here for you, Marisol. But I can't survive an act of God. If something else happens, take the knife. Go to the port. Find a way to get back to Elio and the girls."

"Dino..."

"You did it once. You're smart and very, very resilient, Marisol. More fuckin' resilient than I think anyone realizes. You can do it again, and you might need to stab someone to get there. If you need to stab them, remember—"

"Neck. Groin. Legs. Liver. Gut," I say, adding one.

Dino nods. "The gut would be good. Especially with all this dirt around. It'll be septic in a hot fuckin' second."

If I could feel my own skin, that would worry me, because I'd be concerned about dirt getting into my own wounds.

But I can't.

And I'm not.

The calm is the strangest part. I guess that I do remember feeling like this, once.

When I gave birth to the twins.

Adrenaline, my brain tells me. *Fight, flight, flee, or fawn.*

Clearly, I'm a fighter.

"Let's go get back to our girls," Dino says softly.

One word.

Three letters.

And it stops me in my tracks more effectively than any river of mud.

I blink at him, the rain bringing mud into my eyes. I hastily scrub it out, blinking rapidly against the grit that's gathered underneath my eyelids.

"Our?" I say.

I hate that the word sounds shaky, and that it's almost lost in the cascade of the rain.

Dino reaches for my hand, grabbing the one that doesn't hold a knife.

He nods.

"Yeah, baby. Our girls."

I have no idea where we're going.

The road is gone. The jungle is gone. There's no way to know which way we're headed, only that occasionally the rain lifts long enough for us to see the glittering lights of Brasilia, which is somewhere around fifteen miles away.

From Brasilia, we need to take a boat to the coast. Or, we need to catch a flight.

I have no passport and I look like the mountain spit me out. There's no way that anyone is going to put me on a plane...

"Give me your hand," Dino says roughly.

Automatically, I put my fingers in his.

He hauls me up against his firm chest, tugging me over some rocks that I hadn't really noticed.

"Thanks," I mutter.

Dino grunts.

We continue in silence, picking our way through the mountain, through the jungle, and Dino keeps startling like a cat every time he hears something other than the steady fall of rain.

Finally, I can't take the silence anymore.

"Why do you keep looking over your shoulder?"

He sighs. "More landslides. Moretti. Your father, coming after us with his men."

I stop. "My father?"

Dino looks at me, his eyes shining in the dark. "I found him," he says quietly.

"Was he alive?"

He looks away. "Not for long. I'm sorry," he says hoarsely.

I... don't know what to say.

"Um. I... Thank you. I think," I say.

Dino is quiet.

Instead of my brain whirling around this information alone, I start to just... say it out loud.

"I'm not close with my father. He's a monster. He's been the boogeyman that I've been afraid of for most of my life. So I'm not sad. I'm not. But he... I think he saved me," I say hollowly. "He pushed me aside right as the mud swept away the side of the house where I was standing. He helped me. And lately he'd been talking to me like... like he cared about me."

I heave in a huge breath, confusing thoughts rushing through me like a tidal wave.

"He's always been a bad man. The worst man. But how can he be a bad man and one that wanted to save me?"

"People are complicated," Dino says softly. "Everyone seems to have their reasons for doing shit, and sometimes it's hard to know what the fuck they mean by it."

Dino's words are bitter.

Like he's been grappling with this too.

"What were you doing? When I found you?" I ask.

Dino glances at me. "You want to do this here?"

"Yeah," I say.

"Marisol. We need to get off the fucking mountain. It's at least a fifteen mile walk back to the city. You're cold, and we're covered in mud that might contain the next fucking plague."

"I'm not cold," I say defiantly.

Almost on cue, my shoulders start to shake.

Dino's face pinches with concern. "I think you're going into shock. We need to get out of the fuckin' rain like... now," he growls.

"Dino..."

But he's ignoring me. He grabs my hand, tugging me forward, and we follow the path of the mud as it wiped away the jungle down the mountainside.

After walking for a while, I realize that I am, in fact, really cold.

More than that, I'm... freezing.

I can't stop my teeth from chattering. My legs feel like lead, like I can't move them forward because every step is painful. I'm actually not sure that I can keep up, because my head is pounding and my vision is kind of fuzzy.

It isn't until the darkness creeps at the edges of my vision, though, that I fall behind.

Dino turns, looking at me with concern. "Marisol? Are you okay?"

"I..." I'm trying to tell him that I'm okay, that I just need to get the rest of the way down the mountain.

But I never get a chance to.

Darkness swims over my eyes, and everything stops.

I'm warm.

I must be dead, because there's no way that I'm this warm exposed to the rain.

If I'm dead though...

I'll never see the girls again.

The thought spurs something in me, and grief spears through me like a knife. Slowly, I'm aware of tears that feel like they're burning against my face, leaving wet trails down my cheeks that scald me like fire.

"Marisol?" I hear a raspy, familiar voice.

Dino.

Is Dino dead too?

Oh my god, the girls are orphans. Please let my mom find them. Please let them be safe with Caterina and Elio and Gia. Please...

"Marisol, wake up. Please, love," Dino says.

Wake up?

I feel something on my face. A thumb. Brushing the tracks of the tears.

"Wake up, please," he whispers.

I'm trying.

It feels like trudging through layers of sand, each one thicker than the last. Finally, when I start to see light behind my eyes, I gasp.

When I finally open them, everything seems too... *bright.*

I can't see around me. All I see is brightness, that kind of flickers. I struggle, trying to get my elbows underneath me.

"Easy," Dino murmurs, his hands on my sides. "Take it easy, Marisol."

I blink.

Slowly, the room comes into focus. It's small, with an earth-packed floor that is surprisingly dry, considering how much rain has fallen, and a little stove that contains a fire that's merrily flickering, throwing heat into the small room.

Looking over at Dino, my lips purse together. I want to ask him where we are, but nothing but a croak comes out of it.

"Here," he says, tipping a metal cup to my lips.

I drink.

The water is good. Clean. Not full of mud. I take a sip then use some of it to swish around my mouth, getting rid of dirt and mud and whatever else is in there, before I spit it over the side of my makeshift bed and onto the dirt floor.

I look up at Dino. "Where are we?"

He shrugs. "I have no idea. After you passed out I picked you up and just... ran."

"Ran?" I ask.

He nods. "Eventually I came to this hut. There wasn't anyone in it, but it was clean and dry. I think maybe this might have been an outpost, or something that someone built to spy on your father. There's a fence, or the remains of a fence, that we crossed before we came here. That fuckin' fence marks the edge of your father's property," Dino says.

When he's trying to whisper, his voice is so low.

It's sexy.

This is a terrible time to think of anything sexual, Marisol.

I nod. "Can you help me up?"

Dino slowly helps me to my feet.

I stretch, trying to check and see if anything is broken.

"How do you feel?"

Nodding, I look back at him. "Fine."

"You passed out from shock," he says quietly.

I sigh. "I figured."

"When I say that you're sick or in trouble, Marisol, I fuckin' mean it," Dino growls.

The wound is just too new. The attitude. The argument.

I turn on Dino with the full force of the anger that's been sitting in my chest for far too long now.

"You don't know me better than I know myself."

He freezes.

There's no stopping me now, though. I'm a fighter. I'm not someone who freezes under stress. I'm someone who can stab a dead body to make sure it's dead. I'm someone who can give birth to twins.

And I'm not going to take this anymore.

"I'm so tired of the men in my life seeing me as fragile. Delicate. I'm not fragile or delicate, damn it!" I practically yell. "I'm a mother. I'm tough. I'm the one who has figured out how to handle my father. I'm the one who came here to protect my mother and my children. I am not delicate, and you don't know anything about me that I don't know about myself!"

Dino nods. "I know."

I blink.

"One of the things I like about you, Marisol, is that you're brave. You're fuckin' cute as hell and you make me want to tuck you into bed so I can fuck you senseless for weeks, but you're brave. You're smart. You can figure shit out faster than I can, and you're fuckin' good at it. You're the best mom I've ever met, and I fuckin…" he pauses.

My heart is thundering in my chest.

What was he going to say next?

"I'm not tryin' to say I know more than you. But people in shock don't really know they're in shock," he says calmly. "I wasn't tryin' to tell you what to do, Marisol. Fuck no," he says with a little rasp. "I was fuckin' warning you, since it's pretty common for people in shock to not know what's happening for them."

"Oh," I say quietly.

Dino nods.

"Well. Um. Okay."

"I respect the hell out of you, baby," he says. "I'm proud as hell that my girl is like a fuckin' tiger, she's so fierce."

I flush with his words. "A tiger?"

Dino grins.

"Hell yeah, baby."

27

DINO

We can't stay here forever.

Much as I'd be happy to just keep Marisol here, dry, warm, and completely isolated from the outside world, I know we need to move on. The rain is still coming down, and any minute the dirt floor is going to start to ooze, or the mud is going to come down the mountain and take us with it.

But, the image of her fainting?

That's something that keeps me glued right here, where I can fuckin' see her and hold onto her.

Where I can know that she's safe, and that she isn't going to collapse in the middle of the fucking jungle again.

The memory of that sends another chill through me, and I tuck her closer.

We're both lying on the cot that was already in the little hut when we arrived. It's tiny, cramped, and half of my body is hanging off the back, but fuck it.

I need to make sure she's okay.

Hell.

I need to *know* that she's okay, and the only way for me to do that right now is to just... touch her.

Marisol rolls in my arms, peering up at me. "You really see me as brave?"

I laugh softly. "Hell yes I do."

"Why are you so..." she curls her lip, a mock-snarl that gives me the tiniest bit of joy.

Squeezing her close to me, I press a kiss onto her forehead. "Because, Marisol, I'm not gentle. I'm not sweet. It wouldn't matter if you walked around fully armed to the teeth all the time. I'm proud of you and want the world to know you're mine, so I'm gonna fuckin' act like you're mine, no matter how capable you are of taking care of yourself. Hell, I think it works even better because I know that if you ever need me, it's because you really fuckin' need me. I just want to be the man you need, even if I can't be the man you deserve," I murmur.

She frowns. "Who do I deserve?"

Possessiveness rumbles through my chest. "Don't fuckin' matter. I'm who you got."

"Dino," she scolds.

I sigh. "Fine. You deserve someone who can... walk into a room and not already have a beef with half the people in it. Someone who can fuckin' write poetry or some shit. Someone who can wear a fucking suit and sit in a chair and create a world just for you to live in it."

Marisol's quiet just for a minute.

"That sounds like my dad."

"What?"

She straightens, her brown eyes looking directly into mine. "You're describing my dad. Or Marco, or Elio, if you're not describing someone quite as vicious as Benicio."

I frown.

Marisol sighs. "Dino, you're who you are. I didn't ask you to be Elio or Marco or my father... or yours," she says softly. "I've had enough smooth-talking mafia men to last me a lifetime. I don't want elegance and suits and all of that. I just want someone who sees me for who I am, and who chooses me. Someone that could look at the whole world, and every treasure or pleasure it offered, and turn them down to be with me."

Fucking hell.

Her words make my heart ache.

I know how bad it feels to just... want someone to see you.

"I've had enough of people using me or trying to manipulate me. I've had enough of people assuming who I am. I've had enough of people looking at me and seeing something they want to see, instead of the real person I am," Marisol says bitterly.

I lean forward, pressing my forehead to hers. "I see you, baby. I fuckin' see you," I whisper.

Marisol breathes, her shoulders shrugging like it's a huge weight that's gone from them.

I don't know how long we lay there. Long enough, I guess, for both of us to fall asleep. When I wake up, the fire is low in the little hearth, and Marisol has her head tucked into my shoulder.

Seeing her there brings me so much joy it fuckin' hurts.

I know that she says I don't need to be anyone else. But, deeper than that, I still have a question that beats at my ribcage.

I don't know who I am, either.

Her words resonated with me, but it picked at this scab, bringing it up until I can't ignore it any longer.

How can Marisol choose me, out of anyone in the world, if I don't have a fuckin' clue who I am either?

My whole life, I've been whatever my brothers are not. If Marco was calm and collected, I was a fuckin' mess. If Sal was smart and strategic, I was loud and ready to solve every fuckin' problem with a hammer.

Even Caterina was the only person allowed to be kind. The only person I could picture being actually nice, in our fuckin' shit-show of a family.

I've spent so much time trying to be just... *different*. Whatever that meant, whatever it took, didn't matter. As long as I wasn't like anyone in my family, I had done what I wanted to do.

Thinking about who I am, though, on my own?

Not a fuckin' clue.

I know that I want Marisol. I know that she's the perfect one for me, that I'll never meet anyone like her.

But someday, she's gonna figure out that I'm hollow.

There's nothing inside me. The only thing that keeps me going, the only thing that's driven me ever since I found out about the twins... it's just *her*.

I don't have anything to offer her. I can choose her all day, every day, but the outcome will be the same.

I don't know if I'm a good father. I don't know if I'd be a good husband for her.

Marisol can't pick me, even if she wanted to.

Because me? The person I am?

It doesn't fuckin' exist without her.

And that shit scares me... more than it should.

When the sun starts to drift through the walls of the hut, Marisol sits up.

She looks down at me. "The rain. It stopped."

Holy fucking shit.

It has.

We both scramble out of the cot.

Marisol puts her shoes back on, and the outer layers of the sweatsuit she had on finally dry from the fire. Cautiously, we head out into the forest, which is, in fact, a hell of a lot drier than it was.

"Brasilia isn't meant to get this much rain," Marisol says, surveying the scene around us. "It's not the Amazon. We're not supposed to have this."

"Fuckin' climate change, I guess," I mutter.

We survey the scene in front of us.

It's clear where there's been a mudslide, or the rain has washed something away. The trees and landscape have clear scars on them, and the sun is bright in the spaces that have been left behind.

I blink.

Something moves at my side, and I startle.

"Easy," Marisol murmurs. "I was just trying to hold your hand."

My chest tightens, and I wrap my hand around hers.

"Why is your hand so small?" I mutter.

She gives me a little squeeze. "Who cares, Dino. It fits, doesn't it?"

Her words make my mind go to a very different place.

This is not the fuckin' time. We're both covered in mud that's probably toxic as hell. Marisol fainted, and neither of us has had any food for I don't know how long.

But damn.

"Come on. Mind out of the gutter. We need to go," she says.

"You don't know what I was thinkin'," I growl.

She laughs. It feels just as bright as the sunshine around us. "Yes, Dino. When you look at me like that, I know exactly what you're thinking."

I start walking.

The world around us is too quiet, especially when you're used to a forest of sounds coming at you from every angle. When we hear the rumble of a truck, we both flinch.

"Hide," I rasp, looking around for somewhere to tuck both of us.

Marisol nods, heading for the side of the road. She finds a fallen tree and crouches behind the roots, and I do my best to cover her with my body.

When the sound of a speaker screeches, we both jump.

I can't speak Portuguese, but some kind of message is being blasted from the truck.

Beneath me, Marisol twitches, wiggling to get up. When I don't let her, she looks up at me. "Dino. They're from the government. My father would never have anything to do with them. They're looking to rescue people and take them into town."

"No," I grunt.

The speaker blares again, the unfamiliar words clashing against my eardrums.

"Dino. Seriously. This could be our way to get back to the girls."

The desperation in her voice makes my chest knot. "Marisol..."

"I'll tell them that I'm pregnant. They'll take us straight into town. Please," she begs.

Fucking hell.

The word *pregnant* throws me off, and my brain is scrambled for a second.

"Please, Dino. Trust me," Marisol whispers. "I know what I'm doing."

Shit.

Even though everything in me is screaming to keep her hidden, she's right.

Marisol is smart. She's a fucking survivor.

And I need to trust her.

I straighten. She looks back at me, her face flooding with relief. "I'll do all the talking."

"That would be good," I grunt.

She pauses for a minute, then scoops some mud off the ground and smears it on my tattoos on my neck. I raise an eyebrow, and she shrugs.

"Just in case. They're not exactly subtle."

I wish I could laugh at that.

Slowly, I follow Marisol over to the truck, which has paused as soon as she waved. She flags them down, a torrent of words coming out of her. She clutches her belly, then waves at me, maybe explaining something about why I don't speak.

The soldiers don't even blink.

We're loaded into the truck, along with a couple of other people who are just as mud-soaked and fucked-up as we are. One of the soldiers smacks the side of the truck, which lumbers away...

Back down the road, toward the city.

I'm tense. I have no fucking clue who else is loaded into this thing, and I don't want to make fuckin' enemies or find someone who would give us right back to Benicio.

I might not have won the competition, but I don't give a fuck about that.

I won the only thing I cared about, which was Marisol.

I'm staring out the side of the open truck when Marisol sits on my lap. She cuddles against me, her lips near my ear.

"No one here is going to hurt us, Dino."

"Easy for you to say," I grunt, trying to hide my mouth as well. I don't know if it matters, but giving away that I only speak English is probably not a great way to keep a disguise.

"All these people were working the farms nearby when the mudslides happened. They're in the same boat as us... just trying to get out of here."

"Yeah, and what about when they pull your father and his men out of the mud and we're fuckin' fighting with them?"

"Benicio Souza lost us when we walked out," Marisol whispers. "And the rest of them..."

She lets her voice trail off, and I sigh. I know what she means. Even if there are any men left alive, it's going to be an all-out war to establish a new leader if Benicio...

"He might be dead," she says softly.

Yeah.

That.

"How do you feel about that?"

"I don't know," she says honestly. "I really don't."

I nod.

I know what it's like to have complicated feelings about your father, living or dead. I tuck her closer, resting my chin on her head.

You have no idea how to be a fuckin' dad, man.

I don't.

Marisol wants me to be the father of our children. But how am I supposed to do that when I have no fuckin' clue how?

You can't give her what she wants.

The truck rumbles down the hill, and the thoughts circle my mind like vultures.

Now that we made it out, I don't know what I'm doing. Marisol is mine. I have her. She's tucked safely in my arms, and we're just two people trying to get dry and warm after a natural disaster. Right now, I have her.

But do I have what it takes to fuckin' keep her?

28

MARISOL

There's a little relief village set up on the outskirts of the capital. Dino and I are given a tent, access to space to bathe, and food.

I've never been so grateful for anything in my life.

The tent isn't shared; we're put in there together, because I keep explaining to anyone who will listen that my new husband and I are together.

That we were on our honeymoon, going to visit the ecological park nearby.

That I'm pregnant.

It's weird how easily the lies fall from my lips, and occasionally as I'm saying them, I glance over at Dino.

He has no idea what I'm saying.

I wonder, if he knew, what his reaction would be.

Once we're finally alone in the little tent, I sigh, sitting down on the small bed that's been set up on top of some old wooden crates. "I want a shower."

Dino growls. "I can't watch over you there, Marisol."

"You're going to have to deal with it," I say.

Well.

I snap.

Clearly, the mud has gotten to me.

Dino glares, but I shake my head. "You can wait right outside. Or, you can shower in the men's area. Either way, I need to get clean, and you do too," I give him a meaningful look at the mud that I plastered on his neck.

His nostrils flare, but he doesn't say anything.

Eventually we agree to a timed system. I'll take exactly sixteen minutes from the time I walk into the women's bathing area to come back out. He'll be out in less than that time. If I'm not out when the sixteen minutes is up, he's free to tear the place apart to find me.

Needless to say, the shower is fast.

There aren't many people here yet. The soldiers said that the majority of the damage was in a remote area, which means that it was mostly around my father's compound.

I try not to think about that.

Fifteen minutes and forty seconds later, I meet Dino, and we head back to the little tent.

Inside, I collapse onto the bed. "Dios. That's magical," I sigh.

It feels so good to be clean.

I prop myself up on my elbows, blinking at Dino, who is glowering in the corner.

The clothing they provided for us is basically a prison uniform. Tan pants, tan shirt, somewhere between scrubs and a canvas sack.

But Dino makes it look… sexy.

"There's room for two," I say, patting on the bed next to me.

Dino eyes the wooden supports, made from wooden crates, suspiciously.

I stand. "Or, we could just put it on the floor."

Silently, Dino moves the bed off of the crates, the flimsy cot-like mattress so thin, I can feel the floor through it.

I wrinkle my nose. "I'm not sure that's better…"

Dino plops down next to me and pulls me close.

It's better.

I inhale deeply, my nose in his chest. He smells good. Clean, like the sanitizing soap, but also…

Like Dino.

I huff again, trying to get closer, wiggling my hips against his.

Dino rumbles. "Marisol…"

"Yes?"

"Stop."

I freeze. "Why?"

He takes a minute to respond. "Because you… this isn't the time."

"For what?"

I know I'm playing innocent, even though I understand what he's saying now. I can't help it, though.

After all that?

I want a reminder that I'm alive. That I made it out of the mud.

And that I'm heading home, to my girls.

I wiggle closer again, my lips just brushing his chest.

"Marisol," he grunts. His fingers pull my chin up, until I'm meeting his eyes. "Stop."

"No," I whisper, defiant.

His nostrils flare, and I can see a muscle work in his jaw. "Are you sure?" he rasps.

God.

I love that sexy rasp.

"I'm sure. Think of it as a little honeymoon, because I've been telling everyone we're..."

I don't get to finish that sentence.

Because Dino's lips cover mine, and I groan into his kiss.

It takes two seconds for me to go from playful and cute to panting beneath him. Dino's hands are rough and covered in calluses, but they scrape so gently against my skin as he tugs me closer, consuming me with his kiss. I break the kiss and tug at his shirt, desperate for him to take it off.

Desperate to see more of him.

He leans back, and I watch as he rips the shirt open. He tosses it aside and I run my hands over his muscles, watching them jump and twitch under my fingers. The canvas of tattoos on his body is something that I trace, line by line, watching him flex under my touch.

They linger on a new scar.

I look up at him. "Did you get hurt?"

Dino's pupils are blown wide, and it takes a minute for him to process the question. "What?"

"Did you get hurt. In the mudslide?"

"No," he grunts.

I smile.

"Good."

I lean up, digging my nails into his shoulders to tug his mouth down to mine.

I'm not gentle. I do it *hard*.

Dino responds.

I don't know what's happening, but I know this is what I needed. My shirt follows his. My rough canvas-ish pants go next, and when he tugs them down, he hooks his hands in my extremely unflattering government-issued panties, bringing them down as well.

When one of his thick fingers enters me, I arch up.

"Fuck me, Marisol," Dino grunts. "You're so fucking tight."

I want him to stretch me. I remember how big he was, when I touched him in the rain, when I found him in the pool, and I know exactly how much that's going to stretch me.

I remember.

When he bites against my shoulder, I gasp.

Yes.

"More," I pant against his shoulder. "I want more, Dino."

"You want my cock, Marisol?"

"Yes," I practically whine. The words feel like they're harsh, but I know Dino. He's *my* Dino, and even if he's a little rough around the edges, I know his heart.

"Do you need it?"

"Please, Dino," I murmur. I don't even care that I'm begging him for it.

I want more.

He pulls back, leaning up so he can take off his own rough tan pants. He pauses, looking down at me.

"Fucking hell Marisol. You make me fucking crazy."

I love to hear that.

I try to open my legs wider for him, because I'm probably going to have to.

Dino's eyes graze my core, and he shuts them. His jaw works, the muscle in it twitching as he stares at me.

"Fuck. Marisol. You... I'm... I'm fucking clean," he grunts.

I freeze.

This is what happened the first time. When we...

I gulp.

"Well. It's not like we don't already have kids," I murmur. "Nothing wrong with adding to the group, no?"

Dino's eyes flash. "Another baby?"

I shrug. "Why not? We're already a family. If you want," I say quickly.

We haven't talked about any of this. A future. An identity.

Being a family.

Dino's eyes shutter, slightly, and he looks away. "I want what you want, Marisol," he says.

But the words feel kind of... off.

"I'm fine if you're fine," I whisper.

Dino looks back at me.

Slowly, I run a hand up my torso, watching his eyes as they drag along the path of my fingers.

"I want you," I whisper.

It's the truth.

I want him. I want us to be a family. Dino sees me in a way that no one else has. He *wants* me.

Me.

Not my father's daughter. Me. Marisol.

And I believe him when he says that I'm his.

There's no time to talk about it. There are more days where we can negotiate the specifics.

For now?

We just have to trust each other.

It's a tense moment, and I break it by saying one word.

"Please," I say.

Dino takes over. He leans forward, notching himself at my entrance. I gasp at the intrusion.

"Holy hell, Dino. You're..."

"You're gonna take me, Marisol. You're gonna take me just fuckin' fine," he murmurs. "You already did it once, baby. You can do it again."

Damn.

I mean damn.

Slowly, Dino pushes himself inside me. It doesn't matter that we're on the thinnest mattress known to man... I might as well be in a five-star hotel, with how reverently and carefully he treats me. Hands delicately tracing my skin, he moves so slowly, and so intentionally, that I gasp at the first delicious stretch. My eyes roll back in my head at the sensation of being filled by him. One of his hands drifts up to massage my breast, his fingertips lightly gripping my nipple as he does so.

God.

"You're doing so good, Marisol," Dino grunts. "You take me so fucking well."

I blush at his compliment.

Dino telling me that I'm doing a good job is...

Okay.

It's really damn good.

"You like being told how good you are, don't you Marisol?"

Dino says in that dark, gravelly voice that has my entire body screaming for more.

I don't want to tell him yes.

Not yet.

I want to make him work for it a little more.

"Answer me," he says in that dark voice.

"Yes," I pant, my body automatically responding to the demand. "Yes, I like it, okay?"

"Good. I want you to feel good, Marisol," he rumbles.

Well, he's doing great at that part.

Dino starts to flex the thick muscles around his hips, pumping in and out of me slowly as he does. I gasp, my hand flying to brace myself.

He's so fucking powerful.

So vicious.

So... *big*.

The vision of him, gentling all that muscle and all that power, in order to make sure that I'm okay, that I'm enjoying him and enjoying this...

I shut my eyes.

My orgasm is already pressing at the edges of my awareness, and I don't want this to stop anytime soon.

It's all I can do to focus on not coming all over Dino's enormous cock.

"Marisol," Dino snaps, his voice pulling my focus. "Look at me."

I do.

He looks like some kind of ancient, primal god right now. The tent is dark, and I can see the outline of him silhouetted slightly. His torso gleams with sweat, and seeing it move in the dim light makes something break in me.

I feel wild. Open. Completely and totally under his spell.

And completely powerful, to have a man like this.

"I want you to look at me when you come, Marisol," Dino groans. "Can you do that for me?"

Heck yes.

He starts moving faster, the pace a little erratic. I roll my eyes back. The change in tempo is hitting something inside of me that I honestly didn't think existed until now.

I've heard of it, of course. But feeling it?

Totally different.

"Dino," I gasp, my body clenching around him prematurely. "Dino I..."

"Watch me, Marisol. Stay with me, baby," he groans.

I lock eyes with him.

One of Dino's big hands traces down my torso, and his thumb rests on my clit. I don't think he needs to do that, based on the feelings rippling through me, but I...

I lose my train of thought when the orgasm crashes over me.

I lose all ability to think, actually.

My body feels like it's floating, a bundle of nerves that I am only loosely associated with. The point of connection, the one thing I can feel through the storm of sensations wracking through me, is Dino.

And when he grunts, lashing me with heat from the inside, I swear that I can feel it through every nerve in my body.

This.

I missed this.

I *wanted* this.

Always.

Dino collapses on top of me eventually. He moves so that his arms are tucked kind of under my head, so he's cradling me at the same time as he leans down, his breath sawing harshly in and out of his mouth next to my ear.

He hasn't pulled out yet.

And I'm kind of weirded out by how much I like that.

I shift. "Well. That's one way to feel alive."

Dino laughs, and the sound makes my chest feel tight.

"You've been telling people what, about us, exactly?" he murmurs.

"That we're married. You're my husband and I'm your wife and we were here on our honeymoon."

He stiffens.

Too much, Marisol. Too much.

"It's just something I'm telling people. Just to make sure we can get out of here and no one is looking for us."

"I see," he says.

Dino shifts back, and I feel the loss of him everywhere.

I frown. "Did I say something wrong?"

Dino sighs and runs his hands through his hair. "What if I'm a shitty husband?"

Well, we haven't really talked about that as an option yet...

"What if I'm a shitty father, Marisol? It's not like I had a good model," he murmurs.

My heart aches. "Dino. Everyone has to learn to be a parent. It doesn't really matter who taught you... you have to learn on your own."

"You want that? Being my wife. More kids," he says.

His voice sounds hollow.

I raise an eyebrow. "Yeah. I mean. Isn't that what you want? You keep saying I'm yours..."

"You are," he growls.

"That's what it means to me," I say quietly.

Dino looks at me.

I have no idea what his expression holds. There are so many emotions there, they're hard to pull apart.

I don't know what to ask him. How to ask it.

How to get him back. How to keep him from going thousands of miles away from me in his mind.

How to show him that he can be a good dad, a good husband...

If he wants to.

My stomach, however, rumbles, breaking the moment.

Dino looks down. "You're hungry."

"No, I'm fine, I…"

He pulls back, dragging his pants on, and bringing my clothes to me. "Let's go eat," he says.

The air, warm from our bodies still, suddenly feels cold.

I dress, then follow Dino out of the tent.

My heart is heavy. Dino doesn't think he can be a parent, or a partner.

And I don't know what that means for me…

Or for us.

The food, predictably, is plain. Easy. Nothing to write home about. Dino and I sit by ourselves, off in the corner. His eyes are roaming the crowd behind us, seeking out the crowd.

I'm focused on his words.

Or, the lack thereof.

I need to talk to him about it. To ask him if he sees a future with me. Because if not…

There's a loud sound behind us.

I'm on my feet, turning to look, but Dino is faster. He shoves me behind him, and as soon as I peek from around his shoulder.

There's a mud covered man.

Holding a gun.

Walking straight for us.

The soldiers are scrambling, but no one has weapons on an aid mission. The man comes closer, and my heart skips to a thousand miles a minute.

Underneath the mud, a familiar cold face glints back at me.

"Andrei," I breathe.

"Stay back," Dino barks at me.

Andrei comes closer, gun steady. He blinks, his eyes red and staring as he comes to point-blank range.

"Give her to me," he growls.

Dino stiffens. "Fuck off," he snarls.

"Give her to me," Andrei repeats.

"No," Dino growls.

Andrei shrugs.

Everything moves in slow motion after that. I hear the gun cock, see his finger on the trigger. My eyes go wide and a scream poses in my throat.

He's going to shoot Dino.

I push, hoping Dino makes it out of the way in time, but he's made of stone...

The sound of a gunshot shatters the moment, and everything moves at once.

People scream around us. The camp is in chaos.

I'm holding onto Dino, hoping to God that he's okay, that he's not hurt too bad. I look over at Andrei, ready to beg for Dino's life, when my jaw drops.

Andrei is on the ground.

He's moaning, his hand clutching his shoulder.

Dino, next to me, standing, unhurt, is still as a statue.

"Dino?" I ask.

"Bernadino Drakos?" an unfamiliar voice calls.

I turn.

One of the soldiers, a tall, dark-haired man with silver dashed through his thick hair, is staring at us with curiosity.

There's a gun in his hand, but it's pointed down.

He shot Andrei.

"I'm Dino. De Luca," Dino says.

The man's eyebrows raise. "Is that the name you choose?"

I swear I can hear Dino's heart beating in his chest.

Slowly, he moves. "My father... my biological father... might have been a Drakos," he murmurs. "But I don't know what that has to fuckin' do with you."

The man stares for a minute longer.

Then, his face breaks into a huge smile, and he says something...

In Greek.

"English, fucker," Dino snarls.

The man winks, and something about his face sets my heart at ease a little. He moves closer, and Dino steps in front of me.

The man pauses, noticing the gesture, then bows slightly. "Ah, I heard that you only speak English. Pity. My name is Nico Drakos. It's nice to meet you...

Cousin."

29

DINO

Cousin.

The world is roaring around me. Andrei still moans, writhing on the ground, but it's a background sound compared to the blood rushing in my ears.

Cousin.

"The fuck are you doing here?" I snarl at him.

Nico, who looks to be a little older than me, bows. "Oh, your brother sent me."

"Brother?"

For a second I'm confused. Do I have another fucking brother to deal with?

"Yes. Marco?" Nico says.

My jaw is on the fuckin' ground.

"Anyway. Marco got in touch with me, and I am here to take you to Greece with me."

Oh.

Fuck no.

"Hell fucking no," I growl. "I'm not going fucking anywhere with you."

"Can you get us back to New York?" Marisol peeps from behind me.

"Naí, beautiful lady," Nico practically purrs.

I'm going to punch this motherfucker's lights out.

Growling, I move to do that, but Marisol's hand on my elbow keeps me still.

"Dino," she whispers. "He can take us back to the girls."

"I will take you wherever you want to go, beautiful, so long as we leave this place right now. I fear my disguise is ah... done," he says.

Sure enough, there's shouting nearby, and I have a feeling that those soldiers are going to come ripping through the camp at any moment.

Fuck.

"Dino," Marisol says softly.

She doesn't need to beg.

"Fucking hell. If you fuck with us, I'll rip your stomach out and feed it to you," I snarl at Nico.

He smiles, his grin broadening. "I like you."

"Fuck off," I snap.

I grab Marisol's hand, and we follow my... *cousin*.

I'm still not used to the words in my mouth, and they taste like ash sitting there.

Nico, however, leads us on a winding path through the tents and workers of the relief camp, until we pop out the edge. There's a Jeep there, stashed underneath a tarp, and he whips it off and starts the Jeep quickly.

"In!" he yells at me.

I help Marisol into the back seat, then get into the passenger side.

As soon as the door snaps shut, he slams on the accelerator and the Jeep roars away.

"How do I fuckin'know you're who you say you are?" I say once we're rolling through the city.

Nico shrugs. "You could probably check my passport, if you needed to."

"I fuckin' need to."

"Good. This type of attitude is very nice. It's going to work out for us," he says calmly. He rifles through the center console, handing me a gun in the process, and then whips out a passport.

Sure enough.

"Nicolas Drakos," I read. I look up at him. "Did you forge this shit?"

"It's nice that you think we have enough money for a quality fake," Nico remarks dryly.

I narrow my eyes. "The fuck does that mean?"

"It means, dear cousin, that you, and your connections to the Rossi family, are the only lifeline that our small family has to survive."

What the fuck?

Marisol leans forward from the backseat. "What do you mean?"

Nico sighs. "The story goes that my uncle, your father, was desperately in love with the woman who would marry the De Luca heir. She found him favorable enough, it seems, but the De Lucas ruined us in an attempt to bring her back into the fold. She caved, bringing my beloved cousin with her, and leaving us completely... broke," Nico announces.

"Broke?"

He turns, winking. "We'll be flying coach back to New York."

"With what money?"

"The cash that your dear brother, my cousin.... Once removed? Ah, I don't know," he mutters something in Greek. "It doesn't matter. Marco has offered us an alliance that was altogether too enticing."

"Of course he fucking did," I growl.

Nico glances at me. "You did not want to be saved? I probably will not take you back to the camp because I rather wish to not be shot by Brazilian soldiers, but I can take you if you wish."

I open my mouth, but Nico laughs. "Actually no, I cannot do that. Marco has offered a lifeline."

"He fuckin' sold me to you, didn't he?" I say bitterly.

"No."

"Then what's the fuckin' deal?"

Nico gives me a sideways look. "To talk to you. Take you where you want to go. So that you can make… an informed decision about your future."

I bristle.

Marisol leans back. "I just want to get back to my children," she says quietly.

Softening, Nico looks at her. "You are so close, beauty. So close."

"Shut your fucking mouth when you talk to her," I snap.

His eyes wrinkle with something that looks an awful lot like he's happy. "That would be quite hard, no? How do I talk to this lovely creature with my mouth shut?"

"YOU don't. I do. Fuckwit," I growl.

Nico laughs. "Oh, cousin. I am so glad to know you."

"I'm not."

"Marco told me of your demeanor. How you are… what did he say? A ray of sunshine," he grins.

I'm going to kill him.

And Marco too.

"Dino is wonderful. He's just a little tired and stressed right now," Marisol says from the backseat. "He's going to be just fine once we get the hell out of here."

"And that, we shall, beauty."

Eventually, the Jeep rolls up to… the airport. Like the full on, actual airport. Nico gives us passports, wallets, and smiles.

"Shall we?"

I have no fuckin' clue how he pulled this shit off.

Plane tickets. Passports. Border questions. Nico is a polyglot, just like Marisol, and the two of them sound like fuckin' kittens as they chat in Portuguese with the border patrol agents. The documents, though, are good, and they pass inspection.

The tickets are first class. We have an entire section to ourselves. The seat folds out into a bed.

Because Marco, apparently, has a sense of fuckin' humor.

We're on the plane, hours into the flight, when Marisol finally falls asleep.

I shuffle her slightly, so she's tucked into her long sleeping seat against the window. I turn to Nico sidling in next to him in the empty seat, my voice low.

"You, motherfucker, are going to tell me exactly what the hell is going on? No games. No fuckin' questions. Got it?"

He pulls his sleeping mask off, and takes his seat out of the reclined position.

"Why do you have a problem with your brother helping?"

"Because Marco's help doesn't come without a fuckin' price," I growl.

Nico nods. "He thought you would say that. Here," he says, handing me a phone.

I blink.

"In the videos. He made you one. Play it," Nico says, handing me headphones.

I don't want to.

But my fingers put the headsets into my ears. My hands shake, but I find the video, the only one, and I press play.

Marco's face fills the screen.

He doesn't smile. As per usual. He gazes solemnly at the camera, and speaks.

"I know you're pissed. I know that right now, you're probably thinking of ways to remove Nico's spine, and shove it somewhere that spines shouldn't go. I know, Dino. And I know you're mad at me.

But I had to.

I'm not trying to fish you out of this, brother. You chose to go to Benicio, you chose to take on the competition.

I'm proud of you."

That sentence, somehow, pokes at something in my chest.

"I'm proud of you, Dino. I always have been. You had the courage to do something I could never do, which is to forge your own path. You and Sal both have made your way in the world, and even though I interfered with that at various points, you had the courage to tell me to fuck off. To tell dad to fuck off. I admire that, and I wish I hadn't seen that as something bad. You are who you are without any concerns, and I'm... I wish I could present myself to the world as you do."

There's a strange, grim regret in his eyes, and for a second I wonder what the fuck that's about.

He sighs, continuing. *"Nico is your cousin on your father's side. I offered them a million dollars to retrieve you, but you'd be interested to know that they turned it down at first. He wanted to get you himself, because he said he wanted to get to know his cousin. The money, I will give them, but don't let Nico fool you. He was more interested in you than the money, and I think it's because he's an idiot who has no interest in running the dredges of the Drakos family."*

I snort at that, casting a glance at Nico. I don't think he's an idiot, by any means, but I absolutely can see that Nico has no interest in being a head of family.

He's far too happy for that.

"You have a chance to make your own path, this time, again. A family to start over with. I know we weren't the family you wanted.... That I wasn't the brother you wanted," his voice trails off, and regret clutches my stomach.

"But, I hope this could be a chance for you. You can forge your own path with the Drakos family. See what you can do. We'll be here if you need us, but you're better than an enforcer for Elio. Better than a dock supervisor for me. You are my little brother, and I love you. If you need me, you know how to find me," Marco says.

The video ends.

I stare at the screen until it goes blank.

So many emotions swirl through me, I don't even know where to begin. I fucking hate it, because I don't know what to do.

Marco said he loved me. That he was proud of me. Some very small part of me, a little boy inside my chest, is beaming and parading like a fuckin' show pony.

I hate that it matters so much.

I don't fuckin' trust Nico. Not by a longshot. I agree with Marco's assessment that he's not interested in being head of his family, just in the few hours we've been around each other, but I need to know a couple of things before I decide what to do.

I poke Nico, pulling my headphones out.

He yawns, pulling the sleep mask up off his eyes again. "Your manners could use some work, cousin—"

"Are you head of the Drakos family?"

Nico stills. "What?"

"Right now. Are you head of family?"

"I am," he says, his normally cavalier voice guarded.

"Do you fuckin' want to be?"

For the first time, all the humor and goofy-ass shit falls from his face.

"No," Nico says, his voice honest.

"Why?" I demand.

"Because I don't have the stomach for it."

I raise an eyebrow.

Nico sighs, his voice low as he leans forward.

"After the De Luca family financially ruined us, your father disappeared. We do not know if he is dead or alive, but we presume him to be dead. My father did not recover from the loss of his brother, his twin. He succumbed to a heart attack nearly a year ago. I have been searching for help since then. I do not want this," he says fiercely. "I do not want to be in charge of a failing empire. I do not want to walk into a room and have to... I am not made for it."

"What are you made for?"

Nico gives the ghost of a grin. "I run a bar."

"A fuckin' bar?" I growl.

He nods. "A tourist bar. On an island. The island is our home; it's been in the family for generations and it is the last thing we have. I love the bar. It's easy work. The women?" he makes a little kissing face. "Plentiful. Bountiful. I do not care about the Drakos name, so much as I care about the pursuit of things I like. Good wine, good food, beautiful women," he winks. "I think we have this in common, no?"

"If you talk about Marisol again, I'll fucking kill you," I snap.

He sighs. "Relax. Your wife is safe."

"She's not..."

Nico looks at me.

I look away. "Mind your fuckin' business. What do you want from me, in all this?"

He leans in. "The million dollars your brother promised."

"And?"

Nico assesses me. "And, for you to take the mantle of head of family. We are small. There is only you and I. A handful of enforcers, older than dirt, and some lingering business interests that involve selling tourists fake pieces of the Greek monuments. We were once... mighty. But we are no longer. I have no interest in running the ruins of our empire, or making them into palaces once again."

Palaces.

I look over at Marisol.

She's perfect.

My Marisol.

My woman.

My queen.

And for her, and the girls, I can only think of how good they'd look in a crown.

I turn back to Nico. "Palaces, huh?"

He nods.

I sit back in the chair. "Tell me everything."

Nico grins, and begins to talk.

30

MARISOL

Dino is awfully quiet the rest of the way back.

He doesn't let me out of his sight. Whether it's his hand on mine, or his arm around my waist, or any possible way, he touches me the entire time as we head back to New York.

I like it.

But, I haven't had any chance to actually talk to him. There's so much more we need to talk about.

So much more that needs to be said.

Decided.

What did you mean when you said I was yours?

Nico, on the other hand, is an endless fountain of information.

He never stops talking. Literally. I'm entertained by it, and he's definitely a good conversationalist, but the contrast with Dino's stony silence is almost striking.

It's hard to see them as related.

Until, of course, I look at them.

From Nico, I learn that Dino's father and his father were twins. I can see it. Underneath all the scars and tattoos, they definitely look alike. They have the same broad shoulders, the same lean but honed physique. They even have the same hair, except Nico seems to be going grey a little faster than he should.

"My mother's side," he explains when I ask. "It's said that they were cursed by the gods."

"What's the curse?"

He laughs. "Essentially, 'here for a good time, not for a long time.' Most of them have died young, so I'm happy with the grey. It means I have broken the curse."

That, I think, might just be Nico in a nutshell.

We make it past customs, which Nico literally flirts to secure our way through, and into the private car that Marco sent for us.

Dino still hasn't spoken.

Soon, the road looks familiar. I see the winding dirt that leads up to Elio's mansion, and my heart starts to pound.

I'm so close.

So close to seeing my children again.

My girls.

My angels.

So close to being a family.

I turn. I need to ask Dino. "Dino, what…"

"We're here," he cuts me off.

Oh.

I try not to be disappointed.

I asked for this, didn't I? I wanted to go back to the girls.

Dino never promised anything other than that.

Maybe I read too much into it. Maybe he doesn't want… to be a family with me.

Maybe…

I shut my thoughts down.

All that matters right now is getting back to my girls.

The car door opens, and I run out. I don't wait for Dino. I don't wait for Nico. Elio and Gia and Sal are at the front door, but I don't stop.

I briefly look at Caterina. "The girls?"

She smiles. "Playroom."

It's all the encouragement I need.

I fly down the hall, my feet barely touching the ground. Soon, I'm at the playroom door. I push it open, slowly.

"Mamá?"

I can't see. My eyes are flooded with tears. Words catch in my throat, and I can't get them out.

I don't need to.

The girls are in my arms. I'm holding them.

I lose myself in the moment.

Time passes, but I have no idea how much. Eventually they wiggle out of my arms, chattering and tugging at my hands, begging me to come see their dolls and their artwork and a million other things.

I follow them.

"Oh good. You made it," I hear a familiar voice.

I turn, sagging with relief. "Mãe."

My mother smiles, tugging me in close. "I told you I would find them, didn't I?"

I don't have a response. Because instead of using words, I let the tears that I've been holding back for weeks loose.

And I lose it.

Eventually, I stop crying, the girls and my mom all staring at me. My mother is gently patting my head, and I wipe my eyes, taking a tissue when she offers me one.

"So. He was that bad?" she asks.

I look at the girls.

My mother sighs. She asks the girls to go play, the Spanish rolling off her tongue, then turns back to me.

"Tell me."

In Portuguese, I slowly start. "I don't know. I don't think he was as bad as he could be. As bad as he was. He assigned Moretti to follow me around like some kind of guard dog, and Moretti... he wanted to marry me, to be father's heir."

My mother snorts and cusses in Spanish.

"Mãe," I chide, looking at the girls.

She waves her hand. "I have been working on their Spanish, but they don't know that word yet."

"They'll figure it out," I whisper.

She shrugs. "Continue, please."

"He... father... he made it seem like he loved me. Loved you," I say quietly.

My mother's eyebrows pinch together. "Loved?"

I take a deep breath.

Then, I tell her about the mud. About the mountain.

About him pushing me away.

And, what he told Dino.

As the story unfolds, my mother's face goes pale. When I reach the part about Dino seeing father die, she winces.

"I was afraid of this."

Curious, I tilt my head and look at her.

She shakes her head. "Benicio and I... We are like the moon and the sun. Destined to be apart, forever. If we were together too long, the world would stop spinning. A while back, I woke up in the night feeling... like I had lost the moon," she whispers.

"Mãe," I say, my voice breaking on the word.

She waves her hand at me. "Benicio was not an easy man. But I am not an easy woman. What we have... I will hold. I will keep. I do not expect anyone to know about it, I do not expect anyone to understand. But as happy as I am to see him dead, I will miss him with every piece of my soul."

I don't know what to say to that.

Other than to just hold her hand.

We stay like that, together, watching the girls play. My mother mourning the loss of her moon.

And me, wondering if I ever had mine to begin with.

I leave the playroom.

Eventually.

Seeing my mom mourn my father, while also hating him, has created an energy that galvanizes me to move forward.

I have to know if Dino wants to have a life with me.

I have to know if he will be with me, or the girls.

Or, if I need to start mourning the loss of him, in addition to the father I wonder if I could have had.

After making small talk with Elio, Caterina, Gia, and Sal, who are all more or less completely charmed by Nico, I look at Caterina. "Where is he?" I ask.

She sighs, and points to the patio.

I walk outside.

The air isn't cold, but it also isn't warm, exactly. My skin prickles at the chill, but it could also be goosebumps from the conversation I'm about to have.

The conversation that needs to happen.

Which could either be the beginning of everything...

Or the end.

I head out onto the porch, then walk into the yard. Dino is sitting on a swing that's attached to one of the huge trees out back. There are so many toys in the backyard, it's like a minefield.

I sit next to Dino, looking at the giant playhouse that's sitting in front of us. "That's new."

"I'm not shocked. Elio probably jumped at the chance to get a new toy for the kids."

"He definitely seems to be a family man," I say.

Good. At least we know what we're here to talk about.

Dino looks at me, and I sit on the swing next to him.

"We need to talk," I say quietly.

His silence is the confirmation that I need to keep going.

"I need to know if there's a future with us. With the girls. If you don't have a future with us Dino, then..."

"I want you, Marisol. I do," he says, cutting me off.

I look at him.

"My whole life I didn't think I belonged in my family. I spent my childhood fighting everyone. My dad. Marco. Sal. Every fucking body that I could. I was angry, all the time. I don't know what it means to be part of a family like you are. That you want to make. I don't know how to be a dad," he rasps.

My heart sinks.

"I don't... Nico, he said that he wants me to take over. To be the head of the Drakos family."

My jaw drops. "Dino. Do you want that?"

"I don't know. I know that if I build that empire, then I'll have something to give you and the girls."

"Dino, you don't—"

"I need to know that I can give you something, Marisol. Something more than how I feel about you. If I think about myself as a father, as a partner, then I need to be able to provide. Protect. I need to..."

"I don't need you to do that!" I yell.

Dino stares at me.

I take a deep breath. "Dino, if you want to take over that role, you should do it. For yourself. But not for me. The girls and I just need *you*," my voice breaks.

I feel like I'm begging him.

Just to be with me.

That thought makes my jaw snap shut.

I will not beg anyone to be with me.

I won't.

Dino looks at me. "Come with me."

"What?"

"Come with me. To Greece."

"Dino. No," I blurt out. "The girls, they just got settled here, we can't..."

"Okay," Dino says quietly.

There's nothing left to say.

I stand up, the swing creaking as I step away. I take two steps, then look back.

Dino is staring at me so intensely, it makes my heart ache.

But I won't beg him to be with me. To choose me.

Choose us.

I tuck my shoulders, keeping my head high.

And I go back into the house.

When I wake up, Dino is gone.

The house is quiet. The girls are asleep in their beds, where I spent the night as well. They had questions about Dino, but I dodged the answers.

I didn't sleep.

Not even a little.

I'm making coffee when my mother comes into the kitchen. "Morning, Mãe," I murmur.

"Do you mean to tell me you let the girls' father walk away?"

I turn.

She's in her pajamas, her hair in rollers. She has on an eye mask, and she's glaring at me through it.

"I'm not going to beg him to be with me."

"I didn't tell you to do that," she snaps. "I asked, did you just let him walk away?"

"Yes."

She lets out a long string of curses in Spanish.

"Mother. Please," I say in English. "There are babies in this house."

"And they'd say the same thing if they knew the words. What the hell are you thinking!"

"That I'm not going to beg him to be with me! If he wants to choose me, he can!"

"And you think that him choosing a future that you can live in isn't choosing you?"

I raise an eyebrow.

She collapses into a chair, her eyes trained on me. "I have been talking to the women. Listening. Hearing about this Dino, the father of my grandchildren. He reminds me so much of your father—"

"Oh, no. Then I definitely need to run," I snap.

She holds up a hand. "Let me speak, because I am your mother and I will not be talked to like this."

My mother rarely scolds me, and it shocks me into silence.

"He has a fire in him that reminds me of your father. But unlike your father, that fire has not burned him alive. When I fell in love with Benicio, there was merely an ember. He lived in the blackened shell of himself, and he had done things that were... that were beyond repair. I loved the man Benicio was. I did not love the things Benicio did to fill the darkness in his heart."

My heart aches. "Dino has darkness, Mãe."

"Not like your father did. He is choosing to build you a life, Marisol. He's going to make you a queen."

"I don't want to be a queen," I whisper. "I just want to be loved."

My mother's face falls, and she stands. Slowly, she tugs me into a hug.

"Why can't you have both?"

I look up at her.

"Those things are not exclusive, my love. Your father did not know how to do both. Like I said, the fire in him had burned away much of the person Benicio could be. I loved him, even if I didn't always like him, even when I knew that loving him would burn me too. But Dino... he loves you. It is clear. He loves you, and what he does, he does for you and the girls."

"Then why did he leave?"

She rolls her eyes. "Have you been in this house? There are too many men. They make the air thick with their machismo. A man like Dino who is full of so much dynamite will explode. But if he channels that into a place where he can make his own action, he will carve an empire out of the very bones of the earth. He means to change the shape of the world. For you," she whispers.

I frown.

"He has always loved you, Marisol. He has just waited to see if you would love him too."

I blink.

Could that be true?

If it is, then I have made a terrible, terrible mistake.

I look up at my mother. "Mãe…"

She smiles.

"Go. I will watch the girls. And when we come to Greece? I want a villa all of my own," she smiles.

I take a Range Rover. I don't know whose it is. But I peel out of Elio's garage, hoping that I can beat Dino to the private airfield that Gia told me he was headed toward.

Please don't let it be too late.

I'm barreling down the road, barely around the corner of the turn, when I slam my foot on the brakes.

There's another car.

Heading up the road.

Just as fast.

And I recognize the driver.

Slowly, I get out.

Dino mirrors my movements. We walk to the front of our respective vehicles, eyes locked, drawn to each other.

Like the moon and the sun.

Except Dino and I are like the sun and the earth. The moon and the stars.

We belong *together*.

Always.

He has just waited to see if you love him too.

Dino opens his mouth. "Marisol..."

"I love you," I blurt.

Dino reels like I slapped him.

"I love you. I love you so much that I'm afraid you'll take this and just walk away from me. That you'll abandon me and the girls. I love you and I don't know how to handle it because my mom loved my dad and he turned out to be... him," I gasp. "And I want you and I to have so much more than they did, and I love you so much and I don't..."

I stop talking when his lips cover mine.

Dino and I have kissed many times. So many times that I remember all of them. Each one feels unique to me, special in a way that I'm sure I'm never going to forget.

Before this, each kiss felt like a treasure. Something to hold onto when I felt lonely.

Not now.

We've never kissed like this.

This kiss is life. It's all the promise of a future. All the passion that we've kept for each other, everything that we haven't been able to say.

It's here.

When it finally ends, I pull back, gasping.

Dino smiles. "I love you, Marisol. I've loved you since the second I met you on that fuckin' beach."

"So why did you wait?" I laugh.

"Because I didn't think I deserved you. You deserved to be happy, and I'm…" he stops at my look.

"I'm the man who loves you, and I'm going to make you happy," he finishes.

My smile feels like it stretches across my entire body. "That sounds about right."

Dino presses a kiss to the top of my head. "I love you, Marisol. Will you please come to Greece with me?"

I hum. "My mother wants a villa."

"Done."

"The girls are going to need to go to school."

"On it," Dino grins. "I'll build you a fucking palace, Marisol, I—"

"You are my palace, Dino," I whisper. "You're the home I need. Where you are, I am home. Just be there, and I'll be happy."

Dino doesn't say anything.

He presses a kiss on my head.

"My heart is yours. My home is yours. And I'm yours," he murmurs.

I tug him close.

Dino is mine. I'm his.

And together, we're going to build the future we've always dreamed of.

EPILOGUE: DINO

Six months later

I'm going to kill that motherfucker.

I slam the door to my office open, the wood shaking as it cracks against the frame. With all the emotions raging through me, I can't hardly hold myself upright.

The light breeze smells like lemons and lavender.

It's fucking nice.

I can hear laughter out by the pool, and I know where he is.

My feet stomp on the teak floor around the pool deck. Nico and Marisol are watching the girls play in the pool. I can see Marisol's mom, napping on her own chair under an umbrella.

My target, though, is my fucking cousin.

"Nico!" I bark

He turns from where he's laid out, lounging in one of the chairs. "Yes, cousin?"

"Did you order fucking French wine for your goddamn bar?"

"Language," Marisol sings gently.

I flare my nostrils. "Did you order freaking French wine for your bar?" I repeat softer.

The girls are still playing in the pool, clearly completely oblivious to the fact that I'm standing on the deck about to rip my cousin in half.

"French wine is for a higher-paying client," Nico says, the smile curling across his lips.

Fucker. "You don't have higher-playing clients."

"But I want them."

"Your bar was on the 'Best Budget Travel' for college student's list. Your clients are university students from London, who are using their parents' pin money to f…fund their vacations where they can fu… chase after anything that moves," I seethe.

Fucking language. Editing my words is hard.

"Dino," Marisol says softly. I release a breath as her hands drift over my shoulders, and I shudder into her touch. "Come hang out with us. You've been working all day."

"It's noon," I grunt.

"And you woke up at four-fifteen this morning."

I feel guilty about that, because when I woke up at four-fifteen, I woke Marisol up too.

"Sorry," I mutter.

She leans in and presses a kiss to my cheek. "It was a really nice way to wake up," she whispers.

Nico coughs something out in Greek, and I glare at him. "Don't you have some fucking French wine to peddle to European teenagers?"

"The bar doesn't open until..."

"Beat it," I bark.

Nico rolls his eyes, but stands. He gives Marisol a kiss on the cheek before giving me a rude gesture.

I watch him go, my eyes narrow.

"Give him some credit, my love. He's trying his best."

"He isn't doing shit," I mutter. "He flirts with women who are barely legal."

Marisol makes a sound and gently tugs my hand down, so we're sitting on the lounge chair together. "A week ago I went down to bring him some dinner, and he was kicking out a group of men who were harassing a girl. He beat the hell out of them, without calling you for help. I think he's doing his best," she smiles.

That makes me feel a little better.

"Still doesn't give him the excuse to bill me for a fuckin' million dollars of French wine," I grunt.

Marisol sighs and stretches out, facing the pool. I lean with her, pulling her against my chest.

"He'll sell the wine. You know he will."

I don't respond to that.

In the six months since we've moved to Greece, I'll admit that Nico has made some fairly decent progress on all of this shit. All of his investments in the bar so far have been approved, and he's even to the point where he could, in theory, make an actual profit this year.

Considering that we had to renovate so much of this shithole to even get it to a place where we could *entertain* some fucking tourists, he better turn that shit around very, very quickly.

"You're both doing great, my love," she murmurs.

Yeah.

"I don't feel like I am," I say.

The girls shriek in the pool, and it startles Marisol's mom awake. She yawns and waves at us, then heads down to sit next to the girls.

I nod at her. "Your mom seems happy."

"She just likes the villa," Marisol snorts.

I don't think it's the villa.

Greece is an adventure. Different than we thought it would be, but I don't fucking hate it, that's for sure.

Without my brothers and sister around all the time, I can finally fuckin' breathe.

And, I can do something that I've never tried to do before.

I can be my fuckin' self.

I'm not bad at it either.

Since coming to Greece, I've forcibly retired four unhelpful uncles, and supported two more with coming into the business. Nico, for all his flaws, has actually been fuckin' helpful with that. He's not part of the family business in that sense, but I appreciate that he hasn't left me high and dry, exactly.

But he is ordering millions of dollars of French wine.

Having connections with Elio and Marco is, unfortunately, pretty fuckin' helpful. I see Sal and Gia every now and then, but Marco…

He's Marco.

He fuckin' appears when he wants something, or when he has something to say. Then, he goes on his mysterious fuckin' way, and I can't exactly say that I'm in a place where we're going to do game nights or shit like that.

But right now it's… peaceful.

My attention returns to where Marisol is tucked against my side. She sighs, and I lean so I can whisper in her ear. "We won't be able to fit together on this much longer."

Marisol laughs, and my hand slides around over her belly.

"Someday, we'll have a kid that isn't a complete surprise," she sighs.

I kiss her neck. "It's kind of fun this way though, right?"

"You can say that when you're the one hauling around your giant babies," she murmurs.

I smile.

Yeah.

I should enjoy the peace while I can.

I know that I'm not going to be a dad like Elio. Or Sal. Or anyone, really. But all I need to do is be the dad that loves the girls.

That loves our new baby.

And if I swear a little too much? Fuck it.

I love them enough to make up for it.

My phone buzzes, throwing off the peace that I'm so happy with.

"What," I bark into it.

Iason, one of the uncles that I've tasked with security, is on the line. "Boss. You're gonna want to come to the front door."

My eyes narrow. "Why?"

"Someone's here. Says it's for your wife?"

Fucking.

Hell.

Five minutes later, the man stands in front of both Marisol and me.

I have a gun in my lap. Iason stands behind him with a pistol cocked at his side.

But looking at the guy in front of us...

A fucking heavy breeze could knock him out.

"What do you want?" I snarl.

The man winces.

Marisol gives me a look. "How can we help you, Mr...."

"Rodriguez. I'm your father's attorney," he says quietly.

Marisol freezes.

"Say that again?" I rasp.

Looking for all the world like he's about to get fucking dental work done, the man takes off his glasses and cleans them on his shirt. "I'm Benicio Souza's attorney."

"My father had an attorney?" Marisol asks, kind of dazed.

He nods. "Of course. He was a businessman, wasn't he?"

"Well.. Yeah.. and... a criminal," Marisol blurts.

The lawyer shrugs. "I specialize in very nuanced clientele."

"That's one way to fuckin' say it,' I mutter.

The man gives me a look, then turns back to Marisol. "I'm here to read your father's will."

She blinks. "What?"

"Your father had a considerable estate. It's been six months since he passed, which you have my condolences for, by the way. I know how hard it can be to lose a parent who is so devoted," he murmurs.

Marisol and I exchange a look.

"Get to the fuckin' point, asshole," I snarl.

Mr. Rodriguez gives me a look that's usually only reserved for vermin, but continues. "Like I said. Your father's estate has passed the legal six-month period, which it needed to hold steady for during that time to settle any of his outstanding debts."

Fuck.

My mind races. If he's trying to keep us on the hook for all of Benicio's shit, I'm sure there's a way out of it. Unless Marisol, as his last surviving child, is the one who has to hold all of the debt...

"Debt?" Marisol says.

The lawyer tilts his head. "Well. Those have been resolved, you see, during the six-month period that the estate was held in escrow. So debt was a part of that process, yes."

Marisol droops a little. "He had a bunch of those, didn't he?"

The lawyer frowns. "I'm not certain what you mean, madam. But I assure you that your father's estate was in a very healthy place. It's why I'm here today."

It takes me a second to process what the small, drab man says.

Somehow, he takes the silence as some kind of an indication of our acceptance. He bends down, pulling a sheaf of papers out of his briefcase.

Both Iason and I jump, and the lawyer sighs again when he straightens.

"Not every problem can be solved with a gun, you know," he mutters, giving us a reproachful glance.

Fuck him.

The papers go on the desk, and he clears his throat. "You, Dino Drakos, and Iason Drakos, are willing to witness this will?"

I nod.

He sighs. "I, Benicio Souza, of sound mind and health, and of my own free will, do give the following assets upon my death..." he starts to read.

The words coming out of this guy's mouth are impossible.

Im-fucking-possible.

I don't know how long we listen for, but by the time he's done, my jaw is on the floor and I'm not sure that anything is real anymore.

Rodriguez looks up. "Do you have any questions?"

Beside me, Marisol takes a deep, deep breath.

"Let me make sure I understand. My father was not broke at all. I thought that he needed to marry me off in order to make sure that he could pay people off. But you're saying that wasn't true?"

Rodriguez chuckles. "Well, while your father may have had certain cash flow constrictions, he certainly had assets that made up for it. I would say that his overall business had been in a more... reduced capacity, but his plan to train an heir is one that wasn't poorly constructed at all."

"And that plan to train an heir... it wasn't about giving the organization to my potential husband?" Marisol says softly.

Rodriguez shakes his head. "I can't see how that would make sense, given that he left the entire...business, as it were, to you."

That's the part that I can't fuckin' wrap my mind around.

If what the lawyer said is right, there was never any reason for him to find someone to take over for him. Benicio Souza wasn't looking for a son.

He was doing something else.

But Marisol was his heir.

The whole time.

"When did he write this?" Marisol demands.

"Ten years ago. We revised it recently, as is pertinent, of course, but I assure you he chose you, and only you, as his heir," Rodriguez looks at Marisol, a smile on his lips. "You, Ms. Souza, are the only inheritor of his estate."

"Drakos," she murmurs. "Marisol Drakos."

"Ah. Well. It should be noted that the business in its entirety has been given to you, Mrs. Drakos. Your husband may provide input, and you may, of course, choose to make business decisions for the two of you that may be pertinent to the business, but the organization... it's yours."

Marisol blinks.

The lawyer leans down to pick up his papers, then stops. "Oh. Before I forget, your father did leave you with this," he hands Marisol an envelope.

She takes it, tucking it in her hands.

Rodriguez bows. "Well. I'll be off then. You'll be contacted by all the necessary accountants as we go."

With that, he leaves.

Stunned, I look at Marisol. "So. Um. What the fuck?"

She glances down at the letter. "I think I need a minute, love," she whispers.

I want to be with her. But I know that she's not going to be able to focus on me and the letter at the same time.

I squeeze her hand.

"I'll be ready when you are."

Marisol

My eyes go over the letter again.

And again.

And again.

I've already read it a million times. For hours, actually. I know that my mom got the girls inside and fed, and that Dino put them to bed.

But all I can do is sit at the side of the pool.

Looking at the letter.

It's so dark that I can't read it again.

I have no idea what to do with this information.

"I know I said I'd wait," Dino says quietly from behind me. "But I'm worried you need to eat, baby."

I lean back, smiling at him. "I'm okay. I promise."

"You wanna talk?"

I pat the seat, and Dino comes to sit with me.

"What does it say?" he looks at the letter.

I don't know how to explain this.

So I take a deep breath, my eyes drifting over the letter.

"He wasn't broke, Dino. He wanted to find someone for me to fall in love with. It's kind of fucked up, but he was worried about me. He wanted someone to marry me so that I'd be safe, and taken care of, so that I wouldn't have to physically fight the world when I got to the business, but he wanted me to take everything over."

"What about loved?" He asks.

I shrug. "I think he wanted that too, but I'm still not sure he knew what it meant. I mean, the love of his life was my mom, and she shot him in the chest with a shotgun, remember?"

"Yeah, promise me you'll tell me before you shoot me, love," Dino murmurs.

I laugh softly. "I don't think it will get to that point."

He sighs. "Are you okay?"

I don't know.

"I just found out that my father was a monster who loved me in a really, really fucked up way. I'm the heir to a criminal organization worth millions. I'm also six months pregnant, so I'm pretty sure my brain is going to explode," I murmur.

Dino kisses my neck. "That's a lot."

"It's a lot!" I say.

"But you know what? If there's anyone in the world who can handle all that shit, baby... it's you," he whispers.

I turn. "You think so?"

Dino smiles. "I know so."

"Shoot," I whisper.

Dino holds me close, I sigh into his arms.

This is a mess.

But as I lean back, my father's letter in my hands, my world reforming around me, I realize something.

I can do this.

I have everything I ever wanted. Dino. The girls. My mom. All safe. I have everything I dreamed of.

But now?

I look down at the letter, and smile.

Maybe there are some new dreams.

And with Dino, with my family?

Maybe it's time to see what other joys the future holds for me.

I've never really thought that another life is possible for me.

However...

I'm ready for the adventure.

EXTENDED EPILOGUE: MARISOL

FIVE YEARS LATER

"Okay. Everyone get together for a picture!" I yell.

Trying to wrangle our brood of children, however, is way harder than just telling them to get in for a picture.

Especially with all the cousins.

And today, since the combined Rossi and De Luca clans are all here?

There's really a lot of cousins.

The twins and Luna have the most attitude, of course. Well into their tween years, I dread to know what they're going to be like as teenagers.

Really.

It's going to be a nightmare.

"Listen. All you little... kids," Dino snarls. "Listen to Marisol! She wants a freakin' picture!"

Begrudgingly, they all move together.

"Okay!" I yell, putting the camera on the self-timer feature. "Here we go!"

I dash over to the group, hoping we all get in the frame.

The flash blinks a couple of times, and I swear, if we didn't get this picture...

"I'm going swimming!" I hear a voice shriek.

I look at Dino, who's mouth compresses into a tight line, and he nods.

Then, he races off after our son, who at four has decided he's more or less completely invincible.

And he's definitely not supposed to swim without his life jacket when he's swimming in the ocean.

We're on the island that Dino inherited when he took over the family. Once a year, we close all the hotels and the restaurants down, and we invite family.

All.

Of.

The.

Family.

It's a lot. But it's a good break.

Dino and I work really hard most of the time, so for a few weeks out of each year (if you count the holidays and all of that as well), it's nice to just be here.

Together.

On an island that's currently heavily guarded by the combined security forces of four very prominent mafia families.

I ended up choosing to take on the role as my father's heir. I wasn't sure if I needed to do it, or wanted to do it, but I wanted to challenge myself.

So, pregnant with our baby boy, I took over my father's organization.

With Dino's support.

Which did, in fact, sometimes look like him beating the crap out of people. But after the first couple of people, he just had to lurk behind me, menacingly, and people pretty much got the picture.

It wasn't even that hard of a transition, honestly.

But it is a lot of work.

At six months pregnant, and then seven, and then eight...

It was a lot.

But between the two of us, we made it work.

Now, we're doing... well.

I've cleaned up some of the less savory aspects of my father's business. Made them into something a little easier to manage, and things that aren't quite as morally repulsive for me.

Most of them, anyway.

The children run screaming to the beach, with a variety of adults running after them. I stay back, picking up my phone and looking at the picture.

It's awful.

Half the people in it aren't looking at the camera. The other half have an eye closed, or a mouth open, or a tongue out.

It's pure chaos.

But I guess I wouldn't have it any other way.

"How'd it turn out?" Caterina smiles.

I shrug. "Exactly how you'd expect."

She chuckles. Her hand drifts over her belly, which is definitely looking uncomfortably large at seven months pregnant. "Well, I don't think any of us were thinking that things would turn out like this."

She's right.

I reach out and grab my sister-in-law's hand. "I'm happy you could make it."

"Elio absolutely freaked out about it, but that's not new. You'd think that after three pregnancies, he'd stop."

I roll my eyes. "The day Elio stops freaking out about you will be a cold day in hell."

She laughs.

"Thank you, Caterina," I say quietly.

She smiles. "For what?"

"For being so wonderful when I needed you. For being someone who believed in me and the girls right away. And for someone who... believed in Dino."

When no one else did are the words that I'm not saying.

But over the years, Dino told me the story of every scar. Every single one.

Including the one across his throat.

The smile fades slightly. "You know, it makes me sad that Dino never felt this accepted with us. I wish that he could have had this peace with us. But I'm so grateful that he found it with you. Dino... he's never been easy, exactly. But he's loveable. He deserves love. And you've given him that, for years and years, and I'm so thankful for you," she says.

The tears on her cheeks are going to make me cry.

Absolutely.

"Listen, girl, if you cry I'm going to cry so you better stop it right now," I whisper.

Caterina laughs and pulls me in for a hug. "Then I guess we'll cry together."

I hold on to my sister-in-law for a while. I'm sure that it's the pregnancy hormones on her part, but I really am so happy that I met her.

So happy that this family became mine, because it's everything I wanted.

Caterina pulls back and winks. "I'll see you in a bit."

I watch her go.

Dino sidles up behind me and presses a kiss on my temple. "You good, baby?"

"Yeah, I'm good. How's the perimeter?" I ask.

Chuckling, Dino pulls me in. "You really are a mob boss now, aren't you Marisol?"

I blush. "What makes you say that?"

"We're here, having a family vacation, and you're still thinking about security."

I roll my eyes. "We're kind of a high profile target right now. And, there's that business with…" my voice trails off.

Dino's eyes darken.

Moretti, somehow, survived the mudslide five years ago. No one knows how. But I inherited his contract from my father, which was apparently a lifetime contract that he signed more or less willingly.

And Andrei Moretti has been pissed about that ever since.

He never came back to serve it. We get reports of him, every now and then, or he takes contracts, usually with those that are trying to oppose us.

"He wouldn't fucking dare come after us, Marisol," he growls. "He just wouldn't fucking dare."

I sigh. "Maybe there's another solution to this problem."

"Like what?"

I cast him a look. "You know, love has been a really good thing for you…"

"If you're comparing me to that fucking asshole, then I think you should probably stop," he growls.

"Dino," I reprimand him. "Come on. He was pretty hell-bent on marrying me five years ago. What if he didn't want to just marry me, and he wanted something like… love? Or family? What if he wants the thing that we already had?"

"Come on, Marisol. You don't really think…"

I kiss Dino lightly on the lips. "I do, actually think that."

He blinks.

"Think about it, Dino. If we offered Andrei an alliance of some kind, then he'd be bound to us. He couldn't make a move against us."

"We can't just assign some poor girl to marry him," Dino growls.

I pointedly look at Caterina, who is laughing with Elio.

Dino sighs. "Who the fuck would marry him? We have to have someone volunteer. I'm not doing to some girl like my parents did my sister. She has to agree to it."

I tap my finger against my lips. "Doesn't Stassi have a cousin?"

Dino stills.

Bingo.

"Marisol. She has to agree to it," he growls.

I smile at him. "I know. She will. I know she will."

"Moretti is a loose fuckin' cannon..."

"He is. But lots of people said that about you too, my love," I kiss him.

Dino's eyes flash.

"Look, let's really think about it. I don't want to put someone in harm's way. But until Andrei has something worth fighting for, he's going to keep coming for us."

"Why?"

"Because he wants what we have, my love," I whisper.

Dino sighs. "So what are you going to offer him?"

I smile. "I have some thoughts. You set up the meeting, and I'll talk to Stassi's cousin."

He shakes his head and leans in. "Again. You're a real mob boss, Marisol Drakos."

"I learned from the best, Dino Drakos," I murmur back.

The kiss is full of warmth. I lean into it, appreciating Dino as he wraps his arms around me.

I won't let anyone threaten what we have.

Peace.

Happiness.

The type of business that will keep our children safe.

I'm Marisol Drakos, the leader of the Souza family.

Dino's wife.

Mother of many sassy, annoying children.

And I'm not going to let anyone take what I've built.

Thank you for reading Dino and Marisol's story, if you enjoyed it, kindly leave me your review.

Your next read starts here- you will absolutely adore Elio and Caterina's story in Mafia King's Secret Baby, An Arranged Marriage, Enemies To Lovers Romance. You will fall in-love with their little daughter Luna, Here is an a little taste...

31

MAFIA KING'S SECRET BABY

Elio Rossi and Caterina De Luca's Story

Chapter 1

CATERINA

"It's not a death sentence, Caterina. It's a wedding."

I grit my teeth. My brother Marco, six years older than me and my self-appointed life ruiner, is sitting behind his huge desk with his hands folded like he's some kind of supervillain.

To be fair.

He kind of is.

At least, he is to me right now.

"Marco," I say slowly, my breath hissing through my teeth. "It's not just a wedding. You know full well that the Rossi family murdered our parents. Do you really think that history isn't going to repeat itself, especially given the circumstances?"

The circumstances, of course, are too similar to ignore. It was six years ago that our parents died in a tragic accident on the way back from an engagement party.

My engagement party.

To the same man that Marco is asking me to marry again.

He huffs out a breath and steeples his fingers, and I resist the urge to roll my eyes. "Caterina, this is the only way. I can't keep the business afloat without the contracts that the Rossi's bring in. If we can't keep the business afloat, we can't—"

"Find out what happened to Mom and Dad," I interrupt him. "I know, Marco."

We stare at each other across the desk.

Marco is the oldest of the four of us. Unfortunately, he's not my only brother. There are two more, Dino and Sal, born close enough that anyone who can count would be a little suspicious, and then me.

The baby.

A title that Marco, at least, has taken seriously.

Sal, who is closest to me in age, at least treats me like a human being. I haven't seen him in months; Marco has him on some kind of overseas connection for us since he speaks the best Italian.

Marco is also fluent, of course, and Dino can get by.

I can order ice cream and ask to see the beach, and that's about it. Mostly I just make vowel sounds and look angry if people are using Italian around me, and it seems to work pretty effectively. Then again, I've never been to Italy, so I could be wrong.

But it hasn't failed me yet.

Marco blinks at me. "Caterina."

"Marco," I respond. It's not fair that he doesn't have a longer name I can make him angry about. He knows that I hate being called Caterina, but he insists that Cat is too American.

As though we haven't been American for at least four generations.

I fold my arms. "Do you really think that *he* is going to honor this stupid contract anyway?"

"He has to." Marco's face grows dark and shadowed as the specter of who we're referring to enters the conversation.

Him. Elio Rossi.

Marco's former childhood friend.

My one-time future husband.

And our current biggest enemy.

"Marriage contracts simply can't be legally binding anymore," I argue. "That has to be a thing that went the way of the dinosaurs in the '60s."

"Dad wouldn't have negotiated it if that were the case," he says with a frown.

Marco frowns a lot these days.

For a split second, my heart aches for my older brother.

He was only twenty-eight when he was suddenly the head of everything. The legal business. The illegal business. Dad was a healthy man, and no one expected him to die.

Then again, I was only twenty-two when I became a mom so...

I guess no one got what they were hoping for.

Life has a way of doing that, I guess. Not in the sunshine and roses 'everything works out in the end' type of way.

No, for people like us, it's mostly the 'die-or-go-to-jail-for-a-long-time' way.

Or, in my case, have a baby when you're still a baby, and spend your life trying to hide her from her father, because if he finds out...

I shiver. That's the other reason that I'm here begging my brother to call it off.

Elio cannot know about his daughter.

Because if he finds out, I think he's probably going to kill us both.

Marco, however, thinks our family's dwindling resources will be enough to keep Elio and his goons at bay until I can figure out the evidence that we need to prove that Elio and the rest of the Rossi family had our parents killed.

I think this is a terrible plan.

He has entirely too much faith in me, our security, our Aunt Rosa, and our ability to pin the murder on Elio and his siblings.

I have faith in nothing anymore. My only hope is to keep my daughter safe. And you can't do that based on faith.

"Marco. This is a shitty plan."

"Language, Caterina."

I do roll my eyes then. "I'm a grown woman. I've had a literal child. I can cuss if I want to."

"Not if you're going to play the part of a good Italian wife you won't."

I'm pretty sure that Marco's ideas of a 'good Italian wife' are based on mob movies and Grandpa's tales of mob life in the '60s, but I don't point that out.

To my knowledge, which is based on the internet and no other experience, Italian women have moved into the modern world with the rest of us.

Then again, families like ours and the Rossi's go way back in history so...

Maybe old habits die hard.

"Luna will be just fine," he says with a genuine smile.

I don't return it.

He notices and the smile fades. "Caterina, seriously. You think that I would let my favorite niece come to any harm? If Elio finds her, he's a dead man," Marco says with a drop in his voice that makes me shiver.

Sometimes I forget that my brothers, while being my brothers, are also gangsters.

And they can be pretty freaking scary if they need to.

"I don't doubt that. I know how much you love Luna. But Marco..." I squeeze my eyes shut against the tears that prick at the edges of my vision.

"Sorellina, I know. I know what I'm asking of you. I promise you that if I thought you or Luna would be in danger, I wouldn't do it. It's our only course of action, yes. But more than that, it's a plan that will work," he emphasizes the last word softly.

I shut my eyes tighter as the tears flood me. "Please don't make me do this," I whisper.

I really am begging now.

I hate it.

I don't beg. Not to Marco, not my two other brothers. Not to anyone.

But I don't want to see Elio ever again. Let alone marry him.

"Caterina, I swear to you. It's a foolproof plan. We just need—"

"Zietto Marco!" a small voice squeaks.

Instantly I steel myself. Luna can't see me cry.

I won't let her know how hard this is.

To her knowledge, she's just going to stay with Nonna Mia for a while, my grandmother's ancient half-sister. Nonna Mia is a black sheep in many ways, and since her connection to the family is tenuous at best, we figure she would be the best spot to hide Luna while we try and bring down Elio and the Rossis.

Also, she lives on a farm and has goats. Luna will be charmed the entire time.

There's a blur of dark hair and light-up shoes, and my child throws herself in Marco's lap. He laughs, then stands and swings her around. Her delighted shrieks are a balm to my nerves, but only slightly.

Any guilt that I've had over the years about Luna not having a father is entirely erased when she's around my brothers. The three of them are protective as hell, and they spoil her better than any father could. They're perfect together.

All the more reason that we don't need Elio to be a part of our lives. Now, in the future, or ever again.

"Zietto, did you know that the outside of your door is seven feet and three and one four inches tall?"

I grin while Marco pretends to be surprised and engages with Luna.

Luna has been really into measuring things lately. I would blame her kindergarten teacher, but I love it. Her school does a lot of experiential learning, and a local hardware store gifted them all tape measures.

Luna has always loved to build and construct, so she's been really interested in understanding how things are put together. There's no doubt that she's been outside of the office carefully measuring the doorframe for this entire conversation.

There's also no doubt in my mind that she was blissfully unaware of what we were talking about.

Being five is a blessing, and Luna is an even bigger one.

"We should go," I whisper. It's not safe for Luna and me to be around the main house; there's no doubt that Elio and his spies have eyes all over this place.

Luckily, my grandfather was a wildly paranoid man, and Luna and I could use the tunnel system that he installed to our advantage.

Elio hasn't found out about her yet. He appears to have no

interest in me whatsoever past that night, which is fine with me.

I'm done hating him for his indifference.

Apparently, my brothers and I have moved into a much colder phase of our feelings for Elio.

Revenge.

"One week, sorellina. Then we begin."

I gulp.

One week of waiting. And then it's time to marry my worst enemy.

And the father of my child.

The drive back to our townhouse is quick. I live close enough to the main house that I'm easy to get to if needed, and so that the security that Marco pays for can easily zip back and forth if required to.

Hans, my personal bodyguard, is German, unusual for a mafia hire, but he's a great guy and a fantastic bodyguard. I wave at him as we walk in. He waves back; he and his wife are expecting a little girl in a few months, and he's been asking a lot of questions about Luna's birth in order to prepare to be supportive.

I love that. It's exactly the kind of father a kid needs.

After I settle Luna in for bed, I pour a glass of the Prosecco that I'm trying to bring to market and go out to my balcony. I linger, just for a minute, and grab the locket that I never take off.

Its only contents are a picture of my mom and me.

"I miss you, Mamma," I whisper at the sky.

My mother was a ray of sunshine. She had been against the marriage contract with Elio from the beginning and had only agreed when the last of her uncles was thrown in jail, right before I was born.

I wasn't certain what the exact terms of the contract were. My dad and Elio's dad had come up with them while they were out drinking and carousing in Atlantic City, of all places, and they had ensured that neither one of their families had access to the safe deposit box.

A brilliant plan.

My mother thought so as well. She berated both of them, but at the time, I hadn't been born yet. The deal was to have Giovanni Rossi's first son marry Antonio De Luca's oldest daughter.

Who turned out to be me.

To my knowledge, Marco still hasn't seen the original document, and neither has Elio. The location of the original contract is still a mystery.

But the terms aren't.

The Rossi family runs a shipping empire. They import luxury goods from every corner of the globe, but mostly through Europe.

Those goods come into ports that were, at one time, staffed by De Luca workers. The De Lucas would then take the goods, along with anything else that showed up in those crates, and turn them into cash, which the Rossi's would get a cut of.

A healthy cut of goods that were both legal and illegal.

The Rossi family is Italian. Like, Elio and all of his siblings except one were born in Italy and they only have citizenship in America because of some slick dealings and greased palms.

The De Lucas, via my great-grandfather and great-grandmother, came to the United States around the turn of the century. At first, we did quite well; there's a whole section dedicated to us in The Mob Museum in Las Vegas. I've never been, but Dino says that it's a hoot.

Then, along with the rest of organized crime in America, the feds got smarter than we were, and one by one, De Lucas filled up prisons from sea to shining sea.

With the lack of manpower came a decline in our ability to be the pin in the Rossi flow of goods. We still have a solid presence on the docks in the Port of New York, but it's nowhere near what it used to be.

My dad and Elio's dad must have been drunk on some prime shit, reminiscing about some old times, in order to dream up this ridiculous arrangement.

With the unification of the families, the Rossi's agreed to only use De Luca docks and De Luca distributors to sell. This is a terrible plan because the amount of goods that Rossi Industries brings in would vastly overwhelm our workforce.

I have no idea what Elio gets out of this deal.

Well... I did once. I grimace and sip my Prosecco.

Me.

There was a time when Elio and I would have been good for each other. I was a wide-eyed girl, just starting my junior year of college. He was handsome; he was my brother's age, and they had been friends since grade school.

I can't remember how handsome he is.

Physically, I'm capable of remembering. I see his unusual grey eyes every time I look at my daughter's face. I see the slope of his cheeks, the tilt of his nose. There's no doubt that she has Elio's face.

Thank God it's a pretty face, for both of their sakes.

And thank God even more for the fact that her personality is all mine.

I'm capable of remembering how handsome Elio is for sure.

But I *can't* remember it.

Because if I think about how attractive he is, how he makes my knees feel soft and wobbly when he smiles that dimpled smile, I'm going to do something stupid.

And I can't be stupid.

Not in this.

Not when so much is riding on it.

Elio Rossi made me very, very stupid once.

And I'm never going to be that girl again.

Elio

There's only one week left until I finally get my revenge on Marco De Luca.

It's going to be the longest fucking week of my life.

Since I dislike spending any time stewing in my own dread, I've decided to spend the week at my villa in Tivoli as a way to avoid the impending disaster of the marriage contract.

It's a little treat. Something I'm giving myself before my life totally goes to hell, and I turn into the villain in so many stories.

It's a price I'm willing to pay if it means that our parents will finally be avenged.

I take a deep breath, inhaling the light scent of the orange blossoms from the trees that are scattered through my property.

I love it here. This is the only one of our many familial properties and holdings that is truly and completely mine. I bought it seven years ago, intending for the villa to be a wedding gift for the beautiful and young Caterina De Luca.

She never saw it, so it became a gift to me. It's a haven, of sorts, that I have used many times since that horrible night.

If I had to, however, I'd trade it to have my parents back in a heartbeat.

I'm brought from my reverie by the crisp sound of heels clicking down the marble hallway to my office. "Boss," my twin sister Gia, knocks on the doorframe in a very cursory gesture of respect before entering my space. "New intel."

I grimace.

First, Gia only calls me 'boss' when she's got some really fucking bad news.

Second, if the intel is new, I don't want it.

The plan was perfect as I had it. If there are any adjustments, any pivots...

That perfection is gone.

And I demand nothing but perfection.

Softly I curse in Italian before looking at my sister. "What, Gia?"

She raises her eyebrows, and her hands crack like she's holding back from punching me in the face.

Well.

That makes two of us, I guess.

"Your bride-to-be is suspicious as hell."

I snort. I know that's the truth: for years she was simply beneath my notice, and so I didn't invest any time into finding or keeping her in one place.

Quite honestly, I never wanted to lay eyes on Caterina De Luca ever again.

And yet.

I sigh.

Being a Rossi is a sacrifice. It costs us everything and gives us everything.

I'm sure my father didn't intend for that to include the cost of his life when he said it, but here we are.

Both of our lives, gone.

Given to the family. To the business. Given in service of a deal with the devil that wore the face of a friend.

The De Lucas were close with us once. American, though their ancestors had come from Italy, they were my family's 'in' to the ocean of untapped buyers that the States offered us.

Somehow, every last one of them landed behind bars. Which meant their ability to operate ports and find markets for our particular brand of exports diminished.

Which meant their usefulness to us ended.

It never made sense to me that Father had entered into such a stupid bargain with the De Lucas. We didn't need them.

After their grip on the Port of New York loosened, we found other pathways. The Russians. The Japanese. Hell, even the Irish offered a more promising route to American markets than the De Lucas did.

But after one weekend in Atlantic City, my father came back and declared that he and Antonio De Luca had made an agreement. An arrangement. Binding the two families together.

An oldest son for an oldest daughter.

The irony, of course, is that the oldest daughter was also the youngest daughter. Six years younger than me, Caterina De Luca started out as my friend Marco's little sister.

That's how I thought of her. For years. I had known, of course, that we would be married at some point.

My father made it very clear to me when I entered my teens that any female companionship that I managed to wrangle would have to be non-committal at best, because Caterina De Luca would be my wife someday.

As with all of the men in my family, my father had a healthy appreciation for sex workers and mistresses, and while he did not discourage the use of either, he did encourage me to keep it quiet. I didn't need to be told twice, and it wasn't like I could mess around too much anyway.

After all, for every private party or club I went to, my bride's older brother was right there next to me.

I would miss Marco, I supposed.

If I did not hate him so violently.

"What is the intel, Gia," I say with exactly as much exasperation as I feel.

She slaps down a packet of pictures. "Bodyguard. On her 24/7. Looks like just one though. A condo. I think she nannies for a little girl in the family. Any of the brothers have a good time they forgot to keep under wraps?"

Gia's puns will be the death of me.

Provided, of course, that any of the other multitude of actors slavering for my demise don't work out.

"Marco probably not. I imagine he got the same level of emphasis that I did about accidental… mishaps."

"The others?" she prompts.

I frown. "Dino and…"

"Sal. The hot one," she clarifies.

"Gia. He is three years younger than you."

She arches an eyebrow. "Hotness doesn't have an age."

Ugh. She sounds so *American.* "He is the son of the man who killed our parents."

"Yeah, yeah. He's still hot. Anyway. Either one of them have a surprise baby?"

I sigh. "We should look into it. That type of leverage could be useful."

"More useful than being married to their precious baby angel younger sister?"

Her tone is sharp. I know she doesn't approve of this plan.

It is, however, the best option.

"We will have a backup. If the child proves useful, we will make use of it. If Caterina is the most useful, we will make use of her. Find out who is the father, and we will go from there."

Gia gathers the pictures and taps them sharply, collecting them back into one pile. "You know," she says with a pause. "You don't have to do this."

I close my eyes. "Not this again, Gia."

"Listen. We can send Enzo. He can work his way up in the organization..."

"Enzo, who is nearly identical to Father at that age?"

Gia shakes her head. "They don't know. It's not like there's a picture of him lying around the De Luca estate or anything."

"Marco will know. He spent plenty of time with Father and I."

"I know, but if we can just find the contract..."

I slam my fist down on my desk. "Enough, Gia!"

The hurt in her eyes cuts me, but I hold her gaze. Gia and I are fraternal twins, but our looks are so similar that when we were both tiny and sported terrible bowl cuts, people would mistake us for each other.

She is my sister. My best friend. My closest confidante.

And even to her, I am a monster.

Sacrifice. "We are not looking for the contract, Gia. There's no point. The only way for us to get Marco and the De Lucas to admit that they killed our parents is to use their greatest weakness against them.

"Caterina is young. She's naïve. She's been sheltered by three older brothers who would do anything for her, and she's the person who will hurt them the most when we take her."

Gia's expression morphs into something hard. Her lips draw tight, and the corners of her eyes look pinched.

"I understand, boss."

With that, she leaves.

I sit back in my chair. My head is pounding now, and I lean forward to pinch the bridge of my nose between my fingers. The orange blossom-scented air reaches out to me again, and I inhale deeply, letting it soothe me as I try to think around the pulsing in my mind.

Everything that I said about Caterina is true.

She is the youngest of the De Lucas. She's been painfully sheltered by her three older brothers to the point where her innocence is so obvious on her face that it's almost palpable.

After Marco and I graduated from business school, I moved back to Italy. An American education through young adulthood was plenty for my family, but the promise of a business degree had been mine.

The last time I saw Caterina prior to our engagement party, she was fourteen. She was all legs and glasses and frizzy, wild curls. Remembering Gia at that age, I had been polite but indifferent. I had kept a wide berth from her, because she was a child.

When I saw her again at our engagement party, I had been expecting that child.

But instead, a woman had shown up.

I think Marco may have pinched me a little too hard when his sister, on the arms of Sal, the brother closest to her in age, walked into the room.

I breathe in the citrus blossoms again. Dio santo, I remember everything about that night.

Her dress. A lilac color that made her look like some kind of fairy tale princess.

The way her skin glowed in the candlelight.

The way her lips had rounded on my name, shaping it into syllables that I knew, but hearing them from her made me feel reborn.

The way her eyes glittered when we danced.

My jaw works as I try to stop myself from remembering more.

Because there is so much more to remember.

The sweet surprise of her lips as I parted them with my tongue. The little noises she made when I pushed the gown off of her shoulders, releasing her pert breasts to the cool night air.

The way she gasped my name, first as she came around my fingers, next as she came...

Read Mafia King's Secret Baby FREE With Kindle Unlimited and available on Paperback.

ABOUT THE AUTHOR

VIVY SKYS the author of Steamy Contemporary Romance novels, featuring smart, strong, sassy and witty female characters that command the attention of strong protective alpha males, from Off limits, age gap, bossy billionaires, single dads next door, royalty, dark mafia and beyond Vivy's pen will deliver.

[Follow Vivy Skys on Amazon](#) to be the first to know when her next book becomes available.

Printed in Great Britain
by Amazon